Freed's Man

A Novel of the Umea Bakearen

By Rick Rossing
Copyright 2016 Rick Rossing

Table of Contents

Chapter 1: The End of the Tour 5

Chapter 2: Interview 9

Chapter 3: Orientation 13

Chapter 4: Training..25

Chapter 5: The Umea Bakearen 37

Chapter 6: Business as Usual 49

Chapter 7: UnionCon 2025 GCE..55

Chapter 8: Crash and Burn? 61

Chapter 9: The Falls of Polaris, 2026 GCE 69

Chapter 10: The White Forest of Aldebaran 75

Chapter 11: Ben's Wedding..87

Chapter 12: Hiatus 93

Chapter 13: Too Good to Last...101

Chapter 14: *Enpresa*...113

Chapter 15: In Council 119

Chapter 16: The Waiting 123

Chapter 17: Another Crisis 127

Chapter 18: Deneb's Southern Continent............................ 137

Chapter 19: Relocation and Redemption............................. 145

Chapter 20: Freehold 155

Chapter 21: Some Guys Get All The Luck..............................161

Chapter 22: Lost... And Found 175

Chapter 23: Learning To Fly 187

Chapter 24: Preparations 195

Chapter 25: The Way to UnionCon 203

Chapter 26: Admission Day Crisis 211

Chapter 27: Changes 223

Chapter 28: A New Beginning 235

Author's Note 237

About the Author..237

Chapter 1: The End of the Tour

I suppose most historians are going to say Desert Storm was more of a slight drizzle, but it was still combat. War is never trivial. Still, it came as a bit of a surprise how quickly it ended.

"Nice flying, Diego. Congratulations, you're done."

"Done, sir?"

The flight commander shrugged and handed me an envelope. "New orders. You're going home."

"Home? Don't you like my work?"

"We've met our objective. Saddam's out of Kuwait."

I unsealed the orders. "Reserves? But I'm here on the ROTC schedule. I've got at least six more years in my contract. How am I supposed to meet my obligation in the Reserves?"

"You do what the DOD says you do. If they want to put you in the Reserves, that's where you go."

"Yes, Sir I'll still get to fly, right?"

"Not for me to decide, son. If the USAF needs you to fly, you'll fly. Otherwise, you work in the private sector. You have considered life after service, haven't you?"

I shrugged. "I hadn't really thought about it that much, Sir. I still had a job to do here. I figured there would be time."

He laughed. "Good point, Lieutenant. Don't worry, you're smart. I'm sure you'll find a way to pay the bills."

***

Later, in the base mess, Jack sat beside me. "I got orders, too, bro. What're you planning to do?"

Jack wasn't my brother, but he had been my best friend since...hell, I couldn't even remember. We had almost always been classmates. We had double-dated in high school, signed up in ROTC together, even deployed to Iraq together. Jack wasn't my brother by blood, but he was the closest thing I had to one.

"It would be nice if I could keep flying," I said, "but I'm told that it's not that easy to get a job with an airline, especially with so much time left on my contract."

Jack shrugged. "There's other stuff besides flying."

"Get thee behind me, Satan!" I said, making a sign of the cross with my fingers. "Pilots fly. It's all I ever wanted to do!"

"Take it easy," he said, "I'm not saying you'll never fly again. Who knows what kind of stuff is out there? Me, I hear they have openings in the State Department." Jack leaned forward. "Diplomatic Security."

"You mean, like taking a bullet for the President?"

Jack shook his head. "Tony, Tony, Tony, didn't you ever pay any attention in Government? That's the Secret Service, and they're run by the Treasury Department. I'm talking DSS! Protecting Ambassadors. Travelling the world!"

"I've travelled the world," I said.

"Germany and the Middle East is hardly the world, Tony."

"I did Canada, too," I retorted.

Jack rolled his eyes. "For someone who really wants to fly, you sure don't seem to have much in the way of wanderlust."

"Speaking of lust," I said, "You want to try to pick up a couple of *chicas* later?"

"I didn't say 'lust'," said Jack, shaking his head. "You are incorrigible."

"That wasn't a no."

Jack swatted the back of my head. "Think about it, bro. I've got an interview in three days. You should come with. They said there were plenty of positions available. Not many people go for it."

"That might be because it's boring work," I said. "Standing around, trying to keep Idi Amin alive."

"I don't know if he's even alive anymore," said Jack. "He's been out of power since '79, and you'd know that if you didn't sleep through History. C'mon, man! It's honest work! And you get to carry a gun."

"Will I get to fly?"

"Don't know. I hear it pays pretty good, though. Maybe you can buy yourself a Cessna in a couple of years."

"I'll think about it," I said.

"Don't hurt yourself," said Jack, grinning wryly. "When's the last time you thought about anything? Besides picking up girls, I mean."

I blinked at him. "What else is there?"

"I'm beginning to think there's no hope for you, Diego."

"When did you ever think there was?"

Jack laughed. "Good point."

***

The next morning, we strapped into a couple of seats on the Herc that would take us back to DC. Jack leaned back and promptly fell asleep. He always could sleep anywhere. Struggling to get comfortable, I ended up just sitting there studying all the others who were going home. Jackson was planning to open up a burger joint in Mississippi, assuming he could get a GI loan. Mack was going back to Mississippi, too, though he never said what his plans were. Snake wrangling, probably.

The plane rumbled as the engines started up. I felt the jostling of movement as we built up speed for the takeoff.

I shifted in my seat again and looked for some source of natural light. "Would it have been too much to ask to put a few windows in down here?"

"What does a cargo plane need windows for?" said a woman's voice from a seat diagonally behind me.

I turned to face her. "I don't believe we've met," I said. "Diego, Tony. Pilot, Warthog. I'm not cargo."

The woman laughed. "Moss, Kayla. Pilot, Hercules. On this trip, you are, flyboy."

"You fly these tubs?"

"Used to," she said. "Once this baby touches down at Andrews, I'm done. Same as you."

"Aren't you sad about that?"

She cracked a smile that seemed to brighten the dark hold where we all sat. "Hell, no. Sure, I won't get to pilot one of these guys again, but I'll still get to fly. My folks run a small courier service. We have a couple of Metroliners, though my dad still has a DC-3 he keeps running. Now, that's a tub."

"Will you marry me?"

"Hell, no," she said.

"Well, do you think I might fly with you? I mean, work for your folks?"

"Look, Diego, I don't know you from Adam. If you want to work for my folks, you're going to have to impress them yourself. Your marriage proposal has already lost you brownie points, so don't think I'll be recommending you."

"Bummer. I meet the girl of my dreams, and blow it "

Kayla rolled her eyes. "I'd think you'd be used to that by now, if you don't have any better lines than that."

I clutched my chest. "You wound me. You think it's easy, talking to a pretty girl?"

"I'd think someone like you would have the routine down pat. Let me make this as plain as I possibly can. Not. Interested."

"We'll see," I said.

"I doubt it." She leaned back and closed her eyes.

"Crash and burn," said Jack, his eyes still closed. "Too bad for you, bro. She's pretty."

"Was she?" I said. I looked back over my shoulder. Kayla's flight suit did not adequately hide her curves. Her helmet could not completely hide her golden hair. Though she wore no makeup, her pouty lips glistened in the low light of the cargo hold.

"Damn, I hate it when you're right, Jack."

Chapter 2: Interview

Against my better judgment, I went with Jack to the DSS office. "Uh, I'm here to apply," I said to the receptionist. "Mr. Forbes here said I might have an opportunity?"

"Lucky for you, Mr. Forbes is correct," she said, handing me a short stack of paper. "Fill these out. Were you military, or law enforcement?"

"Uh, military." I looked over the stack. "Are those the only kinds of people you take?"

She shook her head, smiling. "No, but it does fast-track you. Assuming you had a clean service record. There's a background check, you see. If you're military, you've already had one. Is there anything on it we should know about?"

"God, I hope not," I said. "I've always tried to behave. I'm a pilot."

The receptionist smiled again. "Pilot. I might have known. I should warn you that dating co-workers is strictly prohibited."

I gave her a wink. "Would we be co-workers?"

"Only if you get the job, Mr. Diego. Shall I tear up your application?"

"I'm not certain how to properly answer that, Miss—" I looked at the name badge clipped to her waist, "—Campbell. Either I flatter you and lose the job, or I hurt your feelings. Neither option appeals to me."

"I like you," she said. "I guess that means I'm off limits, as far as you're concerned."

"More's the pity," I said, grinning. "I promise to keep our relationship professional. Assuming I get the job, of course."

Jack shook his head. "You'll have to forgive my friend. He's...well, he's Tony."

"No problem," said Campbell. "This place is full of them. Mr. Biggs will see you now, Mr. Forbes."

Filling out forms was every bit as interesting as one might expect. As I looked over the pages of questions, I heard a now-familiar voice say, "Oh, it's you."

I looked up. "Moss? I thought you were going to fly for your parents."

"I never said that," said Kayla, sitting down in the seat beside me. "I just said I'd get the chance to fly again. Tell me you're not applying for DSS."

"It so happens, I am," I said. "That's not a problem, is it? It is possible for me to have a professional relationship with a beautiful woman. Is that not correct, Miss Campbell?"

Without even looking up from her computer screen, Campbell replied. "Yep. You'd better check page seven, paragraph four, though. It's improper to use terms such as 'beautiful,' 'handsome,' 'sexy,' 'ugly,' or any other superficial characteristics when talking to, or discussing, one's co-workers. You get one warning. That was it. This agency has a strict sexual harassment policy."

"Yikes! I'll keep that in mind."

"I certainly hope so," said Kayla. "I'd hate to see what they do to offenders."

"Firing squad," said Campbell.

"Seriously?" I said, quickly turning to page seven.

Campbell smiled mischievously. "No, but after a few sensitivity training sessions, you might prefer it."

After a while, Jack came back out to the waiting area and sat down. He nodded to Kayla. "Moss, was it? Good to see you."

She nodded back. "Forbes, right? How did it go?"

"Not so bad. Agent Biggs is slightly intimidating, but he seems a fair judge of character."

"Moss," said Campbell, "You're up. Good luck."

Jack watched me finish up my paperwork. "You all right? You don't look so good."

"Come on, Jack, you know how much I like to flirt with the ladies. I'm liable to get my ass handed to me before too long. I've never been so scared in all my life!"

Jack laughed. "You've flown Warthogs, Tony. You've survived flak, missiles, and at least one irate father. And you're afraid of sensitivity training?"

"I've got to be me. I'm afraid that might not be good enough, here."

Miss Campbell looked up from her desk. "I think there might be hope for you yet, Mr. Diego."

***

My own interview with Agent Biggs went well. "Your service record is pretty impressive, Diego. How many sorties have you flown?"

"Twenty or thirty, Sir," I said.

"You don't have to call me sir," said Biggs. "My final rank in the Marines was Master Gunnery Sergeant. You technically outrank me, Lieutenant."

I chuckled. "Then shouldn't you call me sir?"

The look Biggs gave me chilled me down to the bone. "We're not active military anymore, are we, Diego?"

"No, Sir," I said. "I mean, uh, Boss?"

Biggs grinned. "Boss works, if that's what makes you most comfortable."

"I can't say that comfort is the word I'd use, Boss. Does this mean I'm in?"

"You're probationary, but yeah," he said, extending his hand. "Welcome aboard, Diego."

I shook his hand. "I hope I don't disappoint you, Boss."

"We'll see. Before I let you go, I need to ask you one more question." Biggs looked me square in the eyes, and said, "How do you feel about aliens?"

I shook my head. "My family were immigrants," I said. "Besides, what kind of DSS agent would I be if I were afraid of foreigners?"

Biggs grinned slightly, but his expression remained serious. "I don't mean foreign nationals, Diego. I mean extra-terrestrials."

"Little green men from Mars? You can't be serious."

"Just answer the question."

"You are serious," I said. "What did I just sign up for?"

Biggs smiled. "Diplomatic Security Service, like it says on the outside of the building. But there are all kinds of diplomats, and not all of them are of this Earth."

"Yeah, right," I said.

Biggs raised an eyebrow.

"Uh, I mean, 'Yeah, right, Boss.' Okay, I'll play along. If I ever do see a little green man, I promise I won't shoot first and ask questions later."

"Fair enough," said Biggs. "Keep in mind that one of the forms you signed is a confidentiality agreement. You are strictly forbidden from discussing any part of your work with anyone not directly associated with DSS. Not your friends, not your family, heck, not even your dog."

"Sure, because my dog might be a spy."

"You jest, but it has happened."

What the hell was I getting myself into? "Okay, I get it."

Biggs's face was totally unreadable as he handed me a card with an address and a time. "Be there tomorrow morning. Don't be late. If you miss the bus, you won't get another chance. You won't even remember getting this one."

I was about to make a snide remark, but something in Biggs' tone told me it was best if I shut up, so I did. "Tomorrow morning, 0700. Got it. Uh, what should I wear?"

"You're the first today to ask that question," said Biggs, smiling almost imperceptibly. "You might be smarter than you look. Business casual will be fine, for now. Part of the orientation will deal with our dress code."

"Uh, okay then. See you tomorrow, Boss."

Chapter 3: Orientation

Jack and I parked in front of an Armed Forces Recruiting Office in a local strip mall. The schedule in the window revealed that the center wouldn't open for two more hours.

I checked the card again. "This is the correct address, all right. What time do you have?"

"Ten to seven. We're not late."

"You'd think someone would be here to meet us," I said, looking around."

Jack shrugged. "Biggs seemed like the punctual type to me, don't you think? He'll probably get here right at seven."

A white Firebird pulled into the lot. Kayla Moss climbed out and nodded toward us. "Morning."

She wore a knee-length gray tweed skirt and a neatly pressed white blouse. Unlike her flight suit, which could not adequately hide her curves, this outfit accentuated them.

"Morning." I tried not to stare at her hips as she walked. How bad could sensitivity training possibly be, I wondered.

She looked around. "Where are we supposed to go, exactly?"

"Your guess is as good as mine," I said. "Biggs did mention a bus at my interview. I thought he was just being figurative. Maybe this is just a good meeting spot."

Another car pulled in and a dark haired woman stepped out. "You must be the new guys Biggs told me about. I'm Rita Cruz."

We barely had time to introduce ourselves before a black passenger van pulled up. Biggs hopped out and opened up the side door. "Good. You're all on time. Get in, find a seat, and we'll get underway."

Jack and I climbed into the back row, while Rita and Kayla sat in front of us. Biggs climbed up next to the driver of the van and said something to him in a language I didn't recognize.

The van pulled away from the curb and into traffic. Leroy turned around to face us. "You've all flown before, right?"

We all nodded, even Rita. That surprised me, because I had assumed that Biggs already knew her.

"Are we heading back to Andrews?" I asked.

Biggs shook his head and smiled rather mischievously. "That's need-to-know, Diego. Why don't you just sit back and enjoy the ride?"

DC traffic was always heaviest during the morning rush hour, so I knew enjoying the ride wasn't really going to be an option. I looked out the window. I looked around the van. I looked at the back of Kayla's head.

"You really need to learn to relax, Tony," said Jack. "You're making me nervous with all your fidgeting."

"I do not fidget," I said. "I just never much cared for traffic."

The driver snorted. "I agree with you on that point, Agent." He said something to Biggs in the odd language.

"Rules are rules," said Biggs. He said something else that made the driver chuckle.

"You know, it's not very nice to speak in languages we don't all understand," I said. "How do I know you're not making jokes about us?"

Jack laughed. "Now you know how it feels, bro. Every time we visit your folks, you start speaking Spanish!"

"Damn, I do, don't I? Sorry, man. I'll watch my tongue next time. What language is that, anyway?"

"Euskara," replied the driver. "It is my native tongue."

"Where do they speak Euskara?"

"Deneb."

"Where's that? Europe?"

The driver looked at Biggs. "Is he serious, Leroy?"

Biggs cleared his throat. "Turn into Rock Creek Park, Zeru. This time of day, it ought to be safe. Mostly."

"Safe for what?" said Rita. "Where are we going?"

"Groom Lake," said Biggs.

"Never heard of it," I said.

"I have," said Jack. "It's in Nevada. You guys might know it as Area 51."

"Nevada?" said Kayla. "Via Rock Creek Park?"

"Area 51?" I said. "You weren't just pulling my chain, Boss? We're going to meet a real live ET?"

"You already have, Diego. This is Zeru Petra. He's the pilot of one of the Denebian vessels stationed there."

"So, Deneb's not in Europe, then."

"Give the man a sitar," said Zeru. "I guess he is pretty

sharp after all."

I shook my head. "Uh, that's 'a cigar,' Zeru. Or do your people receive musical instruments as prizes? That would probably be a healthier option. A lot more expensive, I imagine."

Kayla shook her head. "You talk too much, Diego."

"I've been told that, yeah. Sorry. No offense, Zeru. Your English is better than my Euskara, I'm sure."

Zeru laughed. "Correct, again."

Inside the park, there were very few vehicles. After a quick look around, Biggs gave Zeru a nod. "Punch it."

"The button is quite sensitive, Leroy," said Zeru. "I do not need to hit it with much force."

Biggs chuckled. "Whatever you say, Zeru."

Zeru leaned down and touched a switch. The trees outside the van suddenly vanished. I yelped and looked out the window. The trees were still where they had been, much to my relief. We had merely risen several hundred feet above them, and we were still rising.

"What the hell?" shouted Kayla. "This thing flies!"

"Does it ever," agreed Jack. "It looks like we're already halfway across West Virginia. We must be supersonic already. How is that even possible?"

Zeru began describing the technology. Jack seemed to follow what he was saying, and Rita, too, but as far as I was concerned, Zeru might as well have been speaking Euskara. One look at Kayla and I could tell she had no idea what Zeru was saying either.

By the time Zeru had finished his discourse, we were flying over St. Louis. "Look, kids, the Gateway Arch!" I said, pointing at the ground. "Never mind. It's gone."

"We are just passing the halfway point," said Zeru. "Ten more minutes."

"We must be going over seven thousand miles an hour!" said Kayla.

Biggs nodded. "Yep, about that."

"That's over Mach 9! Nothing goes that fast!"

"Nothing built on Earth does," said Zeru.

"Where can I get one of these?" I asked.

"Unless you're DSS," said Biggs, "You can't. The tech still hasn't been approved for Earth yet. Wayne is working on it."

"Wayne who?"

Zeru gasped. "You do not know your own *Umea Bakearen*?"

"Are you insulting me, spaceman? You saying I don't know my own backside?"

Zeru looked back at me wide-eyed. "I meant no insult, Tony!"

"*Umea Bakearen* is Wayne Freed's title, Tony," said Biggs. "It literally means 'Peace Child'."

"Wayne Freed?" said Jack. "I think I know the man. Well, I know of him. He was at Georgetown, Tony. The guy with the pink-haired girlfriend?"

"There were several pink-haired girls on campus, Jack," I said. "How do you know his name?"

"I was a computer science major," Jack said, as if that would be explanation enough.

"You hacked the student records?"

"Of course not," said Jack, his face reddening. "And I'll deny it if you tell anyone!"

Rita laughed. "You stalked his girlfriend."

"Not exactly. I just wanted to know her name, was all."

"Did you find it?"

"Janet Clarke," said Jack. "She grew up in Oklahoma City, practically next door to Freed."

"That's in his dossier," said Biggs. "Nice work, Forbes. That is, it would be if it wasn't just a little bit illegal."

"I didn't do anything with the information," said Jack, his voice quavering. "Is this going to hurt my standing?"

Biggs cracked a smile. "Not in my team, it won't. Just don't do any unauthorized snooping on the clock, got it?"

Jack breathed a heavy sigh. "Got it, Boss."

"One more thing," said Biggs. "If Wayne should happen to marry this Janet, that's not going to be a problem, is it?"

Jack shook his head. "I've never even spoken to her. It's bad form to try to poach another man's girl. She doesn't know me from Adam."

"I just thought you were afraid," I said.

"Just because you throw yourself at every pretty girl you see doesn't mean that's the way all men are," said Kayla.

"I do not throw myself at every pretty girl!"

Kayla looked at me with one raised eyebrow. "No? You hit on me, and you hit on Miss Campbell."

"You hit on Jess Campbell?" said Rita. "You must have *cojones* of steel, my friend. I'm surprised she didn't tear up your application."

"She almost did," I said.

"No one has ever gotten past the Campbell trap before. You must be special."

"Do you think I have a chance with her, then?"

Kayla punched my arm. "About as much chance as you have with me, buddy."

"Not even," said Rita. "Jess prefers women."

"See, Kay?" I said. "You wouldn't have any competition."

"Only friends get to call me Kay, Diego. I haven't made my mind up about you."

"Ah, so I still have a chance."

"I wouldn't go that far," said Kayla, crossing her arms.

"I'd be careful if I were you," said Biggs. "As long as you're both on my team, you will keep your relationship professional."

"Got it," I said. "So why is Freed so important?"

Zeru shook his head. "How can people not know?"

"It's not Diego's fault," said Biggs. "Only a few people know. It's classified information here."

Zeru sighed. "Yes, of course. But surely people responsible for his safety must know why, yes?"

"That's why we're going to Groom Lake," said Biggs. "These four are joining the Sol-Deneb Task Force. This trip is part of their orientation."

"Could you not have done that before now?"

Biggs shook his head, smiling. "If, for some reason, they can't handle the truth, we need to be able to undo the damage."

"Uh, by undo, you mean wipe our memories, don't you?" I said.

Biggs nodded. "But I think you'll make the cut, Diego. I'm pretty sure about all four of you."

"I thought Rita was already in," said Jack.

"I've been in the DSS for several years," said Rita, "but I've never been a part of the SDTF."

"So what are you doing here?"

Rita smiled. "I'm not at liberty to say."

"She hacked my PC," said Biggs. "Initiative like that ought to be rewarded, so I promised not to turn her in right away."

Zeru shook his head. "I am not certain that you appreciate how important the *Umea Bakearen* is to the survival of this planet. You recruit rookies and potential security leaks?"

Biggs laughed. "It will be up to Dok Fil to decide, not me."

"Uh, who is Dok Fil?" I asked, raising my hand.

Zeru laughed. "You will soon find out, Diego. We are on final approach to Groom Lake."

There were half a dozen large, vaguely cylindrical objects sitting on the tarmac where we landed. One of them appeared to fade in and out of sight.

"What's going on down there?"

Zeru looked out. "Oh, that? The guys are trying to repair the cloak. Not to worry, though. They will get it working before we even attempt to fly that vessel again. In the meantime, there are still five fully functional cruisers available to us."

"Uh-huh," I said, not entirely satisfied with the answer. "Boss, what are we doing here, anyway?"

"This is a training run," said Biggs. "You're here to meet Dok Fil, Mediator of the Galactic Union, and his associate, Professor John Remington. We're going to accompany the Professor to Deneb, where he'll be spending several months teaching linguistics to a bunch of college students."

"We're going to be gone for several months?"

"Negative," said Biggs. "We're dropping the Professor off, then returning to Earth. The round trip will take three weeks, at most."

"I should have stopped the mail."

"Not a problem. DSS has dedicated house-sitters for agents going abroad."

"Are they going to feed my cat, too?" asked Kayla.

Biggs nodded. "They're professionals."

✳✳✳

"I should have known you had a cat," I said, as we walked across the tarmac.

Kayla peered at me through narrow eyes. "You got a problem with that?"

Biggs turned and glared at us. "Am I going to have to separate you two? Because I'll do it. Whatever history you two have, you better resolve it, or I'll have both your memories wiped and your butts deposited at your vehicles."

Jack raised his hand. "Uh, point of order. Tony and I came in my Jeep. I'd rather he didn't drive if his memory gets wiped."

I glared at him. "Way to back me up, bro!"

"It's almost paid for!"

Kayla laughed. "Sorry, Biggs. I know I shouldn't let Tony get to me, but he's..." She trailed off, apparently unsure how to continue.

I extended my hand. "I promise I'll figure out how to behave properly in front of you, even if it kills me."

"That almost sounds like an apology," she said, shaking my hand. "I'll accept it as one."

"See?" I said. "We can play nice."

Biggs grunted and jerked his thumb toward a block-shaped building. "Follow me, all of you. Don't embarrass yourselves when you see the Aldebarans. Got it?"

We all nodded and fell in behind Biggs.

Inside the building, I saw five unusually tall, thin, and very blue-skinned men. The one in the middle looked much older than the others, and they all appeared to defer to him. The old one, I supposed, was Dok Fil.

There were also a few humans present, including the man I recognized as Professor Remington. Jack and I had both been in one of his Language Theory courses at Georgetown. I had barely passed. The man had always scared the spit out of me. He apparently had that effect on almost all his students, because I felt Jack shudder beside me. I desperately hoped he wouldn't remember either of us.

Biggs introduced us first to Dok Fil.

"I am pleased to make your acquaintance," said Dok Fil, bowing graciously. His voice was relaxing, almost musical. The pitch of his voice was at the same time low bass and high tenor, if that makes any sense. His face was gaunt, at least by human standards, but he looked to be in good health for a man of his age, whatever that was. He wore a charcoal gray tailored business suit and a fedora. As he bowed, he removed his hat to reveal several button-horn-like protrusions on his otherwise round, mostly bald head. What little hair he had was white, but it did not appear to be from old age, as the other blue men were also white-haired.

I shook his hand, then stepped back as the others did as well. Looking at the other blue people, I realized that only two of them were male. The two females were slenderer than the males, and they were built pretty much the same as human females, proportionately speaking.

"My associates are Merv, Van Dam, Far Polk, and Fen Gale," said Dok Fil, indicating each as he named them. Each nodded and bowed slightly.

Remington shook all of our hands. If he did recognize either Jack or me, he did not show it, for which I was somewhat thankful.

The other humans were not associated with Remington, I realized, when Biggs introduced them. "This is Kat Jericho, Denebian DipSec; Tanya Orlov, former Russian Navy; and Olav Samuelson, also Denebian DipSec."

"I presume that DipSec is the Denebian equivalent of DSS?"

"It is," said Jericho. "Have you ever left Earth before, Diego?"

I chuckled. "Before about an hour ago, I didn't even know it was possible."

Tanya smiled as she took my hand. "This will be my first extra-terrestrial mission, as well."

"Olav Samuelson sounds like Earth Scandinavian," I said, shaking his hand.

"Earth and Deneb share much in common," said Samuelson. "I would bet that you have never been told that the Sol system was once colonized by Deneb."

I froze mid-shake. "Really? I had no idea."

"That is what the Sol-Deneb Treaty is all about," said Dok Fil. "Have a seat, ladies and gentlemen, and we will give you a brief history lesson."

We did, and Dok Fil began a slideshow. "Approximately twelve thousand years ago, there was an interstellar war. The specifics of the war are unimportant at this point, though the details are available, should anyone choose to research the topic later. What is important is that during the final battle, a planet was destroyed in the Altair system. The aggressors used thermonuclear weapons to eradicate every living thing on the planet. Twelve thousand years later, the once-vibrant Altair II is still a sterile rock in space. Nothing can survive there, and radiation levels are still too lethal for any living beings to safely approach the planet."

"Damn," said Kayla, so silently that only I could hear.

"Damn is right," I whispered back.

Dok Fil continued to speak. "The galactic community was horrified by their use, and immediately passed a resolution forever banning the use, and even the manufacture, of nuclear weaponry. Eventually, other types of weaponry and methods of warfare deemed too cruel or unethical to be used by civilized beings were also banned. This list of banned technologies and methods became known as the Caldera Accord. It is still in effect to this day, and breaching any of its prohibitions carries a death sentence."

I raised my hand. "Uh, Mediator, Earth has nukes. Where does that leave us?"

Dok Fil nodded. "Where, indeed? An excellent question, Agent Diego. After drafting the Caldera Accord, the people sought retribution against those who had destroyed Altair II. The Accord could not be applied retroactively, so they were not summarily executed. In the end, banishment to a remote planet was their fate."

"Let me guess," said Kayla. "The remote planet was Earth, wasn't it?"

Dok Fil pointed to her and nodded, smiling. "Excellent insight, Agent Moss. You are correct. Sol III—that is, the third planet in the Sol system—had been recently discovered. It was habitable, and contained no sentient life. The prisoners were deposited on this planet to colonize on their own. Very little contact was allowed between Sol III and the rest of the galaxy. Generations later, about ten thousand years ago, their descendants staged an uprising, attempting to escape the planet on a stolen supply ship."

"The descendants were still being punished even after multiple generations?" said Rita. "That seems unfair, to me at least."

"Perhaps it was," said Jack, "but their descendants went ahead and built more nukes, didn't we? Maybe the punishment was justified."

"After the uprising, all contact with Sol III was abruptly ceased," said Dok Fil. "The planet was bombarded from orbit until no usable technology remained. Deneb sent scout ships every fifteen years to observe the survivors, but they never contacted the surface again."

"So what is the Sol-Deneb Treaty?"

Dok Fil nodded. "Patience, Agent Diego. I am getting to it, but first you need to know the background behind the Treaty."

"Sorry."

"The observers eventually became quite impressed with the evolution of civilization on Earth. There was even talk of restoring communications before Earth plunged into your First World War, followed by the Second World War. When reports came back of atomic explosions, the Galactic Union began calling for another cleansing of the planet."

Rita cleared her throat. "Um, by 'cleansing', you mean

another orbital bombardment, don't you?"

Dok Fil nodded. "Only Deneb came to Earth's defense in Council. Since Earth was a Denebian territory, Deneb would handle the situation. They had already begun sending more frequent scouting expeditions, so they hoped that they might at least be able to prevent Earth from regaining the ability to reach the stars."

"You interfered with our development?" I said. "What about the Prime Directive?"

"Funny," said Dok Fil. "Wayne said the same thing when he learned the truth. You do know that Star Trek is fiction, yes?"

"Say it ain't so!" I said, clutching my heart in mock horror. The other Terrans in the room laughed, except for Biggs and Remington. The aliens blinked at me in apparent confusion. Or pity.

"Sorry, that was supposed to be funny," I said. "Have any of you ever seen Star Trek?"

Nearly all of them nodded, smiling politely. "I have met Mr. Roddenberry," said Far Polk. "He was quite imaginative..."

I appreciated that she had prevented herself from ending the sentence with, "...for a human."

Smiling sincerely, I said, "I envy you, Far Polk. I wish I could meet him, myself."

"Perhaps I might introduce you to him one day."

"The laws concerning non-interference are not quite as binding as your fictitious 'Prime Directive'," said Dok Fil. "Planets found to have sentient life forms are monitored, but left alone until sociologists determine how disruptive to their culture first contact will be. In the case of Earth, though, since it had once been a colony, it is still a Denebian protectorate. No contact with Earth is allowed unless sanctioned by the Denebian government. As Mediator of the Galactic Council, I am the only Aldebaran—the only nonhuman, really—allowed to make contact without first obtaining express permission. Not that Deneb has ever expressed any desire that I not do so."

"You still haven't told us about the Sol-Deneb Treaty," said Jack. "Is it time, yet?"

Dok Fil smiled. "Yes, it is time. Thank you for your patience up to this point. The Sol-Deneb Treaty stipulates that Deneb will not destroy Earth, so long as the *Umea Bakearen* lives."

"Why would Deneb want to destroy Earth?" I said. "I thought Deneb was protecting us?"

"It was, until the Roswell Incident in your year 1947. One of the Denebian survey ships crashed, killing all three men aboard. That was the beginning of hostilities between the planets. It came to a head in 1967, after the fire that destroyed Apollo 1."

"Why?"

"By then, Deneb had placed observers within the space programs of Earth's most powerful nations. Although the Denebians had nothing to do with the accident, their presence was discovered during the investigation that followed. They were discovered, and detained. In Russia, the observers were tortured, and executed for espionage."

Tanya looked down at the ground. "In my country's defense, it was during Communist rule. Such a thing would not happen today, one would hope."

Dok Fil nodded to Tanya sympathetically. "No blame is placed on your generation, Captain Orlov. But at the time, Denebians became furious. They wished to cleanse Earth once again. My office intervened, and I proposed Sol-Deneb. Wayne Freed of Earth, and his counterpart, Ben Elan of Deneb, had been born at the same hour, millions of light-years apart. Knowing a bit of both planets' traditions, I saw a way to defuse the situation. In Indonesia, warring tribes will sometimes exchange infants in order to avert conflict. Both tribes will protect their Peace Child as a show of trustworthiness. On Deneb, twin children are viewed as special, almost sacred."

I tilted my head. "So Wayne Freed and Ben Elan switched places?"

"They switched identities," said Dok Fil. "The man living on Earth as Wayne Freed was born Ben Elan. He finally learned of his own identity just a few years ago."

"That must have come as a shock to him," said Kayla. "The poor guy must have been lonely. Both of them."

"Actually, both of them are rather famous on Deneb," said Kat. "Wayne received a standing ovation the first time he appeared at UnionCon."

"UnionCon?"

"The ultimate social and political event of the year," said Dok Fil. "Delegates and guests from all around the galaxy come together for three weeks of cultural exchanges, interstellar relations, and entertainment. As DSS agents, one of your duties will be to escort Wayne to UnionCon every year."

"That kind of sounds fun," I said. "Like a nerd convention

on steroids!"

Dok Fil smiled. "I think Wayne will like you, Agent Diego. I truly hope so, because Agent Moss is correct. He has very few—if any —friends on this planet who know his true identity. He will not even allow himself to find happiness in a love bond, not only because of the importance of finishing his law degree, but because he cannot let those he loves know of his true identity. I know that such a role does not normally fall under the purview of security, but your friendship will be as important to him as your protection. This, I have foreseen."

Chapter 4: Training

I was a little thankful that Remington did not seem to require our companionship on the flight to Deneb. He spent most of his time in his own stateroom, venturing out only for meals.

"Aren't we supposed to be escorting the man?" asked Rita.

Biggs shook his head. "Negative. He just happened to need a ride. This is a training flight for the team, to give you all a taste of space travel, and to get you used to working with ETs."

"It's funny," I said. "All my life, I thought it would be exciting to travel to other planets, but now that we're out in space, it seems kind of dull. I've looked out some of the viewports, and all there is to see is black, with white dots. It doesn't even look like we're moving. I thought I might get a look at Jupiter or something, at least."

"That's your first lesson, Tony. Space is routine. The second lesson is that it's also deadly. If this ship suddenly lost pressure, we'd all be dead within seconds."

"Cheerful thought."

"There isn't any traffic in our system, so we aren't likely to be attacked by pirates, but it's possible just about everywhere else." He pointed at his right eye. "This eye is fake. It's a very good fake, but it's a reminder to always be on your guard. I lost it when someone on Betelgeuse thought it would be fun to harpoon the *Umea Bakearen*."

"Ouch," I said.

"Betelgeuse is a great place to lose an eye. They are the best prosthetics designers in the galaxy. My wife doesn't even know it's fake."

"Is it functional?" asked Jack.

Biggs nodded. "I can read a menu from the other side of the restaurant, if I want to. I can program it for night vision, too."

"Like Geordie on *Star Trek*," I said. "Can you do X-ray vision?"

Kayla scoffed. "You would be the one to ask that."

Biggs smirked. "I don't need X-ray vision to see when someone puts their foot in their mouth, Diego. You should probably learn to filter what comes out of yours, or you're liable to lose more than an eye."

"That's not even what I was thinking about!"

"Of course not," said Kayla.

"Honest! I was thinking it would be useful for detecting hidden weapons, you know?"

"That's not a bad idea," said Biggs. "I should probably look into that. I don't even know what all this eye can do."

***

After the training session ended, Biggs took me aside. "I thought you were going to try not to alienate Agent Moss, Diego."

"I am trying, Boss. But she's got it in her head that I'm some kind of frat boy, and nothing I say seems to change her mind about me." I shrugged. "I used to think I knew how to charm women, but she's way out of reach. Like we don't even speak the same language. You know what I mean?"

"I sympathize. My wife was way out of my league, and I knew it."

"How did you get her to marry you, then? I mean, if it's okay to ask."

"Getting up the nerve to even talk to her was the biggest step. I got lucky, though. We were both at a party back in high school, when this guy started pestering her. I got him to leave her alone."

"How did you do that?"

"I asked her to dance with me."

"I thought you might have punched him out or something."

Biggs snorted. "Women don't want to be rescued, Tony. I just gave her the means to rescue herself. She didn't have to dance with me. If she had said no, I would have walked away."

"So she just found you less annoying than the other guy."

"That about sums it up. Romantic, ain't it? While we danced, we talked. After the dance was over, we kept talking. By the end of the night, I wasn't afraid to talk to her anymore. We became friends. One night, after we said goodnight, she kissed me. I married her the day we both graduated college."

"Some guys get all the luck," I said.

"You want Moss to notice you?"

"That would be against company policy," I said. "You said so, yourself."

Biggs nodded. "Yeah, it'll cost one or both of you your jobs. But if you want her, you're going to have to be less annoying than the other guy."

"What other guy?"

"All of them."

"That sounds like a lot of work."

"Well, then, in that case, try to be more irritating than anyone else. I hear that works, too. Maybe alternate strategies. It'll keep her guessing."

"Do you really think that would work?"

Biggs laughed. "No."

"Then why give me that advice?"

"Because I'm often wrong."

"You're no help at all, Boss."

"Truth is, I don't know thing one about women. My wife is the only one I even think I understand most of the time. Maybe that's the key. You're not supposed to understand all women, just the one."

"So, if I ever understand Kayla, she'll love me?"

"No idea," said Biggs. "But you will love her. And that will make all the difference."

***

The ship had long corridors, which followed the outer perimeter of the hull. It wasn't extremely wide, but most of the crew used it as a jogging track. Everyone else had quickly learned to stay on the inside of the corridor to avoid collisions. Everyone, that is, except for the trainees. Jack got the wind knocked out of him twice before he learned the pattern. Kayla and Rita only took one slam each. I was a bit thicker in the head than they were, and I got whacked several times. The last time earned me a trip to the infirmary. Not for myself, but for the poor unfortunate soul who ran into me.

"Nice going, Diego," said Tanya, as I helped her hop and limp along. "Did they not tell you to always stick to the inside rail if you are not running?"

"I said I was sorry," I said, for at least the third time. "No, no one did."

"There are not many ways to exercise on a ship. Naval officers learn very quickly to run counter-clockwise around the deck, keeping to the right. If you are not running, you are supposed to stay out of that lane."

"I was Air Force," I said. "We were not generally encouraged to run around our planes while in flight."

Tanya laughed, in spite of her bruised and swelling knee. "Spaceships do operate more like boats than planes."

***

The ship's doctor was a man named Moses Howard. He had a pretty good bedside manner when dealing with patients. It was far better than his manner in dealing with us idiots who put them there.

"I might have known you were going to put someone in here sooner or later, Diego." He had been one of my previous collisions. "It isn't that hard to figure out. Stay to the inside!"

"Is it broken?" asked Tanya.

Dr. Howard looked at his scanner. "No, it's working just fine."

Tanya laughed, in spite of her pain. "I meant my knee."

"Yes, of course." He opened a cabinet and retrieved an immobilizer and a pair of crutches. "You've a hairline fracture of the patella. I won't cast you, as long as you keep this on. Don't try bearing weight for at least three weeks. Elevate your knee whenever you're sitting or lying down."

"I'm really sorry," I said. "Isn't there some way to make it up to you?"

Tanya sighed. "I forgive you, Tony. Just please remember to stay on the inside curve, okay? The next leg you break might be your own."

***

Kayla shook her head when she saw me bringing Tanya a tray of food in the mess hall. "So, you finally got a woman to fall for you, eh?"

I rolled my eyes. "Is that the best you can do? I feel bad enough already."

"At least he has learned his lesson," said Tanya. "I think he'll not be a menace to any more runners."

"What's the damage?"

"I broke her kneecap," I said.

"The floor did that," said Tanya. "Diego just assisted. But he was kind enough to help me to the infirmary, and he is now acting as my personal valet, so it isn't all bad."

Kayla laughed and sat next to Tanya. "You have a better sense of humor about this than I would have."

"Tony is not a bad man," said Tanya. "An idiot, perhaps, but not bad."

"I'm still here, you know."

"Oh, don't pout," said Tanya. "I did say you are a not bad idiot. Nor am I banishing you from my presence."

"Of course not," I said. "You need me more now than ever before."

Biggs walked into the mess. "Just wanted to let you know that we're jumping in less than an hour."

Tanya pointed at the immobilizer. "I will not be jumping anywhere."

Biggs grinned. "I see that. Nice going, Diego. No, I mean a hyperspace jump. We're near the outer edge of our solar system."

"Will the jump be rough on her knee?" I asked.

Biggs shook his head. "No. You won't even feel the jump. God help you if we need to do an emergency thrust, though."

Tanya glared at me. "No. God help Tony."

***

After dinner, I carried some extra cushions to Tanya's quarters. "Here. To prop your leg up. Is there anything else I can do for you before I turn in?"

Tanya handed me her ice pack. "Would you mind getting fresh ice for me?"

"No problem," I said. "It's the least I can do."

The ice machine was in the galley. I showed the pack to the rather overprotective cook and told him it was for Tanya. Only then would he let me in, but he insisted I stand still while he filled the ice pack. "You have a reputation for getting in the way, Diego. There are sharp things in here."

I rolled my eyes. "So I made one mistake!"

"I heard it was more like three or four," he said. He began counting off on his fingers. "You tripped up Doc Howard. You tripped up Samuelson. You broke poor Tanya's leg. Have I left anything out?"

"I accidentally ran over a squirrel in the road when I was eighteen," I said. "But I swear he was suicidal!"

Cook looked at me for a moment. Then he laughed. "Ah, I suppose you can't be all bad. Just remember to stick to the inside of the perimeter corridor, okay?"

"If someone had mentioned that to us before we got on the ship, none of this wouldn't have happened, you know. I wasn't the only one to trip up a runner." I thought for a moment. "I wasn't even the only one to do it more than once. Forbes did it twice!"

Cook held up three fingers. "You still hold the ship record. Forbes' second collision was not quite his fault, either. The runner was cutting a corner."

"Aha! See? It's not always the pedestrian's fault!"

"No?"

"Okay, all three of mine were my fault. How many times do I have to say I'm sorry?"

"Yeah, I guess you've done enough penance. I'll spread the word to start cutting you some slack. I'll have to warn you, though..."

"I know. Stay to the inside."

"Good. You can learn. There is hope for you, yet."

***

I knocked on Tanya's door. "It's Diego."

"Come in, Tony. The door is not locked."

I opened the door to find her lying in bed, her knee propped up on the cushions.

The immobilizer was the only thing she was wearing.

"Uh, I brought the ice."

Tanya smiled. "Thank you. Please, put it in the cooler. I may desire it later."

"I guess I should go."

"If you wish. I'd rather you stayed. Do you not like what you see?" She smiled. "Ah, I can see that you do."

I blushed. "Uh, won't your roommate be here any minute?"

"Kat is on duty. She will not return until morning."

"I had no idea you loved me, Tanya."

Tanya smiled. "I do not love you, Tony. I want you. Have you never heard of a *maitalea*?"

"I've heard a few of the crewmembers mentioning it, yeah. I didn't realize they were talking about sex."

She laughed. "It is a temporary relationship. We will be lovers until you return to Earth."

"Wouldn't we get in trouble? If it against the rules for co-workers to date, I'm sure sex is right out."

"We are not coworkers, Tony. You work for the American DSS, and I work for Denebian DipSec."

"I thought you were Russian."

"I am Russian. I was a naval officer, until my term of service ended. I now travel to Deneb to begin my new career in DipSec."

"Will I ever see you again?"

"Do you miss me already? We have not even slept together. Do not dwell on the future. A *maitalea* is about the now. Having this thing on my leg will limit the things I can do for you, but I promise that I will satisfy you. I do not doubt that you will satisfy me."

It did not take me very long to come to a decision. "All right. What do you want me to do?"

Tanya smiled. "First, lock the door, in case Kat does return prematurely. After that, I am sure that you will think of something."

I will freely admit that having a *maitalea* did make space travel much less tedious. During our day shifts, we barely saw each other, except during meals. Still feeling responsible for her broken leg, I carried her food trays for her.

And I always kept to the inside curve in the corridors.

***

When we landed on Deneb IV, what struck me as odd was how ordinary the planet seemed.

"Are you sure we're not back on Earth?"

"One of the reasons Earth was colonized was its similarity to Deneb," said Biggs. "Once we get out of the spaceport environs and take to the sky, you'll think you're flying over Napa or Tuscany."

Biggs was right.

"It reminds me of the Rhine wine country," said Kayla.

"Are those really grapevines?"

"Grapes originated on Deneb," said Zeru. "Three of the galaxy's most sought-after wines come from here."

"Huh. I had no idea." I laughed. "I guess that's pretty much a given about lots of things we're going to learn."

Gibbs smiled. "You've a talent for stating the obvious."

"Yeah, I know. 'Shut up, Diego.'"

"Not at all. In our line of work, the ability to see the obvious is a useful talent. We're trained to look for tells, people who seem to be clutching concealed weapons, but if you don't look for the obvious stuff, you'll totally miss the guy openly carrying a harpoon until it's too late."

"Is that what happened to you?"

Gibbs smiled. "That's need-to-know."

***

Tanya sat with her knee propped up on the sofa. "So how was your first day on Deneb?"

I poured her a glass of wine. "I kind of like it here. Deneb City is like D.C., but without the litter. And the cars here fly. Nice place you got here. Do you share it?"

She accepted the glass and sipped. "I expected that I'd have to, but DipSec takes excellent care of its agents. This apartment comes with the position."

"Sweet deal."

"Wait until you see the bed. After those tiny cots in our staterooms, we might have a hard time finding each other. Oh, and there's a tub large enough for us both." She caressed my thigh. "It might make for some interesting games."

I smiled. "I'm sure."

***

Several other *maitalea* bonds had formed between members of the crew. It was common, I learned, for unmarried crew members to form such partnerships while in space. It was, for many, merely another form of entertainment.

Even so, I could not shake the nagging guilt in the back of my mind that I was somehow being unfaithful to Kayla. It was silly,

I knew. We were co-workers, nothing more, nor were we ever likely to be. Kayla had made it quite clear that she was not interested in me whatsoever. It did not even seem to bother her that I spent my nights with Tanya.

Perhaps that was what troubled me.

***

"You sleep with me, but you desire another? Shame on you! You should have formed a *maitalea* with her."

"I'm sorry if I hurt your feelings. I really have enjoyed this."

Tanya rolled over and kissed my neck. "My feelings are not hurt, Tony. We were never meant to be together forever. I have enjoyed our time together, and I will remember our *maitalea* fondly. But I think you would have enjoyed it more if you were with Kayla rather than me. You have settled for second best."

I ran a finger across her breastbone. "You are hardly second best, Tanya."

"Ah, so I am even further down on your list?"

"What? No!" I caught her wry grin and laughed. "You're teasing me."

"You are smarter than many give you credit for, I think. Even I have underestimated you."

After we dressed, Tanya kissed me and led me to the door.

"You are a good man, Tony, and an excellent lover. I hope that one day, you will receive your heart's desire. Until then, you would be a fool to accept another *maitalea*. You might have been a fool to accept this one." She leaned forward on her crutches and kissed me again. "I do not regret that you were my fool. Goodbye, Tony Diego."

"Goodbye, Tanya Orlov."

***

"So that's it?" asked Jack, as we climbed the ramp of the ship that would take us back to Earth. "You spent two weeks together, and it meant nothing?"

"Oh, it meant something, right up until the end. Tanya says that's the way a *maitalea* is supposed to work. Great sex, no commitment."

Jack rolled his eyes. "Whatever works for you."

I watched Kayla and Rita stow their gear and take their seats for launch. "It worked for me this time, but Tanya gave me some advice that I think I'm going to take."

"Oh? What's that?"

"Stay to the inside, for starters."

Jack laughed. "Good advice. What else?"

"Never settle for second place."

"You still have a thing for Kayla, don't you?"

"Can't help it," I said. "I just hope sleeping with Tanya hasn't shut the door forever."

Jack punched my arm. "The door was already shut, bro."

"You are a lousy encourager."

Kayla nodded to us as we took our seats "Did you boys enjoy Deneb?"

"It wasn't that much different from Earth, to be honest," I said.

"At least your nights were enjoyable," said Rita, giving me a wink. "Eh, Diego?"

I smiled. "We had our moments, then she called me a fool, and we parted ways. I have no regrets. She was right."

"I hope everyone is strapped in properly," said Biggs. "It's time for you all to experience your first emergency launch."

"What's the emergency?" I asked, double checking my buckles.

"Some new recruits need some sense knocked into them, is all. This is a drill, but full-power launches are nothing to scoff at, ever. People can, and often do, get hurt if they aren't strapped in. When sirens go off, everyone finds the nearest seat as fast as they can."

Biggs had barely gotten his own strap buckled when the siren went off. "Emergency launch in thirty seconds," came Zeru's voice over the PA speaker.

Exactly thirty seconds later, we were all pressed into our seats. I felt like an elephant was sitting on my chest, and I couldn't raise my own arms. An unfortunate member of the crew flew past us, crashing into the bulkhead behind us. His scream halted abruptly as the wind—and I hoped nothing else—was knocked out of him.

I could not turn my head to see how he was doing, so I just sat, and waited, and watched the digital display counting down to what I hoped would be the end of this body-crushing thrust.

"I don't think I like this very much, Boss."

"Yeah, well how do you think he feels?" was Biggs' reply. "No one likes these things, except maybe pilots. Pilots are bastards!"

"I'm a pilot, Boss."

"Yeah, and someday you'll be up front inflicting this torture on a crew of your own. Can you guess what they'll call you? Bastard, or worse!"

The invisible forces holding us against our seats slowly eased as the digital readout reached zero.

I undid the straps and went back to see to the man who had flown past us. "He's alive, but out cold. Kay, go get a backboard from the infirmary. We should probably stabilize him before we try to move him."

"You got it," she said, and took off.

Once she came back, we strapped the unconscious man to the board and carefully rushed him to Doc Howard.

"Make a hole!" I shouted as we went down the corridor.

The crew responded by flattening themselves against the inside walls.

"I'm glad that worked," I said.

Doc Howard was ready when we got there. Kayla had briefed him when she went to get the backboard. "Pupils dilated. He's got a concussion for sure." He scanned the man's spine. "Two fractured vertebrae. Whoever thought to get the backboard probably saved his life. Definitely prevented him from being a quadriplegic for the rest of his life."

"That would be Tony," said Kayla.

Doc Howard looked at me. "Not bad, Diego. Not bad at all."

***

The rest of the trip was uneventful. Thanks to the injured man, there were no more emergency thrust drills. As word of my so-called heroism spread around the ship, I found more acceptance among the veterans than I had experienced on the way out. Even Kayla stopped treating me like an idiot. She still showed no interest in me beyond a professional acquaintance, but it was a start.

As we all paraded down the ramp, I was stopped by the man who had broken his neck. He wore a halo brace to keep his neck immobile, and used canes to steady himself as he walked, but he walked on his own power.

"I wanted to thank you, Tony," he said. "I might not be here if it weren't for you. My name is Josh Greene. Remember it, because I owe you my life. Once I'm all healed up, if there's ever anything I can do for you, don't hesitate to ask."

"You don't owe me anything, Greene," I said. "I just did my job, like anybody else here would have done. You're staying on, I hope?"

Greene smiled. "I'd nod if I could move my neck right now. I'm going to be on disability for a little while, but I'll be back. I hope I get to serve with you again."

"I hope so, too. Get well soon, Greene. Next time you hear the emergency launch siren, you'll move a little faster, right?"

He shook my hand. "You bet I will."

Biggs chuckled. "Welcome to the DSS, Agent Tony Diego!"

Chapter 5: The Umea Bakearen

My duties as a DSS agent didn't always take me off-planet. I was still a reservist in the Air Force, so I often got sent on routine courier missions. The coolest part about that was that I often got to transport people from Andrews to Groom Lake and back. Every once in a while, I got to do it in the Department van.

Less cool was the fact that I felt like no more than a glorified airline pilot. I once made the mistake of lamenting that fact to Kayla, who was my copilot on one particular routine flight.

"I used to fly Warthogs. I've flown Falcons, too. Now I'm reduced to ferrying VIPs in a Gulfstream."

"At least no one is shooting at us."

"There is that. And at least it's a jet, and not one of those rickety old cargo planes."

"Like the Hercules? Aren't you forgetting that I used to fly those 'rickety old cargo planes?' You ever try dodging flak in a Herc?"

"Whoa, sorry. I didn't mean to imply anything about their pilots. I'm sure you're all just as talented at landing and taking off as a real pilot." As soon as the words left my lips, I knew I was in trouble. "Sorry, I guess I shouldn't have said that."

"Too late, buddy. You don't think I'm a real pilot? I'll bet I could take you on. Just you wait until the next time we're in the sims."

"I really didn't mean anything. I wasn't thinking."

"That's your problem, isn't it? You don't think. You're a big war hero pilot and everyone else is just a crop duster."

"Some of my best friends are crop dusters," I retorted.

"I just bet."

"We're getting close to Tinker," I said. "You'd better call the tower."

Kayla snorted and punched her talk button. "Tinker AFB, this is Uniform Bravo One, requesting instructions."

"Copy that, UB1. You're late."

"Couldn't be helped. Turbulence."

"Not to mention the weather," I added.

"What was that?"

"Nothing, just chatter," said Kayla, glaring at me. "Is the VIP getting restless?"

"No, but my CO was."

"Please convey our apologies."

"Will do, UB1. You're clear to land."

"Very good."

I landed the plane and taxied over to where a Jeep was waiting. Two men got out and stood by, waiting for us to open the door.

"I suppose you want me to get the door, too, O great one?"

"You're not nearly as pretty when you're being sarcastic," I said, sliding out of the seat. "I'll go. Here, you take the pilot's seat for the next leg."

"Oh, thank you, sir."

***

I opened the door and lowered the stairs. "Afternoon, gents. I heard someone needed a lift? Tony Diego, at your service."

"Hi, Tony," said the older man. "I'm Robert Freed, Captain, USAF, Retired. This is my son, Wayne."

"You are the *Umea Bakearen*!" I said, snapping to attention. "Sorry, sir. I should have guessed that from our flight designation. UB1 makes perfect sense now."

Wayne Freed eyed me, smiling. "Not bad. Not everyone gets it right away. So, they don't tell you who you're picking up?"

"No, sir. They just tell us to be somewhere at some time to take on a passenger to go somewhere else."

"You don't have to call me sir. Wayne is perfectly fine with me."

"Yes, sir...uh, I mean, okay, Wayne."

"How many other people do you ferry to Groom Lake, anyway?"

"Huh?"

"You didn't know you were picking me up," said Wayne. "That must mean that others go there too, right?"

"Uh, I'm not sure I should say. It's classified."

"Naturally. If you told me, you'd have to kill me, right?"

"Not on your life!" I felt my face grow hot. "Sorry. I guess you probably have a higher security clearance than me. Most of the time, it's just some brass hat wanting to see the pretty spaceships."

Wayne laughed. "Brass hats, huh? That's one I haven't heard before."

"I probably should not have said that out loud. I'd really appreciate it if you didn't repeat it to anyone. I'm told I tend to ramble a bit when I'm tense. You're the first VIP I've flown who actually deserves the designation, if you know what I mean."

"I don't really feel like a VIP, most of the time. You must have met Dok Fil. He's more important than I am, as far as the galaxy is concerned."

"The galaxy, maybe, but on Earth, it's you. Even if hardly anyone here knows it. Are you ready to go?"

"Let me grab our luggage first," said Wayne. He headed back to the Jeep, where the driver was already opening the trunk. Wayne lifted two rather large suitcases, and brought them back to the plane. "Where should I put these?"

"I'm such an idiot!" I said. "Here, let me get those for you."

"You don't have to, Tony. You aren't my valet, just my pilot."

"Well, at least let me take one of them."

Wayne nodded. "Here, I'll give you Dad's."

"Where are you going, anyway?"

"Have you ever been briefed on UnionCon?"

"I thought UnionCon was always the last three weeks of the year. Wouldn't it be just about over by now?"

Wayne smiled. "Yeah, if they went by our year. The galactic standard year is always exactly 360 days. The end of the GSY is five or six days earlier every Earth year. This year, UnionCon runs through most of January. Next year, it'll mess up my Christmas plans."

"That must mess with your college schedule," I said.

Wayne nodded. "And how. Fortunately, this year it's during the winter break. I won't miss too much this year. Even so, I've got... a friend. She helps me keep up on my work."

"You're talking about Janet, right?"

"Wow," said Wayne. "How did you know that?"

"Her name came up during my first briefing, a couple of months ago."

"I'm not surprised. Just about everything about my life is known by someone, somewhere."

"You could let Janet in," said Robert. "She's always been a friend."

"It would freak her out, Dad. She's my only... I'm afraid she might start avoiding me if she found out I'm an alien."

"I wouldn't worry too much about that," said his father. "Of all the people we know, she's the person I would think would be the most capable of handling the knowledge of life out there."

"What about you, Tony?" asked Wayne. "How did you react when you found out there are aliens on other worlds?"

My eyes got wide. "There are aliens? Out there?"

Wayne looked startled for a moment. After a second or two, he started to laugh. "You're joking, aren't you? You already mentioned meeting Dok Fil, and you knew I am *Umea Bakearen*."

I smiled. "Technically, I didn't mention Dok Fil. You did. But, yeah, I know. How did I take it? I thought Biggs was joking, at first."

Wayne nodded. "Leroy's a good man. He's saved my life at least once or twice. I had hoped I might see him this trip."

"I don't know," I said. "If he were coming, he probably would have flown with us."

"Us? Who's your copilot? I wonder if he's someone I've met."

"No she isn't," said Kayla, stepping out of the cockpit door. "Kayla Moss. I'll be your pilot, Mr. Freed. Tony's taking the second seat on this leg."

Wayne smiled and shook her hand. "Pleased to meet you, Kayla. Call me Wayne, if you don't mind. Mr. Freed is my father."

"That'll be me," said Robert. He shook her hand and said, "You can call me Robert. I never much cared for titles, even when I was my son's proxy at UnionCon."

"Does the rest of your family ever travel with you?" asked Kayla.

Both men shook their heads sadly. "My wife... she doesn't remember the exchange that sealed the Sol-Deneb Treaty, and our daughter has never known."

"I'm sorry to hear that," said Kayla. "That seems hard on both of you."

"It was for the best," said Robert.

"It still sucks," said Wayne.

Kayla frowned. "I'm sorry if I stirred up a sore spot. I was just trying to be friendly."

"It's okay," said Wayne. "Dad and I have this same discussion often. It usually ends the same way. Mom went through a depression while I was still a baby. She knew I wasn't really her son, and it was killing her. Dok Fil erased her memory."

"Not erased," said Robert. "Locked away. If ever the time is right, her memory can be restored."

"What would that take?" I asked. "For the time to be right, I mean."

"Someday, Earth may be ready to see what's out there," said Wayne, gesturing toward the sky. "That's my dream, for this planet to join the interstellar community and the Galactic Union. But they're still not ready. The galaxy is still afraid of what might happen if Terrans, uh, 'got loose', I guess is the best way to put it. I hope that doesn't offend you two."

"I know what you're talking about," I said. "Dok Fil told us about how Earth came to have humans on it. I don't blame the galaxy for fearing our nukes. They scare the crap out of me."

"That sounds weird, coming from a fighter pilot," said Kayla.

"Yeah, well, maybe I am weird."

"No 'maybe' about it! Come on, let's get these folks to their ship."

Once we were in the air, I looked over at Kayla. "Do you really think I'm weird, being afraid of the idea of a nuclear war?"

She sighed. "No, it scares me, too. I hope he succeeds in getting nukes disarmed. I doubt he will, but I hope so."

"I think he likes you," I said.

Kayla blushed. "Why would you tell me that?"

"Because I think you like him."

"I think it doesn't matter," said Kayla, setting her face.

"You heard Dok Fil. He wanted us to be his friends."

"I can't be his friend, any more than I can be your friend, Tony."

I crossed my arms. "All right, Moss, I understand why we can't be lovers, since we're coworkers, and it would be unprofessional—"

"Not to mention disturbing."

"—but why can't we be friends? Jack and I are friends. We have been since we both were kids. Don't you have any friends at the DSS?"

Kayla shrugged. "Sure, I do."

"So why don't you want to be my friend?"

"Do you really want to know, Diego? It's because to you, I'm not a person. You think women are put on Earth—or whatever planet—to please men. You slept with Orlov every night for two whole weeks. Since we returned from Deneb, you haven't even called her once, have you?"

"No. But Tanya hasn't called me, either. We agreed going into it that it was going to last until I came home, and then we would go our separate ways when it was over. She called it a *maitalea*."

"I don't care what she called it," said Kayla. "And yeah, I know there were other couples doing it. That doesn't make it any better."

"I didn't realize I needed your approval, Agent Moss. It wasn't even my idea in the first place. She initiated the whole thing, not me."

"I'll bet it didn't even occur to you to say no."

"What am I supposed to do when a lovely, naked woman invites me into her bed?"

Kayla shook her head and laughed. "Yeah, I'm sure it went exactly like that. You walked into her room and she was just lying there, asking you to take her, right?"

I smiled. "That is kind of how it happened. Why does that surprise you, anyway? You don't think a woman would be attracted to this body?"

"There has to be something more to you than good looks."

"Ah, so you think I'm good-looking?"

Kayla snorted. "Okay, so maybe in your case there isn't. You like my legs, or my butt, or whatever, but you don't know who I am. All you care about is stuff you can see."

I blinked. "How am I supposed to know things I can't see?"

Kayla's eyes burned through my soul. "When you can answer that question, Tony Diego, then, and only then, will I even consider calling you a friend."

"I... guess I'll have to get back to you on that. Uh, if you don't mind, I need to go back and use the rest room."

Kayla cracked a smile. "You should have gone before we left. Go on, I've got things under control."

***

"Everything all right?" asked Wayne as I came back through the passenger compartment. "Your face is really red."

"Huh? No, it's just a little warm up front. Heater seems to be working overtime. Can I get you anything? These VIP planes usually have a pretty-well-stocked bar and fridge."

"No, thanks. What's our ETA, do you know?"

"About two more hours. Sorry the Learjet isn't as fast as one of those special cars."

Robert laughed. "It's no problem. Strictly speaking, we're only supposed to use those under special circumstances. Maybe someday they'll be everywhere on the planet."

I grinned. "That would be nice."

Returning to the cockpit, I handed Kayla a can. "I got you a diet coke from the fridge while I was back there. Since we're on duty, I figured rum would be out of the question."

Kayla blinked. "How do you know I drink rum and diet coke?"

It was pretty much the only drink I had ever seen her order whenever the team relaxed at the lounge. "Lucky guess."

"Thanks," she said. "I'm sorry if I hurt your feelings. I might not like you, but I don't hate you."

I laughed. "I'll take what I can get."

***

Once we arrived at Groom Lake, Kayla and I received new orders from the base commander. "I just received word that you two are to accompany the UB and his father to UnionCon." He handed us envelopes containing the official orders.

"What happened to the assigned detail?" asked Kayla.

The commander shrugged. "No idea. Orders didn't say."

"This is just great," I said. "I didn't bring a change of uniform or anything. I was expecting to fly back to Andrews this afternoon!"

Kayla rolled her eyes. "Didn't Biggs ever tell you to always be prepared? Didn't the Boy Scouts teach you that?"

"I was never a Boy Scout," I grumbled.

"Why am I not surprised? Looks like you'll be doing laundry in your skivvies every night, then. You did at least bring an extra set of those?"

"Um, no."

Kayla sighed, shaking her head. "If you're lucky, maybe the ship's quartermaster will be able to help, Diego. If not, I'll stand guard outside the laundry to protect your dignity."

"Thanks, Moss. That's pretty decent of you. I'll owe you one."

"I'm keeping score."

While Kayla went to retrieve her pack, I went up the ramp into the vessel and asked to see the quartermaster.

Twenty minutes later, I had three full sets of clothing in a new duffel bag, and a credit deficit on my stipend account. I hoped that meals at UnionCon weren't going to be too expensive. I stashed the new gear in my assigned bunk and went for a walk around the ship. And, yes, I kept to the inside of the corridor, even though I suspected no one would be jogging during launch preparation.

I went into the passenger lounge, where Wayne, Robert, and Kayla were already strapped in, ready to launch. I took the empty seat next to Kayla and strapped in. "I got new gear, but I'm going to be eating rice and beans at UnionCon, unless there are bunches of free samples going around."

"Don't worry about that, Tony," said Wayne. "Dad and I will give you both some spending credits once we get there. It's kind of a tradition for us."

"I like traditions," I said, which made the two men laugh. Even Kayla gave a small chuckle at that.

"While you were getting gouged by the quartermaster, I checked in with Biggs," said Kayla. "He said that the regularly scheduled bodyguards were pulled into some high mucky-muck state function at the White House. We lucked out, being halfway to Groom Lake already, because some of the senior agents would have jumped at the chance we're getting."

"Suits me fine," said Wayne. "It's about time I get to hang out with agents closer to my age than Dad's."

"You can request specific agents, given enough advance notice," I said, matter-of-factly.

"Yeah, but I don't like to show favorites," said Wayne. "Unless I get someone I really don't like, I'm satisfied with the rotation. I get to meet more agents that way."

"Have you ever had someone you didn't like?" asked Kayla.

"Not so far. Then again, I only use the DSS once a year, to go to UnionCon."

"You don't have anyone looking out for you here?" I asked. "That seems kind of dangerous. From what I've heard, this whole planet would be sterilized if anything happened to you."

"Well, think about it. I'm pretty much anonymous on Earth. I mean, how many people know who I am? They're all DSS agents or Government officials. Not even my closest friends really know who I am."

"You ever get lonely?"

Wayne cracked a half-smile. "Depends how you define lonely. At least I have some friends. I was kind of a nerd in school. I never had lots of real friends. It's hard to miss what you never had, right?"

Kayla nodded. "Yeah, it is."

"The sad part is that the folks who do know who I am, I only get to see once a year. There are some folks I don't even get to see even that much."

"You're thinking about Phoebe," said Robert.

Wayne nodded. "Yeah."

"Who's Phoebe?" I asked.

"My first love, I guess you could say. By the end of UnionCon, I was half ready to marry the girl. Trouble is, she wasn't human. She never could have come to Earth to be with me. Except for UnionCon, I'm kind of bound to Earth by the Treaty, so I never could have lived on Betelgeuse. I hear it's tough enough trying to carry on a cross-country love affair, let alone cross-galaxy."

"Sounds like hell."

Wayne nodded, sighing. "Yeah, we both decided it was best to go our separate ways. It's been a couple of years. I haven't even tried for a relationship with anyone since then."

"Not even Janet?" asked Kayla.

Wayne eyed us suspiciously. "How much do you both actually know about me and her, anyway? I hope there isn't some dossier on her at the DSS office. That would creep her out for sure."

"I'm not sure I would be allowed to say," I said. It was true enough. I didn't want Jack getting into trouble.

"Janet would most definitely be willing to kick our relationship up a notch, or two." He glanced at his father, his face reddening. "But between keeping up on schoolwork and keeping all this stuff secret, I couldn't handle the stress of letting her get any closer than she already is. If she ever found out all the stuff I've been keeping from her, I really don't want to think about what she'd do. I'd rather keep her as a casual friend than lose her entirely by revealing everything."

"She might take it much better than you think she will," said Kayla. "I know I'd want to stay with a man who cared that much about me."

Wayne grinned. "Well, if it doesn't work out with Janet, I suppose we could give it a try. I mean, you're Terran, you already know who I am, and you have the most beautiful blue eyes."

Kayla blushed a deeper red than I had ever seen. "I'm flattered, really, but I doubt I'd be effective as your bodyguard if we were... I mean, if that happened."

Wayne winked. "I'm kidding, Kayla. Mostly. You do have lovely eyes. But I'm not looking for a permanent relationship with anyone right now, and I'm not the *maitalea* type, either. I would have you as a friend, though."

"I think that can be arranged. I like you, Wayne Freed."

***

Okay, I'll admit that I was a bit jealous of Wayne at that point. Kayla had just told me less than two hours before that she didn't offer her friendship that easily, yet he had won her over after a short conversation. What did he have that I didn't?

My first thought was that she was attracted to his fame. But he had already said that he was anonymous on Earth. Interstellar fame didn't quite resonate with me, and I was fairly certain it didn't faze Kayla, either.

I didn't get it. If Kayla wanted to be friends with Wayne, and not with me, that was her business. I could get any woman I wanted. My *maitalea* with Tanya had proven that.

Except, I reminded myself, I didn't want Tanya.

I wanted Kayla.

I wanted to dislike Wayne, because he could get away with flirting with Kayla, and I couldn't. But Wayne was too damned likeable. Genuine was the word I'd use.

Maybe that was it. Kayla liked Wayne because he was genuine. Heck, I liked him, too.

Was I not? And if not, how could I become genuine?

My head began to hurt. I decided I would figure it out some other time.

***

I'm not sure exactly how I could describe UnionCon, except that it reminded me of a huge comic book or sci-fi convention. There were lots of merchandise vendors, all kinds of strange foods, and people dressed in outlandish costumes. Except, I realized, not all of the makeup was makeup.

"This sure brings back memories," I said. "I used to go to a Con back in Jersey. I hooked up with a girl who dressed as Elvira. Man, she was hot."

Kayla scoffed. "Why am I not surprised? Did you dress up, too?"

"I was Han Solo."

"Also not a surprise."

"Yeah, Jack was Chewbacca. I don't know if he hooked up with anyone."

"Is that your main reason for doing everything? Find some girl to sleep with?"

"No, not every time. Sometimes I crash and burn."

"You are incorrigible."

Chapter 6: Business as Usual

"Looks like you've got friends in high places, Diego," said Biggs, dropping an envelope on my desk. "Wayne Freed has requested that you be on his security detail again this year. Congratulations."

"Really?" I said, opening the envelope. "I wasn't sure he'd even remember me. The whole event was pretty dull, by his standards."

Biggs dropped an envelope on Kayla's desk, too. "You're on the detail, too. Also by Wayne's request."

"Don't forget your duffel bag this time, Diego," said Kayla. "I hear the cost of spare clothes went up this year."

"Oh, haven't you read the orders? This year's UnionCon is on a 'clothing optional' planet. I won't need it."

"You're kidding." she said, quickly tearing open her orders. Once she satisfied herself that I was joking, she breathed a sigh. "Oh, thank God. I certainly didn't want to see you without your clothes. Once was enough!"

I spun in my chair, startled. "When did you...?"

Kayla cocked her finger at me. "In your dreams, Diego! I can't believe you fell for that."

"Boss, isn't that sexual harassment? She ought to get some kind of sensitivity training."

"She has to put up with you for the next month," said Biggs, heading toward the door. "That's about as cruel and unusual as department punishment gets these days."

"This says we have to leave in an hour, Tony," said Kayla "We'd better get moving. With traffic, it's going to take almost that long to get to Andrews!"

"You guys get all the luck," said Jack. "Rita and I still haven't gotten a chance to even meet the guy!"

"I'll send you a postcard," I said. I glanced at Kayla's back as she departed and added, "Wish me luck, bro."

"It'll take more than luck," said Jack, smiling mischievously.

"Have fun, kids!" shouted Rita as I ran after Kayla.

After having to shell out for new uniforms the last time, I had begun keeping the extra uniforms in my locker. After a quick stop to retrieve my bag, I was just as prepared for the trip as Kayla always seemed to be.

An agent drove us to Andrews, where a plane was fueled and ready for us to fly it to Tinker.

"I guess we made an impression on Wayne last time," I said, once we had reached cruising altitude. "Were you surprised?"

"A little," said Kayla. "Then again, he did say that he liked having people his own age around. Maybe that's what prompted him this time. I don't blame him. I don't know if you noticed, but some of the veteran agents just aren't that much fun to be around."

"I'm glad to hear you say that," I said. "I thought it was just me."

Kayla looked at me. "I never said you aren't fun to be around."

"No, I meant, I thought I was the only one who got bored at the office parties." I tilted my head. "So, you think I'm fun to be around?"

She wrinkled her nose. "I didn't say that, either."

I was about to say something indignant when she cracked a smile. "Oh don't get so testy. I'll admit, you're fun to be around. Most of the time."

"Really? When am I not? I mean, just so I can narrow it down."

Kayla shook her head. "If I told you, it would take the fun out of it."

"You frustrate me, sometimes," I said. "Just so you know."

"I'm sorry. I don't mean to. Maybe we just have conflicting goals."

"Okay, why don't we state our goals so that we can work together on them."

"You go first."

I thought about it for a moment. "I'm not sure I can state my goals without violating the strict 'no harassment' policy at the DSS."

Kayla rolled her eyes. "I knew it! After all this time, you're still thinking with your... Damn. I can't finish that sentence."

"The strict 'no harassment' policy makes it tough, doesn't it? Did you know my Uncle Luis used to be Secret Service?"

"Really? No, I didn't."

"When he was active, only men were allowed in certain departments. Even after they started letting women enter the workforce, no department heads worth their salt would put men and women together in a team. Partners like us would have been right out."

"We aren't partners."

"Not all the time," I said, "but we are right now. Pilot and copilot. That makes us partners, at least for the duration of the mission. Even so, we're a team: you, me, Jack, Rita, and Biggs. Back then, that would have never happened."

Kayla grunted. "So, what's your point?"

"There didn't need to be a 'no harassment' policy when there were no mixed partners. The guys could talk about whatever was on their minds. Do you have any idea what was on their minds most of the time?"

"Sex, probably."

I pointed a finger at her. "No! You know why? Because they didn't have to be afraid to talk about it! They would talk about sports teams, or who they thought the next president was going to be."

"So, you're saying that because you aren't allowed to talk about sex, it's all you can think about."

"Is that what I'm saying?" I wrinkled my brow. "Actually, I can't remember what I was trying to get at. Bummer. It was probably profound, too."

Kayla laughed. "Well, there was ten minutes wasted."

"Passing time isn't wasting it." I said, indignantly. "Maybe now you'll understand me a little better."

"I think I understand you pretty well. You've been wanting to get into my pants for almost two years, now."

"Really? Has it been that long?"

"You aren't going to deny it?"

"What's the point? Even if I did deny it, you wouldn't believe me. Besides, I'd be lying."

Kayla rolled her eyes, then laughed, shaking her head. "You're pretty clever, aren't you? You have somehow managed to hit on me in such a way that you would never get in trouble for it."

I grinned. "Yeah, and you want to know the best part? You're going to spend the rest of the flight trying to figure out how I did it. And the only conclusion that you are going to be able to come up with is that maybe our goals don't conflict that much, after all." I stood up. "I'm getting a ginger ale. You want a diet coke?"

"Sure. Thanks."

I took my time getting back to the cockpit. I felt like I had won a victory, and I wanted to relish it, while giving Kayla a chance to mull it over.

***

Wayne was waiting for us on the tarmac.

Kayla gave him a hug. "Hi, Wayne. Just you, this year?"

"Yeah, Dad and I talked it over and he decided that I'm finally old enough to travel on my own." Wayne scoffed. "Can you believe that? I'm twenty-four years old!"

I laughed. "I turned twenty flying combat missions over Iraq."

"You were in Desert Storm?"

"We both were," said Kayla.

"I didn't know they allowed women to fly combat missions."

"Uh, they didn't," I said. "Kayla was a transport pilot."

"Oh, sorry. I hope that's not a sore spot."

Kayla sighed. "No, I'm used to it, by now. I was near the top of my class, and still they wouldn't let me fly combat."

"Sounds like it is still a sore spot. I'm sorry."

"It's okay, Wayne. Not your fault. At least now they're finally changing the rules."

Wayne nodded. "If you were twenty during Desert Storm, you're what, twenty-two now?"

I nodded. "Yup."

We both looked at Kayla.

"What? I don't have to tell you how old I am."

"No," I said, "but I won't stop pestering you until you do."

Kayla exhaled, making a flappy sound with her lips. "You won't stop pestering me, period. Okay, fine. I'm twenty-six!"

I whistled. "No wonder I annoy you. I must be like a little kid to you!"

"Watch it, bucko. You're like a little kid to lots of people."

"Do you have a sister closer to my age?"

"Do you want me to throw something at you?"

"Well, anyway," said Wayne, "I'm glad you're accompanying me again this year. This was the first time I'd ever requested anyone. I wasn't sure DSS would honor it."

I smiled. "I can't speak for Kayla, but I was glad to get the orders."

"Ditto, here," said Kayla. "What made you pick us, anyway? As I remember, last year's UnionCon was kind of dull for you."

Wayne smiled. "Oh, it was, you have no idea. But it was the first time for both of you, wasn't it?"

I coughed. "Uh, say what?"

"Mind in the gutter, again, Diego?" Kayla laughed. "Yeah, it was the first time we had ever been to UnionCon."

Wayne nodded. "I could tell. You reminded me of myself the first time I ever went. After it was over, I got to thinking how much more fun UnionCon is when you're there with folks who don't think of it as just an assignment. I liked having people my own age around, for a change."

"I totally understand," said Kayla.

"We should probably get underway." I headed up to the cockpit without waiting for an answer. I really hated being the youngest person in the room. I figured that was probably the reason she was more attracted to him than to me.

***

We'd been in the air for about half an hour when I decided to stretch my legs. "Be back in a few."

Kayla nodded. "No problem. Bring me back a diet coke, please?"

"Sure."

Wayne was on his computer. "Hey, Tony. Everything all right?"

"Yeah, just getting drinks. You want anything?"

"No, thanks. Tony, can we talk for a minute? Man to man?"

"Sure, Boss, what's up?"

"I've noticed a bit of, I guess tension is the word I'd use, between you and Kayla. Was it a mistake for me to request both of you together?"

I shrugged. "I promise you that whatever friction there is between Kayla and me won't affect our ability to keep you safe."

"I'm not really worried about my safety," said Wayne. "I'm more concerned about... well, I'm not sure exactly how to put it... I hoped we could all have some fun together. If I know Ben, he's going to have a girl on each arm, and he'll think he's doing me a 'favor' by introducing one of them to me. If that happens, then the six of us are going to end up paired off."

"I think I get the picture," I said. "You want to know which one of us ought to pair off with Ben's girl, and who gets stuck with Kayla, right?"

"Well, I don't think I would have used 'stuck with' as the verb, there. Kayla is a pretty woman, don't you think?"

I looked back toward the cockpit. "Really? I hadn't noticed."

"Yeah, right. Of course, Ben might surprise me and only have one date." He chuckled. "On the other hand, he might have two, and keep them both for himself. He always was sort of a ladies' man."

"You know, Boss, it's really not my place to speak for Kayla. Maybe you should ask her how she would want to handle the situation."

"To be honest, I really hope the situation doesn't come up at all. I've told Ben that I'm capable of making my own mistakes when it comes to women."

I laughed. "I hear you, there. Look, as far as Kayla and me are concerned, I'm Chachi to her Joanie."

Wayne laughed. "Before or after the spin-off?"

I sighed. "Before. Definitely before."

Wayne nodded. "Wish I could give you some advice, but I've not exactly been that successful in relationships myself. Just remember that Joanie loved Chachi, in the end."

"Yeah, but it didn't last. One season and out, if I remember right."

"You're not thinking it through, Tony. The show might have been cancelled, but for all we know, they could have lived happily ever after."

"Well, here's hoping. I'd better get our Cokes and go back. Kayla might need me." I smiled. "I wish."

Chapter 7: UnionCon 2025 GCE

Alpha Libra III was host for that year's UnionCon. It was a tropical planet; at least, the region where the convention center was located was tropical. The indigenous population had apparently never developed air conditioning, and instead had adopted a minimal-clothing lifestyle.

"I thought you were kidding when you said the planet was clothing-optional," said Kayla as we stepped off the cruiser's ramp.

"I was totally kidding," I said. "I had no idea, honest!"

Of the three of us, only Wayne had dressed appropriately for the climate. "Don't they give you agents any kind of briefing before they send you out?"

Kayla wiped sweat off her brow. "You'd think so, wouldn't you?"

"You two are going to melt if we don't get you into lighter clothing. Let's find a shop."

"You really don't need to do this," Kayla protested.

"It's my pleasure, really. I'm embarrassed to say how much I get paid by the United Nations just to not get killed. I don't have a girlfriend to spend my money on, so why shouldn't I spend it on my friends?"

By the time we were finished shopping, Kayla and I each had a week's worth of tropical weather garb.

Wayne smiled. "Now you look much more comfortable."

Kayla frowned. "I don't feel very professional in this." She wore a silk hula skirt, a bikini top, and tennis shoes.

"I suppose it depends on one's profession," I said. My new outfit consisted of a tank top, cargo shorts, and sandals.

"You're enjoying this, aren't you?"

I raised my hands defensively. "I plead the fifth."

***

Ben Elan met Wayne in front of the UnionCon Center. Kayla and I followed at a discreet distance, close enough to intervene should the need arise without looking like hired goons.

I heard Kayla inhale sharply and turned to see what was wrong. She had regained her composure and put on a neutral expression, but I could tell she was less than comfortable with something. "What's wrong?"

"Nothing's wrong. I just spotted Elan's escort."

I followed Kayla's eyes until I spotted Tanya Orlov strolling toward us. Though her attire was similar to Kayla's, her skirt had a slightly higher slit that showed more leg as she walked. Her bikini top seemed to reveal a lot more than it covered.

"Hello, Tony Diego. You are handsome as ever, even if you are a bit overdressed for my taste. Are you still keeping to the inside?"

I smiled. "Hi, Tanya. You look amazing, as always. Yeah, no one else has fallen for me like you did."

Tanya winked. "Not even your lovely partner? A shame. Good to see you again, Agent Moss."

Kayla shook Tanya's hand and nodded. "Likewise, Miss Orlov. Tony, keep an eye on Wayne. I need to use the rest room."

"There is little chance of an incident," said Tanya. "It would not be easy to conceal any kind of weapon under the sorts of garments worn here. I feel practically naked, myself."

I watched Kayla hurry out of the courtyard, fairly certain I had just gotten myself demoted back down to "not hated."

If I was lucky.

I caught up with Wayne. "Uh, Boss, do you mind if I step out for a sec? I think my partner might be ill."

"Go ahead," said Wayne. "I'll be here with Ben and Miss Orlov. We're just waiting for Ben's girlfriend."

I found Kayla sitting on a bench near the ladies' room and approached with caution. She was still carrying a gun, after all. "Are you all right? I didn't think I said anything that inappropriate."

Kayla laughed, which made me feel better, somehow. "I'm not mad at you, Tony."

"Then why did you leave?"

"So I wouldn't punch Orlov in the face. The way she was acting all nonchalant, like you never meant anything to her. You deserve better than that... bitch."

I sat down beside Kayla and gallantly resisted the urge to put an arm around her. "You really don't understand *maitalea* relationships, do you?"

"No, I guess I don't."

I sighed. "Tanya and I enjoyed each other's bodies for a

pre-agreed-upon term. It was more like a contract than a relationship. We literally had no commitment to each other. You must have noticed that we hardly even talked to each other when we weren't in bed."

"I thought that was because you were trying to hide your affair from the crew."

"We would have had to be pretty stupid to think the rest of the crew wouldn't notice." I looked at Kayla sharply. "You really thought I was that stupid, didn't you?"

Kayla looked down at the ground. "I admit, it did make it easier to not like you."

"I guess I deserved that."

"Don't go all noble on me now. Do you still expect me to believe that there isn't a shred of regret where Tanya Orlov is concerned?"

I stood. Of course I felt regret, but I couldn't tell Kayla why, exactly. "I don't care what you believe. I never loved Tanya, and she never loved me. We just had sex. It's not the same thing." As I walked away, I added, "And believe me, I'm the last person I ever would have expected to be saying that out loud!"

I found Wayne, Ben, and Tanya in the food court.

"Is Kayla all right?" asked Wayne.

"She's okay," I said. "I think the heat's getting to her."

"Maybe you ought to bring her something cold to drink," said Ben. "There's a soda fountain just around the corner."

"I could use a drink, myself," I said. "But since I'm on duty, a soda will do."

"I'm going to see if I can find Sonja, then I'll join you." Ben, followed closely by Tanya, headed to one of the elevators.

We got in line behind a rather pretty young woman, with dark hair, a blue bikini top, and a short skirt like Kayla's. Wayne watched her carefully. I almost had the impression that he knew her, or had at least seen her before.

Kayla returned just as the dark-haired girl was ordering a tall grape soda, with extra ice. "I owe you an apology, Diego."

"Forget it," I said. "It's no big deal. You want a diet Coke?"

"Do they have Coke here?"

"There aren't any Earth brands here," said Wayne. "I'm working on it. Still, they do have a fine cola analog. Almost reminds me of this soda shop in Oklahoma."

At the mention of Oklahoma, the dark-haired girl turned to face us, apparently startled. As she did so, she knocked over her tall grape soda with extra ice. It landed right on Wayne.

"Yikes! That's cold!"

"I am so sorry," said the girl. "I just..." She looked up at Wayne and her eyes got wider than I would have thought possible. She put her hands to her mouth, as though she were unable to speak. She looked down at the purple stain on his khaki shorts, gasped, and ran away, almost knocking over a UnionCon sign along the way.

"Wait!" shouted Wayne. "Come back!"

"I can catch her," said Kayla.

Wayne held her arm. "No, the poor girl's frightened enough. What would tackling her accomplish?"

"You're the boss." She looked at Wayne's pants. "It would have to be grape, huh, Wayne?"

Wayne looked down and laughed. "I suppose I need new clothes now, myself." He looked back in the direction the girl had run. "Poor thing. You'd think she had just—"

"Spilled a drink on the *Umea Bakearen*?" I said casually. "The kid probably thinks she just caused a war."

Wayne winced. "I shouldn't have yelled. But it was cold. Did she seem... familiar to you?"

I shook my head. "We've only been to one other UnionCon, Boss."

Kayla closed her eyes. "She had dark hair, blue eyes. She's human. Probably Denebian. She seemed too short to be a Libran. Skin tone was too light, too. She didn't leave a purse or anything behind, did she?"

I looked around. "Negative. She had a fanny pack. Funny, I'd never seen anyone make one of those things look good before. It was monogrammed, though. 'LH.' Sorry, Boss. That's all I got."

"Wow, you guys are still pretty observant."

We returned to Wayne's hotel so he could change clothes. He gave the stained shorts to the concierge, who promised to have them cleaned and delivered to his room.

***

When we finally caught up with Ben an hour later, he looked pale. "What's up?" said Wayne. "You look like you've seen a ghost."

"It's Sonja's sister," said Ben. "She came back to their hotel room sobbing uncontrollably."

"What happened?"

"No idea. Sonja hasn't gotten her to open up about it, yet. She just keeps insisting she wants to go home. I've never seen her so upset. Too bad, too. I was hoping you would get a chance to meet her."

"You were setting me up, weren't you?"

Ben shrugged. "Lynne's a big fan of yours. I figured it couldn't hurt. It doesn't matter, now. They're packing to go home. Maybe next year."

"I told you, I can make my own mistakes, thanks."

"Yeah, but without me setting you up, you won't even give it a try. I'm going to head back up and see if I can help. Try and stay out of trouble without me, all right?"

Wayne grinned. "I have an easier time of it without you, don't I?"

Ben and Tanya headed for the exit.

Kayla put a hand on Wayne's shoulder. "You okay, Wayne?"

"Yeah, I'm fine."

"I won't pester you, but something's troubling you."

Wayne grinned. "That's about as close to pestering as one can get without actually doing it, Kay. I guess I'm a little jealous of Ben. I have to keep all this a secret from my closest friends. Not that I have very many, mind."

Kayla nodded. "Your whole life is 'need to know.'"

"Pretty much. For as long as I've known Ben, he's always had at least one groupie in tow. I never thought he'd get serious about someone."

I laughed. "Ambassadors get groupies? I never would have thought."

Wayne chuckled. "You should have seen the year of the Leia Slaves."

"Do tell," I said.

"I guess it was two or three years ago, now," said Wayne. "I had brought the Star Wars trilogy with me to UnionCon the year before. So just about every female fan of mine came to the autograph table dressed as the Leia Slave."

"Must have been a lot of skin that day," I said.

"Skin, fur, scales, and even feathers. Not all of my fans are human, Tony."

"Right. I should have thought of that."

"Having to resist the temptation to stare at all those bare

midriffs, I wasn't enjoying the day as much as Ben thought I should, so he was totally disgusted with me. But there was this one girl who dressed differently: a female X-Wing pilot. It was a great costume. I practically fell in love right away."

"Yeah, I love a girl in uniform," I said.

Kayla rolled her eyes.

"I never did see her face. The helmet's visor was down. I intended to ask her out, but I made up my mind just in time to see her walking away. I got up to follow her, tripped, and messed up my ankle. I never saw her again, as far as I know."

"Pity," said Kayla. "Maybe she'll show up again someday."

"I suppose. It doesn't matter, anyway. I made a promise to Janet a long time ago that we could finally try to be a normal couple once I was finished with school. By next year, I might even be ready to let her know about all this."

Kayla smiled. "So you've saved yourselves for each other all that time? That is the sweetest thing I've ever heard. Don't you think so, Tony?"

I couldn't help but crack a wry grin. "I don't know. What else have you heard?"

Wayne got to his feet and turned to face us both. "I've been planning to take her out for a romantic date in Chinatown, followed by a sunset stroll around the Reflecting Pool. I've always dreamed of a lovers' kiss beside the Reflecting Pool."

"I wouldn't mind that, myself," said Kayla.

"Well, if it doesn't work out with Janet, I'll give you a call."

Kayla's face went red. "Uh, that's not what I meant. I'm not saying I wouldn't... or that I would."

Wayne laughed. "I'm kidding, Kayla. I know the DSS would frown on such conduct. I don't want you losing your job on my account."

Kayla recovered her composure. "We could always try to keep it a secret. I'm sure Tony wouldn't blow the whistle on our sordid affair, would you, Tony?"

I crossed my arms and pouted. "I find the fact that you are even considering ruining your career on account of any man who isn't me downright disturbing on multiple levels."

Both Kayla and Wayne laughed at that one, for which I was mostly grateful. Wayne sighed. "Ah, well. Looks like we're two ships passing in the night, my dear."

"It's for the best, I'm sure," said Kayla.

Chapter 8: Crash and Burn?

The whole team attended Wayne's graduation. We didn't really expect there to be any trouble, since almost no one on Earth knew who Wayne was. Even so, we couldn't afford having our *Umea Bakearen* killed in some random act of violence, either.

The hardest part, I supposed, was beefing up security without anyone knowing we were doing it, or they might start wondering *why* we were doing it. The best way to do that was to hide in plain sight.

Kayla, Jack, and I all wore our Class A uniforms. Because this was D.C., more than half of the guests on the campus were active or reserve military, so uniforms didn't attract any undue attention. We sat scattered about the area, so that there were no blind spots. The earpieces we wore were so small that detection was virtually impossible; courtesy of our friends at the Denebian DipSec and the Office of the Mediator.

There were Denebian security people there, too, since Ben Elan had chosen to attend Wayne's graduation, as well. Dok Fil had expressed his desire to attend, but Biggs had nixed the idea.

"There is only so much that one can hide with makeup, Mediator. The area will be crowded, and it would be difficult to avoid notice. The best I can do for you is let you watch from a room with windows overlooking the field, but you won't be able to personally congratulate Wayne. I'm sorry."

"I understand," Dok Fil said. "It is disappointing. At least I can be assured that video of the event will be shown at UnionCon."

"That's the spirit," I said. "Wayne will know you're watching. I will make sure of it."

"I am pleased that you have taken my advice and befriended him. He seems much less stressed of late."

"It might have something to do with Janet," said Kayla. "I don't suppose you've heard of his plans for her?"

Dok Fil smiled. "I have. It sounds quite nice. I have toured the Capitol Mall."

"We're going to be watching the whole time," said Jack. "Uh, from a discreet distance, of course. They won't even know we're tailing them."

Dok Fil nodded. "I trust your skill. You all are a credit to your race. I shall go to my observation perch now, if someone would care to show me the way."

Biggs left with Dok Fil, and we filed out to our reserved seats. I sat a couple of rows behind Wayne. He sat beside a pretty pink-haired girl who had to be Janet. Her arm was hooked around his, and they occasionally leaned toward each other to converse.

Wayne had never seemed happier or more relaxed, in my recent memory.

"Cute couple," said Kay's voice in my ear. "Are they talking or kissing? It's hard to tell from this angle."

"You could have sat with me," I said softly. "Then you could see everything I can."

"That would kind of defeat the purpose of spreading out, wouldn't it?" said Biggs. "Cut the chatter, people. Folks sitting next to you are going to think you're crazy, or Secret Service. That would ruin the whole not-creating-a-panic strategy."

"Right, Boss," I said.

Wayne looked around as the president of the university began his speech. He must have noticed one of us, because he started looking around more pointedly until he saw me. He smiled and nodded. I winked back.

Ben sat down in the seat next to mine. "Hi, Diego. I won't bother you sitting here, will I?"

"Hi, Ben," I said. "No, be my guest. Are you here alone?"

"Sadly, yes. Well, apart from my entourage, but they're all scattered, as are your people. Sonja wants nothing to do with me."

"I'm sorry to hear that. What happened, if you don't mind my asking?"

Ben sighed. "She thinks I'm a philanderer."

I laughed. "From what I've heard, that has been your reputation. And one you carry proudly."

"Now you sound like Wayne. I guess you spend enough time with the guy that he's rubbed off on you. Not that I'm saying it's a bad thing. The guy's rubbed off on me, too." Ben shrugged. "It made it very hard to argue the point. Do you have any idea how insincere and unconvincing, 'I'm not like that, anymore!' sounds during an argument?"

I laughed. I had recently had just such an argument with Kayla. "All too well, truth be told."

"How are things going between you and that lovely agent

partner of yours?"

"Keep in mind, I can hear every word you say, Diego," came Kayla's voice once again. "Can you say 'sexual harassment sensitivity training'?"

"Uh, well, she hasn't slapped me with any harassment complaints recently." I pointed to my ear. "I'll be glad to tell you all about it when she—and everyone else—can't listen in."

Ben smiled. "I should have known. The day is still young. Who's the hot babe on Wayne's arm?"

"That's Janet. I'll have to warn you, she knows nothing of the Treaty, so if you do introduce yourself, don't say anything about who you are, or where you're from. Actually, it might be best if you don't say anything at all. Just pretend you have laryngitis and let Wayne do the talking."

"You don't trust me? That hurts. That really hurts."

"No offense intended," I said, apologetically. "But he's got years more experience at keeping a low profile than you have."

"Your point is well taken. This is good, old Terra Incognita. The one place I can go where I don't attract groupies."

"Sorry about that."

"No, you get me wrong. It's refreshing, really. You have no idea what it's like to be recognized everywhere you go."

I mulled that over. "No, I guess I don't. I always thought it would be kind of nice."

"It has its perks," said Ben. "I almost never have trouble finding a date."

"Then why are you here alone?"

Ben was silent for a moment. "I guess it's because I don't want just any girl anymore, and the one girl I do want hates me. You have no idea what that's like."

"The hell I don't," I said. "We're not that different, you know. Well, except I don't have girls falling at my feet."

"Not unless you trip them," said Jack. "Right, Kayla?"

"Shut up, Forbes."

I ignored them. "The point is, I know how you feel. This seems to be the part where I impart some bit of wisdom I've learned about relationships. I really wish I had some. I've gotten some great advice from other folks, but it hasn't done me much good, so far. I don't know if repeating it now would help you or not."

"I'll take what I can get."

"Isn't that kind of what got you in trouble in the first

place?"

Ben was silent for a moment. "You have a point."

***

After the ceremonies were over, Ben and I went over to congratulate Wayne. "Congratulations, Wayne," I said. "We're all proud of you."

"Thanks, Tony, Ben."

"Is this Janet?" I said. I shook her hand. "This guy has told me all about you. I used to think he had to be exaggerating. I apologize for that."

"Why, thank you!" said Janet.

"Where's Sonja?" said Wayne, looking around. "I was hoping I'd get to meet her."

Ben sighed. "Ah, so was I."

"They just broke up," I said.

"Oh. I'm sorry to hear that, Ben," said Wayne. "Are you going to be in town long? We can talk." When Janet grasped his hand, he amended, "Just not tonight, though. I promised Janet we'd celebrate together."

"I'm afraid I must fly out in the morning. But we'll talk again soon, yes?"

"Call me if you need to talk."

Ben nodded. "I thank you, my friend. It is nice to finally meet you, Janet. I hope to see you again soon."

As we walked away, I could hear Janet saying, "They seem like nice people. How do you know them?"

I wondered how Wayne was going to answer her.

"Did I do all right?" asked Ben. "I don't think I revealed anything."

"I think it might have been a mistake for us to go congratulate him, though," I said. "Now Janet has questions."

"I think it more important that Wayne knows he has friends," said Ben. "Don't you think?"

***

Later that evening, the team paired off to provide covert security on Wayne's date with Janet. Kayla and I would pose as a couple walking around the Washington Monument while Rita and Jack watched from a satellite van.

"I feel really odd doing this," Kayla said.

I pinned Kayla's corsage. "I know what you mean. It's their first real date, and we're spying on them."

"No, not that. Why did we have to dress up so formally?"

She wore a cream-colored bandage dress and matching heels. I was in a tux. "We do kind of look like a bride and groom, don't we?"

"In your damn dreams, Diego."

"It's grad night," said Biggs. "You've just come from a party, and you're walking the Mall. You'll look just like any of the hundred or so couples doing the same thing."

I offered Kayla my arm. "We might as well look the part."

Kayla hooked her arm around mine. "All right, let's go."

Once we were on the mall, Kayla bent down to slip off her heels. "If we've been at a party, my feet are tired." She carried them by the straps and walked barefoot.

I looked around and noticed that most of the young women walking around the Mall had done the same. "Nice touch. I don't think I would have thought of that."

"Try wearing heels on a regular basis," she said sourly.

"You ought to at least pretend you're having a good time," I said. "We're supposed to be lovers on a date."

"Well, maybe we just had an argument."

"If so, then maybe I'm apologizing for being a jerk."

"How do you know it was your fault?"

"Isn't it usually?" I said.

Kayla laughed. "I'll concede the point." She hooked her arm around mine. "Apology accepted."

We walked, arm-in-arm, down toward the Reflecting Pool

"There they are," said Kayla, stopping. "We don't want to get too close to them. Since you went and introduced yourself, Janet might recognize you."

"I wanted Wayne to know we were there for him."

"I didn't say I blame you. But it might have been a good idea to have a good cover story, first. Robert was there too. So were Wayne's mother and sister. What if one of them had asked questions?"

"Janet did," I said. "I'm sure Wayne handled it."

"Okay, now suppose Lucy asks and Robert answers. What are the odds both answers match?"

I paused. "I see what you mean. I should have stayed incognito."

"No. We're Wayne's friends. It's good he knew we were proud of him."

We made a point of staying on the opposite side of the pool from Wayne and Janet. They seemed to be enjoying themselves. At one point, they kissed.

"They do look nice together," I said.

When they separated, they both laughed.

"Ah, young love," I said.

"Wayne's a year older than you," said Kayla.

Out of the corner of my eye, I saw Wayne and Janet start to walk toward our position. "Crap. If we try to move, they might see us."

"Kiss me," said Kayla. I kissed her. We continued kissing as Wayne and Janet walked past, holding hands. If either of them saw us, they gave no indication.

They continued up the path until they reached a nice-looking '65 Mustang convertible. Wayne held the door open for Janet, who stepped in. He went around to the driver's side, climbed in, and kissed her cheek before they drove off.

Kayla and I released each other and each took a deep breath. "They're on the move," I said. "Team two, do you have them?"

"Affirmative," said Rita. "It looks like they're heading toward campus again. I guess the date is ending well?"

"It was a nice kiss," I said.

"It wasn't terrible," said Kayla. "We're heading back to the drop point." She removed her ear bud and switched it off.

I switched mine off, too. "What's up?"

"I wanted to talk without any eavesdroppers," said Kayla. "Look, I know you like me, right?"

"I'd be lying if I said otherwise."

"Well, I wish you didn't. We're supposed to be professionals."

"You can be the professional," I said. "I'm childish and immature, and I can't turn off my emotions just because I'm not supposed to date co-workers."

"It's okay to have emotions," said Kayla. "I'd be lying if I said I didn't enjoy kissing you back there. But don't expect me to do it again."

I grinned. "It's more fun if I'm not expecting it."

"I'm serious!"

"Okay. No kissing. Except maybe in an emergency?"

"Okay, I might kiss you again if we're in danger of blowing our cover, but that's as far as it's going to go, okay?"

"I doubt there's any way we might have to sleep together to protect our cover."

To my surprise, Kayla didn't get angry at that. "If it's a life and death situation, maybe."

"So you wouldn't rather die than sleep with me? I have made progress."

Kayla laughed. "I did say 'maybe.' Look, Tanya and I talked about what a *maitalea* is, and I think I understand. I've got to say, though, as far as we're concerned, it's never happening."

"I know."

She stopped walking. "What?"

"I know you're not going to believe this, but I'm not looking for a temporary sexual relationship anymore. Hell, I wasn't even looking for one when Tanya offered."

"Then why did you take her up on it?"

I shrugged. "Because I figured I'd take what I could get."

"That's what Ben said."

"Yep."

"You told him that was what got him in trouble."

"Yep."

"Dammit," said Kayla. "You're learning, aren't you?"

"Not as fast as I would like. Kayla, I like you. I think you're beautiful. And yeah, I want to take you to bed. That's all I know. You keep saying that there's more to it than that. I keep looking for it, but I haven't found it. Not yet. Maybe I will, someday. Maybe I never will."

"I can't say whether I hope you do or don't," said Kayla.

"Why is that?"

"Because if you ever do get that part figured out, there's a really good chance that I am going to find you irresistible." Kayla stopped walking. "I'm not sure I want that."

"Where does that leave us?"

Kayla stood on her toes and kissed my cheek. "It doesn't leave us anywhere, Tony. Not yet, anyway."

She took my arm again, and we walked back to the spot where Leroy would pick us up.

"You know, we don't need to look like a couple anymore. The mission is over."

"I know, but why waste a perfectly good evening?"

I had to smile. "Do you like Chinese?"

"Not particularly. You know where we can get a good corn dog?"

"Marry me," I said.

"Sure. When Hell freezes over."

"It could happen."

"In your dreams, Diego."

Chapter 9: The Falls of Polaris, 2026 GCE

We didn't see Wayne again until it was time to travel to UnionCon once more. We traveled to Tinker, as usual, to pick up Wayne for the flight to Groom Lake.

I expected to see Janet, so I was surprised when Wayne met us, alone, on the Tarmac.

So was Kayla. "Isn't Janet coming? I thought this was going to be the year."

Wayne smiled. "No, I'm still all by my lonesome."

"What happened?" I said. "Did she freak out when she found out? Did Dok Fil have to retcon her?"

Wayne laughed. "No, nothing like that. I still haven't told her. When we kissed on our date, we realized that we had become so comfortable being friends, we didn't need to be lovers. We love each other, but not romantically."

"You seem okay with that," said Kayla.

"She's still my best friend. Once she finishes her law degree, we're going to be partners. Hopefully, I'll be free to share everything with her by then. What about you two? You looked like you were enjoying yourselves when I saw you on my date."

Kay's face took on a rosy hue. "We—we were just trying to maintain our cover."

"Of course. But I saw that kiss. There was real emotion going on, there. You'd make a great couple."

"This is what I've been saying," I said.

Kayla rolled her eyes. "In your dreams, Diego."

I smiled. "All the time."

"Shouldn't we get going?"

"This is what I've been saying."

Kay's face turned even redder. "I meant to Groom Lake! Wayne has a transport to catch."

"Like it's going to leave without him."

Wayne laughed. "I see you're getting along with each other as well as ever. We should have quite the adventure together."

***

Ben Elan met us at the spaceport on Polaris. His DipSec escort consisted of two older gentlemen, rather than the young women I had come to expect.

Wayne shook the man's hand. "You look like hell, Ben. Sonja still won't talk to you, then?"

Ben shook his head. "I can't even reach her phone. She has me totally blocked. I'm still hoping I might at least run into her at UnionCon."

I nodded. "Ah. That's why Miss Orlov isn't with you this year, huh?"

"Precisely. I wanted to show Sonja that I don't need to surround myself with pretty women, not all the time. It's all for naught, though. I don't think she's even coming to UnionCon this year. I haven't been able to find her name on any hotel registries or passenger rosters."

"Oh, bad move," said Kayla. "If she ever found out you're digging that deep to find her, she could file a restraining order."

"I am lost without her. What would you do?"

She shrugged. "Sorry, Ambassador. I wish I had some good advice for you. I've been in as many successful relationships as Diego, here."

I scoffed. "I've had plenty of successful relationships! They've just been short."

"Fine. How about meaningful ones?"

"I suppose that depends on your definition of meaningful."

"You're a real pain in the ass, sometimes."

"I know. I'm working on it. Someday, I hope to be a pain in the ass all the time."

***

The UnionCon center on Polaris was huge; far larger than it looked from the outside. Entire cities were built into caves and tunnels dug into vast cliffs beside the tallest waterfalls I had ever seen. From the observation deck, we could see neither the very top nor the very bottom of the falls. At the base of the falls, I suspected the roar of the rushing water would be deafening.

"Actually," said our tour guide, "by the time the water reaches the base, it sounds like a heavy rainfall. Only a small percentage of the water reaches the base before it evaporates. The water vapor travels up with the winds to fall again as rain, thus perpetuating the cycle."

"I've never seen anything like it," said Kayla.

"Niagara Falls has nothing on Polaris," said Wayne.

"If you think the falls are spectacular now," said Dok Fil, who toured the falls with us, "You should have seen them when I was your age. The falls have dwindled significantly since then."

"I hope they don't keep on dwindling," said Ben. "Polaris would be ruined if the falls dried up. How would they generate power?"

"How, indeed," agreed Dok Fil, looking thoughtful.

The tour guide looked down her nose at us. "You need not worry about Polaris, young sirs. We Polarans are quite capable of handling our own problems."

Ben held up his hands defensively. "I meant no offense, really."

The guide just scowled at him and continued on.

***

Back in the hotel lounge, while Wayne and Ben made plans for their camping trip to the White Forests of Aldebaran, Kayla and I spoke with Dok Fil.

"I understand Wayne and Janet had their long-anticipated date after graduation," said Dok Fil. "Wayne says he isn't bothered by the way it ended. I am wondering if you have observed anything to the contrary."

"No," I said. "Actually, even though they aren't romantically involved, Janet's still around. She's his paralegal assistant."

"They're affectionate," said Kayla. "It's obvious that there is love between them. It's just not what I would call romantic love."

"Does Wayne have any other love interests?"

Kay shrugged. "Not that I'm aware of. It's a pity, if you ask me. He's a sweet man. Any woman who does catch his eye..." she sighed. "Well, let's just say that she had better appreciate him, or she'll have to answer to me."

"Janet, too, I suspect," said I. "Not to mention a million or more fans. Have you ever seen the stats on his UnionCon fan page?"

Dok Fil nodded. "He is only slightly behind Ben Elan as

the most popular diplomatic figure alive today."

"Don't you also have a fan page, Mediator?"

He chuckled. "My popularity has waned as I have gotten older. It is a hazard of having such a long life span. Many of my fans have died of old age. Wayne has fewer fans now, but if he ever finds himself in the public eye as often as Ben does now, he will eclipse Ben."

"That won't threaten their friendship, will it?"

"I seriously doubt it." Dok Fil bent down to speak more intimately. "Those two do not know it, but they share blood. Their mothers were twin sisters."

"How is that even possible?"

"I will tell you, but you must promise to keep the information confidential until such time as they discover it for themselves."

"Why tell us, anyway?"

"You are Wayne's protectors. Moreover, you are his friends, as I had hoped you would become. If he finds the knowledge too much of a shock, I think it will be a benefit to him to have friends who will have a more tempered reaction, because it will no longer be a surprise to you. Agreed?"

"Agreed," we both said together.

Dok Fil nodded. "You have heard of the Roswell Incident, yes?"

"You're the one who told us about it," I said. "Don't you remember?"

Dok Fil smiled. "My memory is not always what it used to be. And I sometimes 'remember' that which has not yet happened, so I can never be certain. One of the dead pilots was a man named Luken Zaio. He was regarded a hero on Deneb."

"I know the name," I said.

"There was a statue of the man at Deneb City Spaceport," said Kay. "In Zaio Square, to be exact."

Dok Fil nodded. "He was their grandfather. Their grandmother was a teenaged Jewish girl he rescued from the Nazis near the beginning of your Second World War. He honored her lost family by taking their name, Stein, as his own when they wed."

"I think I would have liked meeting him," I said.

"I am sure you would. I was quite fond of both him and Ada."

"Was that her name?"

"It still is her name. Ada Stein is alive, living in Paradise."

"What system is that in?"

Dok Fil laughed. "Sol. Paradise is a small town in Pennsylvania. She owns a motel there. She returned to Earth with Wayne."

"How did his mother get to Earth?"

"What do you know about Denebian twins?"

I shrugged. "I've never met any."

"That is because they are extremely rare. So rare, in fact, that many Denebians believe it to be an omen when they are born. You can probably imagine the stress this would put on the children."

"It must be hell," said Kay.

"Imagine the stress of being the twin children of a famous pilot and his widow. Ada did not want her daughters to go through such an ordeal, so when she gave birth, she begged me to take one of them to be raised far from Deneb. I brought the child to Earth, the birthplace of her mother. She was adopted by two loving people, who unfortunately died the same year Wayne was born. It was probably the sorrow of losing her parents that contributed to her emotional breakdown following the exchange of *Umea Bakearen*."

"Then why did her child have to be the one taken?" asked Kay. "That seems cruel to me."

"It had to be Wayne and Ben," said Dok Fil. "Don't you see? Two children born the same hour to twin sisters who themselves were born of people representing both of the very planets involved in the conflict?"

"That's a shit-ton of coincidence," I said. "Pardon my French."

"The term to which you are referring is of Saxon and Germanic origin, Agent Diego," said Dok Fil with a wry grin, which made his blue face and bright yellow eyes almost terrifyingly mischievous. "It does not originate from the French at all."

Kayla laughed. "You know Earth language origins?"

Dok Fil nodded. "I have spent many hours in the company of a certain Terran language professor, if you recall."

"Ah, yes, Remington," she said. "I forgot."

"Tony is correct, however. The order of events was too precise to ignore. I took it as a sign from the One. I now believe that I was correct in my assessment. This coming year is going to be a pivotal year in the Galactic Union, and it will center around those two young gentlemen."

The fear in Kayla's voice chilled me to the bone. "How can you be sure, Mediator? Can you see the future?"

"I sometimes have vague memories of things which have not yet occurred," he said. "It is a gift of the One. Sometimes they are merely shadows of possibilities, and sometimes they are clear as crystal."

"How clear are you on this one?" I asked.

He nodded. "Not as clear as I wish it would be, but clear enough to know that war is coming to the galaxy. The *Umea Bakearen* will be pawns at the beginning, but just as the pawn becomes a powerful piece when it has sufficiently advanced, one of them will be promoted before the endgame. Perhaps both of them. I do not yet know."

"That's heavy," said Kay.

"I apologize for laying this upon you," said Dok Fil, "but as I've said before, I have foreseen that he will need your friendship. And perhaps, you will need his."

Chapter 10: The White Forest of Aldebaran

"Damn it all!" Kayla punch the ceiling of the aircar. "How are we supposed to keep tabs on Wayne if we can't get a signal through these effing trees?"

"I'd love to help," I said, diving to avoid a collision with another of the monstrous flying insects that seemed to infest the upper canopy. "I'm a little busy trying to keep bug guts off the windshield!"

Kayla yelped as one huge barkmoth nearly clipped the front fender. "That was too close!"

"Tell me about it!"

"I'm glad you're flying and not me. I'd be a nervous wreck by now."

"And I'm not?"

"If you repeat a word of what I'm about to say to anyone back at DSS, I will make the rest of your life a living hell." Her face softened. "I think you're a damn good pilot."

"Oh, well, don't worry about me repeating that. They'd all say I was lying."

Kayla laughed. "I'm serious! I think you might be better than me in evasive maneuvers. You're a fighter pilot, while I'm just a cargo jockey."

"You're more than just a cargo jockey, Kay."

"I appreciate you saying that. I've been terrified of flying around critters like this since I hit a flock of geese during a routine training flight."

I made another quick course correction as another critter buzzed the aircar. "What happened?"

"Cracked windscreen, flamed out engine, and a crash landing in a field in the middle of nowhere. It took rescuers at least an hour to get to us." Kay sighed. "My instructor didn't make it. I lucked out: just a broken arm and a concussion."

Another barkmoth tried to mate with the aircar. "Screw this! I'm climbing above these damn bugs!"

"Thank you."

"Don't mention it. You okay?"

"It's been a long time since I've talked about the crash. The review board found no reason to blame me for the incident, and restored me to immediate flight-ready status."

"I'm glad you didn't die."

"Some of my classmates were not. Drake was everyone's favorite instructor. Even if the board cleared me, I still killed him, as far as they were concerned."

"That sucks. It could have happened to anyone."

"Yeah, but it happened to the girl."

"For what it's worth, I think you're a damn fine pilot, too."

"Thanks, Diego. Remember, not one word."

"Scout's honor."

"You were never a Scout. You said so yourself."

I shrugged. "I won't tell if you won't."

***

Zeru Petra laughed when we told him about our experience. "You were trying to dodge barkmoths? That must have been pretty hairy."

"Then what's so funny?" I said.

"Barkmoths won't let themselves get hit by any aircraft. They can sense a pilot's intended path, and they'll stay out of it."

"Well, they sure weren't today!"

"I think they were playing with you," said Zeru. "They probably sensed fear, and tried to bully you a bit."

Kayla blushed, and looked at me pleadingly.

"Who was afraid? I was trying to avoid having to scrape a half ton of bug guts off the car. What would you have done?"

"Just concentrate on going in a straight line. Once they realize they can't intimidate you, they usually leave you alone."

"Good to know," said Kay. She punched Zeru in the arm. "Someone could have told us BEFORE we left the damn ship!"

"It really didn't occur to me," said Zeru, rubbing his arm. "I figured someone would have told you already."

"Veteran pilots are bastards," I said.

Zeru laughed. "I guess we are. I said the same thing, once."

***

The next morning, we flew out to the ranger station nearest

their last known location. "I've got a signal," said Kay. "The campsite must be in a clearing."

I pulled up the holo-map. "Yep. Right there. Should we check in?"

"Nah," said Kay. "Let them be. If they need us, they can call."

We walked around the lot. "The trees are a lot more spectacular looking from the ground, aren't they?"

"And the barkmoths are a lot less menacing, too," she said.

We hadn't been there for more than an hour or two when a huge caterpillar came lumbering out of the woods. There appeared to be two people riding on its back.

"Now there's something you don't see every day," I said.

Kay put up her binoculars. "That's Ben Elan. He's got a girl with him."

"Oh? Maybe he made up with his girlfriend."

"There were six men when they went in," replied Kay. "Wow, Tony, I think you're right! The girl looks familiar. Call an ambulance, Tony, she looks hurt!"

I radioed for an ambulance as Ben rode up to us. "Am I glad to see you two," he said. "Help me get Sonja down, please. Be careful with her. Her ankle is broken."

Kayla and I helped Sonja down. Her ankle was expertly splinted, so we managed to avoid hurting her too much.

"An ambulance is already on the way," I said. "What happened?"

"This guy," said Ben, pointing at the barkmoth caterpillar which was nuzzling his shoulder.

"I tripped over its breathing tube," said Sonja. "I guess we really shouldn't have tried to run."

"Was talking to me really that bad?" said Ben. He sat next to her and helped her prop her foot up on his lap.

"It wasn't just you," said Sonja. "Lynne was afraid to talk to Wayne. After she spilled that drink on Wayne last UnionCon."

"That's why you look so familiar!" said Kay. "You and Lynne are identical twins, right? So there wasn't a rapist lurking around UnionCon last year after all."

"It was a few days before Lynne would talk about it." Sonja winced as a spasm of pain shot through her broken ankle. "By then, Wayne had already gone home."

"There's the ambulance," said Kay. "No, don't get up. Wait for the paramedics. They'll put you on a stretcher."

The medics gently lifted Sonja into the back of the ambulance.

"I can ride with her, can't I?" said Ben.

"Are you family?"

Ben sighed and handed them an ID. "She's my everything."

The paramedics looked at the card, then at each other. "You are Ben Elan, *Umea Bakearen* of Deneb! It is an honor."

"So I can ride with her?"

"Sorry, no. Rules are rules."

"Can't blame me for trying."

"We should wait for Lynne to get down to us," said Sonja. "And Wayne. A few minutes won't matter much to my ankle, will it?"

One of them nodded. "We will wait. But we cannot wait long, for there may be another emergency elsewhere."

"Understood," said Ben.

We watched as the barkmoth caterpillar lumbered back into the trees.

"I think I see them coming out now," said Kay, looking with her binoculars. "They're muddier than you two. Aw, they're holding hands. How sweet!"

"Are they?" said Ben. He took out a camera. "He's going to want a picture for his slideshow."

Sonja saw them walking together and began to cry. "It's about time those two got together."

Ben kissed Sonja. "We'll be right behind you, my dearest."

Sonja nodded. "I love you."

"And I love you. Always."

Ben jumped down and shook hands with the paramedics, who climbed up and sealed the door. As the ambulance lifted off, he took out his phone and called his friends who were still back at the campsite.

"We're going to have to bug out on you guys. I'll tell you all about her next time I see you. No, don't worry about the camping gear. You can have it. No, I insist! Divide it up as you wish. Yeah, the tent too. You're welcome. I'll stop by tomorrow sometime to pick up our clothes and personal stuff. Yeah, you too."

Ben gave Lynne a wink. "I told you he would like you," he said. Lynne's face turned red, and she put her head on Wayne's shoulder. He put his arm around her. They looked like they belonged together.

"There's not enough room for you in our aircar," I said,

apologetically. "It's only a two-seater."

"I've called for a cab," said Kay. "It should be here any minute. There it is now. Shall we follow you?"

"I appreciate you guys having my back," said Wayne. He looked at Lynne. "I think we're going to want a bit of privacy, though."

"No problem," I said. "You won't even know we're tailing you."

Wayne laughed. "Of course. You two should go on a proper date, instead of following us around."

"Our job is following you around," I said.

"Well, you make a cute couple, is all I'm saying."

Kay realized she was still holding onto my arm, and let go. "Not one word, Diego!"

"I wouldn't dream of it."

***

We followed their cab to the hospital and waited for them outside.

"As long as we've got time to kill, what would it take to get you to go on a real date with me? Besides a miracle, that is."

Kay laughed. "How'd you know that's the first thing I was going to say?"

I looked at her. "Seriously? It's the first thing you usually say when I talk about us. I'm not an idiot, you know."

She smiled. "No, I guess you're not. I guess the first thing it would take is for us not to lose our jobs if anyone found out."

"Are you saying that you'd consider it?"

"I said it was the first thing. As long as things are what they are, a date with you just ain't happening, Diego."

"Okay, so, what else?"

"Why are you doing this? I don't want to hurt your feelings."

"I just want an honest opinion, that's all. If I can't have you, maybe I'd still have a shot with someone like you." I winced. "That didn't come out right."

"You think, Diego? What is 'someone like me' like?"

"Well, you have nice... I mean, I like your figure."

"What else?"

"You have pretty eyes, and I like your hair."

"So the top three things on your list are my looks, my looks, and my looks. Is that about it?"

"No, of course not! There's other stuff, too."

"Like what?"

"Let me think."

"Don't hurt yourself. Let me tell you about my looks, all right? When I was in junior high school, I had bad acne, a flat chest, and crooked teeth. How many boys do you think noticed me?"

"I don't know."

"Sure you do. You just don't want to sound shallow. You might not believe this, but that gives me a bit of hope about you. By the time I graduated high school, I had my braces removed, I gained a couple bra sizes, and my acne cleared up. Do you know how many boys asked me to the prom?"

"A higher number, I'm guessing."

"A dozen, at least. I turned them all down, and went with the only boy who had ever liked me when I was ugly. Everyone thought I was insane, because he was a nerd. But he had seen me in a way you can't."

"Where is he now?"

"He owns a software company in Silicon Valley."

"How come you aren't together?"

"After graduation, he came out." Kay sighed. "He and his partner are still together after five years. If it ever becomes legal, they'll probably marry. I have a standing invitation to attend the ceremony whenever it happens."

"Maybe that's what it takes for a guy to like you the way you want. He has to be gay."

"Oh, God, I hope not!" After a short pause, Kay laughed. "You're a nice guy, Tony. I like working with you. I like having you as a friend. I just don't think you're ever going to figure out what a woman really wants."

I said nothing for several minutes.

"See? I've hurt your feelings."

"No, I'm just mulling over what you said."

"And?"

"I still don't get it."

"You're so thick, Diego."

"I know."

Wayne and Lynne came out of the hospital and hailed another cab.

"They're on the move, again," I said. "Let's go."

The cab took them to a hotel on the edge of the White Forest. The big sign out front said "Grand View Lodge."

"Wow, he moves fast," I said as Wayne and Lynne walked arm-in-arm into the lobby.

"Jumping to conclusions, aren't we? Just because that's what you would do."

"You're right," I said. "Let's go in and investigate."

The clerk at the desk was rather short for an Aldebaran, which meant I still had to look up to him. "Hi, there, uh, Quentin. I'm Agent Anthony Diego with the United States Diplomatic Security Service. This is Agent Kayla Moss. We're looking for Wayne Freed. We're supposed to be protecting him."

"Ah, you just missed him, sir," he said, after examining out badges. "Shall I call him for you?"

"Uh, no, that's not necessary," I said. "Did he happen to book a room, or did he go up with his lady friend?"

"He booked his own room, and asked for a tailor."

"Yeah, he was kind of muddy," said Kayla.

I handed him a DSS credit card. "Is there any way we can get a room near his? Preferably between his room and the elevator."

"You're in luck," Quentin said. "There is a suite available on the same floor, it's next to the elevator, and this card appears to have unlimited credit."

"Uh, we're going to need a limousine, too. And some more formal attire than what we're wearing."

"What do we need a limo for?" asked Kay. "And formal clothes?"

"If Wayne wanted a tailor, he's planning to take Lynne out," I said. "A limo is much better than a cab, and if we're driving them, we won't lose them."

"Good thinking, Tony. I'm impressed."

I winked. "Surprised, you mean."

"Same difference, where you're concerned."

"I think I can help you," said Quentin. "I'm afraid the hotel tailor will be occupied with Mr. Freed, but there are several boutiques in the area. I will arrange for your limousine while you shop."

***

Kay looked me over and smiled. "You clean up good, Diego. Very James Bond."

"Dalton, Moore, or Connery?"

"More like Lazenby."

"Ouch. That hurts." I winked. "The fact you even know Lazenby gives me hope for us, though. You look lovely, yourself."

Kay wore a form-fitting red dress and matching pumps. I found myself wishing I could see the outfit lying on the floor beside the bed, but I knew better than to say it out loud.

Back in the hotel lobby, Quentin handed me a set of keys. "Your limousine is parked in space number three out front."

"Thanks, Quentin. How much is the rental?"

"Rental, sir? Limousine dealers do not 'rent' their cars. I'm sorry, I assumed you knew that."

"I own a limo?" I said.

"Correction: DSS owns a limo," Kay said. "I don't want to be you when they audit your expense report."

"The cost was a quite reasonable forty thousand credits. Since your card had no limit, I assumed neither did you."

I shook my head. "I don't blame you, Quentin. I should have specified. I accept full responsibility."

My phone rang almost immediately. "What the hell is going on, Diego?" said Biggs. "Did you just buy a freaking limousine?"

"Uh, it seemed easier to protect the *Umea Bakearen* as his chauffeur than as a tail."

"That explains the tux and dress," said Biggs. "Do you have any idea how much you just cost the department?"

"Sure," I said, "forty thousand, five hundred Union Credits. I'm told it's a quite reasonable price."

"That's a quarter of a million in U.S. bills," said Biggs. "If you're lucky, they'll just let you add a couple decades to your ROTC contract."

"Both of us," said Kayla. "Divide it between us, Biggs."

"I knew I shouldn't have given Tony the credit card," said Biggs. "Congrats, kids. You own a limo. Maybe you can live in it when your houses get foreclosed on."

"He sure didn't sound happy," said Kay.

"I guess I should have cleared it with him first." I opened the front passenger door for Kay and she climbed in.

"Ooh, leather seats. Nice!"

I closed the door, got into my side, and pulled up in front of the hotel just as Wayne and Lynne were coming out of the hotel. "Your car, sir," I said.

"Tony, what are you doing?"

"Making life a little easier on the both of us, Boss." I opened the door for Lynne. "You look beautiful, Miss."

Lynne thanked me and climbed in.

"Nice car," said Wayne, climbing in after her.

I closed the door and got into the driver's seat. "Where to, Boss?"

"I'm not particular, Tony. I'll trust your judgment."

Kay clicked her tongue. "Wayne, you ought to know better than that." She pulled a guide to Aldebaran cuisine out of her purse. "How about a nice steakhouse?"

"Where did you get that?"

"It was in the hotel lobby. Here's one called A Steak Odyssey."

"Good choice, Kayla," said Lynne. "Sonja and I have been there."

I punched the address into the street navigator, and we were off.

***

Across the street from Steak Odyssey, there was a stand that advertised authentic Sol III-style corn dogs. "You've got to be kidding me," I said.

"Why do you think I picked that place?" said Kay. "I figured you might like to know that you could get corn dogs on Aldebaran."

"We're a bit over dressed for a corn dog stand."

"I don't care," she said. "Do you?"

"You sure you don't want to marry me?"

Kay smiled. "Pretty sure. But I'll let you call this a date, if it makes you happy."

As we ate our corn dogs, I said, "Uh, I just realized that I only booked us a single room, Kay."

"You booked a suite, Tony. It probably has a couple of rooms. It most certainly has a couple of beds. But even if it doesn't, I trust you enough to share the bed without sharing a bed."

The thought of lying next to her without touching her was just about as disappointing as one might expect. "Whatever you say, Kay."

After dinner, Wayne and Lynne went dancing at an Aldebaran Jazz club. Kay and I danced together for a couple of the faster songs, just for fun, then sidled up to the bar when the band began playing slower, more romantic tunes.

"I've decided I like Aldebaran jazz," said Kay, sipping her diet Coke and swaying to the music. "It's almost like a fusion of Chicago and Dixieland with a hint of Memphis blues."

"I like it, too," I said, sitting back and watching her body sway from side to side. Her dress was backless from her neck all the way down below the small of her back. "You really had acne in junior high? Because your skin is damn near perfect, now."

"Everything cleared up by the time I finished going through puberty," she said. "What about you? Were you one of the popular kids?"

I scoffed. "Not on your life. Me and Jack, we were geeks, through and through, right up until our senior year of high school. By then we had both decided to go to Georgetown, if we could get ROTC scholarships. Jack went Marines, I went Air Force."

"How did you remain friends, with a rift like that?"

I laughed. "My uncle Luis was a Marine, and my dad was Air Force. I figured if brothers could go separate ways, best friends could, too. You should have seen our dorm room. It was easy to tell whose side was whose. And we both kept the place immaculate, because our CO's could spring inspection at any time. It would not do for the other branch to get better marks. That's when I became a ladies' man, in college. The *chicas* really liked a guy in uniform. It wasn't hard to..." I cleared my throat. "Uh, I don't think I want to say any more about that."

Kay laughed. "You really are learning, aren't you?"

"I'm trying."

∗∗∗

When we finally got back to our suite, I was almost disappointed to learn there were, in fact, two bedrooms, each with a nice, Aldebaran-sized bed.

"Nice suite," said Kay. "We could almost invite the whole crew of the DipSec ship to sleep in here. Almost."

"Which room do you want?" I said.

"I'll take the one on the left," she said.

"All right." I kissed her and said, "Good night."

"Tony? Why did you kiss me?"

"Not sure," I said. "Seemed like the thing to do. We did say we'd call this a date, right?"

"We did, at that," she said. "I guess a kiss goodnight is appropriate. See you in the morning. First one up gets dibs on the shower?"

"Fair enough," I said. "What if it's a tie?"

"In that case," she said, just before closing her door, "we'll just have to share."

"Really?"

Kay laughed. "In your dreams, Diego."

As it turned out, she was right.

Chapter 11: Ben's Wedding

Ben Elan married Sonja Hart in a very small, very private ceremony in her hospital bed. Kay and I waited down in the front lobby, since we were family of neither the bride nor the groom. When Mrs. Elan was released from the hospital, we drove the happy couple back to the hotel in my new limo. There was plenty of room back there for Wayne, Lynne, Ben, Sonja, a pair of crutches, and a wheelchair, with room to spare if we should have happened to pick up any hitchhikers along the way.

"Aldebarans really know how to build roomy interiors," said Ben, who had his bride's surgically reconstructed ankle propped up on his lap. She had an external frame around it, with rods and screws projecting through the bones in her foot to hold the broken pieces in place.

"That really looks painful," said Wayne.

Sonja laughed. "It does look absolutely dreadful, doesn't it? It hurts far less now than it did before the surgery, though. I suppose the pain killers might account for some of that, though."

"I once had to wear a similar contraption on my right arm for a while," said Kayla. "I was nothing short of ecstatic when they finally removed it and put me in a cast."

"I'll bet," said Sonja. "Three weeks, and I should have a proper cast. That will be so much prettier for the public wedding reception. You will come to Deneb for that, won't you?"

Wayne shrugged. "I'll have to let Janet know that I'll be gone much longer than expected, but I trust her to keep the office running. Tony, Kay, is it all right with you?"

"You're the boss, Boss," I said. "Our time frame gets set by your schedule."

Kay nodded. "It's perfectly fine with us. We are driving around a city larger than the entire United States in the most comfortable vehicle I've ever been in. When we finally do get home, we're going to receive the dressing down of our lives for purchasing said limo. We're really in no hurry."

Wayne laughed and nodded. "Then it looks like we'll be going to Deneb for the reception."

"We're going to fly out this afternoon," said Ben. "We've

got arrangements to make."

"You want us to fly you to the spaceport?" I said.

"Thank you, no," said Ben. "Between the two of us, we'll have a lot of baggage. I'll have my ship send a car, so we only have to load and unload once."

I nodded. "Your call."

"This is a very nice vehicle, Tony," said Sonja. "Thank you for your offer."

"I doubt the DSS will let us keep it," I said. "We'll enjoy it while we can."

"Perhaps I could save you from trouble if I bought it," said Wayne. "How much did it cost you?"

"Forty thousand credits," I said. "Quentin said it was a good price. Biggs says it's a quarter million U.S."

"About right," said Wayne. "Worth every penny, too. Leroy and I go back. I'll give him a call. I'm sure I can convince him you were acting at my behest."

When we got back to the hotel, I helped Ben help Sonja out of the car and into her wheelchair. As he pushed her into the hotel, I could not help but think how alike he and Wayne really were, even with their obvious dissimilarities. It was not hard to imagine them being cousins.

A second thought occurred to me. Lynne and Sonja were Denebian, and twin sisters. If Wayne married Lynne—and Kayla and I were both of the opinion that he would, and soon—then the "twin" cousins, who had been born of twin sisters, would be married to twin sisters. Dok Fil's crazy prophecy idea didn't sound that crazy anymore.

One look at Kay told me that she was likely pondering the same thing I was.

***

We stayed on Aldebaran for about three more weeks before we flew to Deneb for the Elan wedding reception.

It was a lovely reception, and it gave me another opportunity to wear my tux, and Kay to wear that gorgeous red dress. I hoped that we might get to share at least one slow dance before the party was over.

Sonja had a cast by then, and she was getting around pretty well on her crutches, but she wasn't going to be able to dance.

Wayne and Lynne acted as their proxies, sharing the first dance as Sonja and Ben watched from their seats. As the music came to an end, Wayne glanced at Ben, who winked at him. He reached into his pocket, and when he and Lynne bowed to each other, he slipped a diamond ring on her finger. She stared at it for a few seconds before she finally comprehended what Wayne had done. He got to his knees and proposed to her. Tears streamed down her cheeks as she nodded and hugged him. The crowd applauded as they kissed.

Kayla, apparently caught up in the moment, grabbed me and kissed me. I held her close, running my hands down her bare back. I relished the touch of her skin under my hands, until I reached the fabric covering her derriere.

I should have stopped at the small of her back. Like the golden coach turning back into a pumpkin at the last stroke of midnight, the magic died.

"Tony," whispered Kayla. "Why are your hands on my ass?"

"I—I got caught up in the moment."

"Would you like to remove them, or shall I?"

I withdrew. "Sorry, Kay."

To her credit, she did not make a scene. She didn't slap me. She didn't throw a drink in my face. She didn't yell. She calmly pickup up her purse and walked out of the room.

Around us, people were still applauding as Sonja hopped over to hug her sister and Ben shook Wayne's hand.

I decided it was best that I also make a quiet exit.

I had barely gone four or five steps out the door when I heard the *whoosh* of an open hand rushing toward my face. I turned my face just in time for Kay's hand to miss it.

"Don't ever do that again!" she shouted.

"What, duck?"

"You were feeling me up!"

"Yeah, I know. I didn't mean it. I'm sorry."

"No you're not, you degenerate! Every time I start thinking you might be a decent human being, you have to go and ruin it!"

"I know," I said. "But you kissed me."

She sat on the curb. "Yeah. Yeah, I guess I did." She looked up at me, the fire renewed. "But that doesn't give you free reign to... it just doesn't!"

I sat down on the curb opposite. "Why did you kiss me, Kay?"

"I just got caught up in the moment, I guess."

"Well, so did I. I'm sorry. I know it was inappropriate. I just forgot where I was."

"Do you think I might have let you get away with it if we weren't in public?"

"I don't know," I said. "But if we weren't in public, I don't think you would have kissed me."

Kay shook her head. "No, probably not."

"What can I say, except I'm sorry? I don't blame you for hating me."

"Tony, I don't hate you."

"Well, that's a relief."

"I like you, Tony. But we can't be partners anymore. When we get back to Earth, I'm leaving."

"You're going to leave the DSS?"

"I can't work with you anymore. If we keep working together, sooner or later we're going to cross the line."

When I was in college, I fell head-over-heels in love with a girl in my forensics class. We started sleeping with each other after our third date. I thought it would last forever. It didn't. On our two-week anniversary, she said I was boring, and she didn't want me anymore. It felt like a knife piercing my heart and twisting.

Kay telling me she didn't want to be my partner anymore felt like six or seven knives.

"Did it ever occur to you that maybe we're not supposed to be partners?" I said. "Maybe we're meant to be lovers."

"Maybe. But I don't think you're ready for that, yet, either. I'm sorry, Tony."

"I'm sorry, too." I wanted to disappear, maybe get drunk. "Do you think we'll ever be ready?"

Kay shrugged. "I don't know, Tony. You still have some growing up to do. Maybe I do, too." After a moment of silence, she smiled. "How did you manage to duck the slap, anyway?"

"I felt the air moving."

"I'm impressed. You move fast."

"Sometimes I move a little too fast."

"Yeah, you do. I'm going to miss working with you."

"Me, too. We ought to go back to the party before anyone misses us." I offered her my arm.

Kay didn't take my arm. She did walk beside me as we re-entered the room. No one there noticed that anything had changed between Kay and me. No one, that is, except Lynne.

As Wayne gave the Best Man's toast, Lynne sat next to me

at the bar. "You all right, Tony?"

"Sure, fine," I said.

"Wayne likes you very much, and I want us to be friends, too. You don't know me yet, so I'm going to tell you something about myself." Lynne's voice was kind, but firm. "I can nearly always tell when someone is lying to me, and I can tell you're not fine. So let's try again. What happened between you and Kayla?"

"Damn, you're good. No wonder he loves you." I sighed, and told her everything. "I know I shouldn't have done it, but I wasn't thinking clearly. Okay, I wasn't thinking at all. Have you ever wanted someone you just couldn't get close to?"

Lynne laughed. "Yes, for years. I'm going to be marrying him in a couple months."

"Seriously? That's why you got so upset when he yelled about the grape soda."

Lynne looked at me with admiration. "You recognized me? You're well suited to your profession. I'm impressed. Wayne hasn't even figured out that was me, yet."

"I notice things," I said. "Right now, I'm noticing Kay's beautiful body, and I'm sad that we can't work together anymore."

"No, you're sad you won't get to see her that much anymore."

"Same difference," I said. "I'm sad."

Lynne kissed my cheek. "I will tell you something I probably shouldn't. She's sad, too, and scared. I'm guessing she's had her heart broken before. That's probably why she's so cautious with you."

"Are you empathic?"

Lynne smiled. "No. But like you, I'm observant."

"Congratulations on your engagement. I don't think it could happen to two nicer people."

"Thanks, Tony." Lynne looked back toward Kayla, who was now talking to Dok Fil and Far Polk. "I hope you both can figure it all out. I think you'll be happier together."

"This is what I'm saying," I said. "I guess we'll see."

Wayne finished toasting the groom and came back over to where we sat. "You weren't listening to my speech, my love. Is something wrong? I'm not boring you already, am I?"

Lynne kissed Wayne. "Never. But I noticed that Tony and Kay seemed upset."

"What's wrong?" said Wayne.

"I got too close to my partner," I said. "Now things are,

well, awkward between us. It will probably be a long time before we do assignments together again, if ever."

"Aw, I'm sorry to hear that, Tony," said Wayne. "Do you think it would help if I talked to her?"

"It would be best if we stayed out of it," said Lynne. "This is something they're going to have to work out on their own. After nearly ruining Ben and Sonja's relationship, I'm all for staying out of other people's business."

"You're probably right, my dear."

"Pardon my curiosity," I said, "but what did you do? I know Ben didn't blame you. He seemed to put the blame squarely on himself."

Lynne smiled. "I helped him catch her attention by feeding him inside information. Sonja got mad at both of us when she found out about it. She thought Ben and I had manipulated her. Which, I suppose, we did. But she had always wanted him. I just removed a few obstacles."

I shrugged. "The road to Hell is paved with good intentions, my Uncle Luis always says."

"Your uncle sounds like a wise man."

I nodded. "I always thought so."

"So what do you think he would tell you to do about Kayla?"

"I don't know. Maybe the next time I see him, I should ask."

Chapter 12: Hiatus

Biggs chewed us both out when we got back to the office at the end of the mission. There had apparently been video of us kissing at the wedding reception, and it had gotten back to him.

"What the hell were you doing? You know the department rules about dating co-workers."

"I know, Boss," I said. "I was stupid."

"Tony can't take all the blame, sir," said Kayla. "He was only responding to signals I was sending him."

Biggs glared at her for a moment before turning back to me. "And you! Using Department funds to buy a limo? Do you have any idea what this sort of thing would do to this office's reputation if it became public knowledge?"

"I don't see how it possibly could, Boss," I said, "seeing as how the whole incident didn't occur, in a place that doesn't exist!"

"Are you getting smart with me, Diego?"

Kay smiled, in spite of herself. "First time for everything."

"You think this is funny?"

"Not anymore, sir."

"I should ground you both, but fortunately for you, Wayne has taken a liking to you. He's intervened, requesting that we take no punitive measures against either of you. And, you'll be glad to know, he has decided to purchase that fine Aldebaran limo. It's to remain at Groom Lake when not in use, just to avoid any temptation to use its unauthorized features. So you're off the hook for that, at least. Just don't let it happen again."

"It won't," said Kay. "I'm leaving the team."

Biggs blinked. "You don't have to go that far, Kayla."

"Yeah, I do."

"If you leave the team, you won't get to go back into space. We're the only ones read into the program. You won't even be allowed to talk about what you've seen working here."

"I understand."

"You have vacation time accrued. Take a break. Go work it out."

"I already have, Biggs. My mind's made up. Revoke my clearance if you have to, but I have to go."

"I can't revoke your clearance without ordering a mind wipe. I won't do it; you're too valuable. It'll be better to have an agent to call on if we ever need backup. Stay safe, Moss."

Kay hugged the team each in turn. She hesitated for just a moment before hugging me, too. "I really am going to miss you," she whispered.

I nodded. "I'm sorry it all went down like this."

"So am I."

Kayla turned and walked out the door. My heart tried to follow; but, being encaged in my chest as it was, it just pounded against my ribs until it was too tired to fight anymore.

"Do you need some time off, Diego?" asked Biggs. "Or are you leaving, too?"

"I'm fine, Boss," I lied. "Put me to work."

The office seemed quiet with Kay gone, but over the next few weeks, I began to settle into the new routine. Almost. I tried not to think about her, but I kept coming back to the question of what it would take to make her want to be with me as much as I wanted to be with her.

I just did not understand women.

***

I received an invitation to Wayne and Lynne's wedding in Oklahoma City. I was slightly surprised that they were marrying so soon after getting engaged, but from what Lynne had told me, she had been a long time waiting for him specifically. Wayne, for his part, felt like he had known her for years.

Which, I had calculated, he had. They had interacted with each other at least twice in my memory, and there were probably a few more times I wasn't aware of. They just hadn't connected.

I sighed. Kay would probably get an invitation, too. Should I not go, so there wouldn't be any awkwardness? But that wasn't any good. What if Kay stayed away too, to avoid running into me? Then neither of us would be at Wayne's wedding, which would probably disappoint him.

I sighed. I couldn't let that happen. Wayne was my friend, and I would be there. If Kay was there too, well, we would just deal with it.

"Hey, Boss," I asked Biggs. "How long do you suppose it takes to get from D.C. to OKC on a motorcycle?"

"Depends how fast you drive, and how far you can go without a rest," he said. "You're Air Force. Why don't you fly? I'm flying."

"Yeah, but I'll bet Kay is, too."

Biggs nodded. "You don't want to run into her, is that it? What went on between you, anyway?"

"I don't want to talk about it."

He shook his head. "All right, I'll lay off. But you're bound to see her at the wedding. What then?"

I shrugged. "I'll think of something."

***

I didn't even see Kayla until the day of the wedding. We ended up coming out to the hotel lobby to catch the same shuttle to the wedding. I thought long and hard for the perfect opening line, something that would perfectly capture everything I had been feeling for the last several weeks.

"Hi."

Hey, I never said I came up with one.

Kay's response was equally appropriate. "Hi."

Biggs walked past and climbed into the shuttle. "I hope you two aren't going to be chattering like that all the way to the chapel. I hate not being able to get a word in edgewise."

Kayla and Biggs had a pleasant enough conversation while I looked out the window and tried to enjoy the view. There were plenty of cows and oil wells to make note of, but not a whole lot of anything else. I guess the best thing I could say about Oklahoma is that it was at least more hilly than Kansas.

I didn't notice Kay's outfit at all. I didn't notice her blue satin sleeveless gown, or the shawl that covered her bare shoulders. I certainly didn't notice her two-inch heels, with the satiny upper, open toe, and sling-back heel. I didn't notice her pearl earrings or the pearl necklace she wore around her neck.

I really couldn't tell you how beautiful she looked. I was watching the cows.

***

After having been to the Elans' reception, I was surprised

by how small and intimate this wedding was in comparison. Ben and Sonja had lots of friends and acquaintances at their wedding, including quite a few Union dignitaries, most of whom could never come to Earth without creating a major panic, I realized. None of Lynne's friends could be here, except for a few of her new friends from France.

"France, huh?" I said, shaking Wayne's hand in the receiving line.

"It's a long story."

I nodded. It probably wasn't that long, I supposed, but this wasn't the time or the place to tell it.

The reception was held in a fellowship hall adjacent to the chapel. Considering how quickly they had to have planned the wedding, I was impressed by how well it all had come together. Lynne and Wayne had put quite a lot of thought into it.

Except for the seating arrangements.

When I got to my assigned table, I found Biggs and Kayla already seated, along with a few people I barely knew or hadn't met. Janet sat on Biggs' other side. Next to her was Lucy, Wayne's sister, and her date, who was introduced to me as Eric. The other two folks were the Chaplain and his wife. The only empty seat left was next to Kayla. I sat down, not taking any notice at all of the light fragrance of Kay's perfume and the little wisp of hair that always seemed to escape whenever she put her hair up.

I really didn't care about her appearance at all.

"Ah, wonderful," said the Chaplain. "Now that we are all here, would anyone be offended if I said 'Grace' before the meal is served? May we all join hands?"

I took Kayla's hand in mine as he prayed a short blessing. When the prayer was over, we kept our hands clasped for just a second longer than everyone else.

After dinner, Wayne made an announcement. "I just wanted to welcome everyone, and thank you for coming on such short notice. I suppose it might seem odd for some of you that I should be so quick to marry someone so soon after meeting her."

"She's not pregnant, is she?" shouted one of Wayne's former classmates, who had apparently had too much to drink already. His own wife was already punching him hard in the arm, her face turning red with embarrassment."

Wayne blushed, and laughed. "No, no, though I wouldn't blame anyone for jumping to that conclusion. Who invited that guy, anyway?"

After the laughter died down, he continued. "As some of you might know, Lynne's sister, Sonja, was recovering from a broken ankle at her wedding just a few weeks ago, so Lynne and I got to share the first dance at their wedding. Now that she's back on her feet again, more or less, we'd like to offer Ben and Sonja Elan the honor of sharing the first dance tonight."

There was applause as Ben led his wife out to the dance floor. They danced alone for a while, oblivious to the world around them. After the first song was over, Wayne and Lynne, as well as a few other couples, joined them. I watched them dance, not even noticing Kay's hand brushing against mine, or the tear rolling down her cheek.

Okay, that I noticed.

I pulled a handkerchief from my pocket and handed it to her.

"Thanks," she said.

"Do you want to dance?" I asked.

"Do you think that's a good idea?"

"No, I think it's a terrible idea. Do you want to dance anyway?"

Kay looked down at the damp handkerchief. "Yeah."

I took her by the hand and led her to the dance floor.

"Are you going to stay mad at me forever, Tony?"

"I'm not mad at you," I said. "I'm just..."

"Just what?"

I mulled it over as we danced. "Hurt, I guess. You left."

"I had to, Tony." She laid her head on my shoulder. "I was starting to—I had feelings for you."

"Yeah, me too. What about now?"

"I've had time to think about it." She didn't say anything more.

I didn't press her. The song ended. "Let's go for a walk," I said, offering her my arm.

She nodded and hooked her arm around mine.

I led her out of the hall and out to the courtyard. There were a few empty park benches, and space heaters to keep away the spring chill. The man who had made the inappropriate comment during Wayne's speech was getting a dressing down from his wife, and another couple were making out in the gazebo. Kay and I claimed a quiet corner and sat down.

"So, how have you been, Tony?"

I cocked a half-grin. "On my best behavior, I have to say. I came on to Jess only once the whole time."

Kay smiled, and my heart soared. "Liar. You know as well as I do that Jess would kill you." She thought for a moment. "Or have it done for her. Nobody messes with Jess. Come on, I'm serious, Tony."

"I've missed you. Even having you constantly angry with me was better than you not being there at all."

"It wouldn't have solved anything," she said.

I shrugged. "Probably not. But walking out doesn't solve anything, either, does it?"

"No," she admitted. "It does, however, create new problems for us. Or solutions, depending on your point of view."

"Oh?"

"You're smart," she said. "Work it out for yourself. I'll wait."

"What, now?"

She nodded.

"We got into trouble because we got too close," I said. "Co-workers can't date. Of course, we weren't dating, we were just... getting too close."

Kay nodded. "Keep going. I like watching you think."

"Too bad it doesn't happen that often, huh?"

Kay laughed and shivered a bit.

I put my jacket around her shoulders. "We're still not dating... but we're no longer co-workers, either, strictly speaking, are we? I mean, we're working for the same agency, but we're in different departments, aren't we?"

"Yes, we are."

"Are you saying you'd like to go on a date with me?"

"I'm not saying anything, Tony. You're supposed to be working it out, remember?"

I crossed my arms. "You're teasing me, aren't you?"

"Maybe, a little. But I need to make sure you're willing to put the necessary effort into making us work. I can't prompt you on this. You have to get there yourself."

"And what will I find when I get there?"

Kay said nothing. She just waited and watched.

I pondered. What exactly did she want me to do? Assume nothing, I thought. She wasn't saying yes to me, but she wasn't saying no, either. Why couldn't she just give me a straight answer?

Then it hit me. I hadn't asked her a straight question.

"Kayla, when are you flying back to DC?"

"My schedule's open-ended at the moment," she said. "I have no concrete plans."

"Would you like to spend the day with me tomorrow? I mean, I don't know what there is to do in Oklahoma City. I'm sure there must be something, or people wouldn't live here, right?"

Kayla smiled. "Yes, I would, Tony."

"Would it bother you terribly much if I kissed you?"

"I don't know, but if you'd like to try it, you have my permission."

I kissed her.

It didn't seem to bother her one bit. I know I enjoyed it.

Chapter 13: Too Good to Last

The days immediately following Wayne's wedding were some of the best I had spent since, well, as far back as I could remember. We spent almost all of Sunday at the zoo, followed by a really good barbecue brisket dinner at a restaurant with a funny name I doubted I would remember later. At the end of the day, as we were walking back to the car to head back to the hotel, I asked Kay if she wanted to spend the night with me. She shook her head.

"Don't get me wrong, Tony," she said. "I like you. I had fun. I'm looking forward to spending tomorrow with you. But I'm not going to sleep with you."

"You confuse me sometimes," I said.

"I'm just not ready, yet. I need to be sure about you before I take that step." She looked up at me. "You... you're not mad at me, are you?"

I looked into her sparkling blue eyes. "How could I be mad at you? I—"

I had almost used the big L-word. *C'mon, Diego, keep it casual*, I thought. *Don't go putting your foot in your mouth already.*

"I'm just glad we got through a whole day without yelling at each other." There. Crisis averted.

Kay smiled. "I know, right? I could get used to this, you know, spending a whole day not wanting to punch you."

"I'll call you in the morning." I kissed her cheek. "Good night, Kay."

On Monday, we toured an art museum and the Cowboy Hall of Fame. We also stopped at a post office in Edmond.

"What are we doing here?" asked Kay.

"I read that this was where the term 'going postal' originated," I said. "It's the site of America's first post office workplace shooting."

"Wow, that's romantic," said Kay, flatly.

"I know, it's not a great romantic site," I said, "but it's history. This event is why they started putting surveillance cameras in federal buildings."

"Really?"

"Well, I'm sure it was a factor," I said. "Anyway, it seemed proper to stop and pay our respects."

"You know, you're right." We saluted the modest memorial there, and then drove on.

"Where do you want to have dinner?" I asked.

"I'm kind of tired after all this walking around. Do you think we could just go to a Sonic or something?"

"Marry me," I said.

"No. Not today. Not yet."

After a couple of chili dogs and tots, we went to a movie.

Back at the hotel, I again invited her to spend the night in my room. Again, she shook her head.

"I do admire your persistence, though," she said, and kissed me goodnight.

Tuesday morning, we had breakfast and drove out to a small airstrip to rent a plane.

Kay put her hands on her hips. "You're not still thinking about the 'mile high club', are you?"

"I'd settle for sea level, honestly." I winked. "No, actually. I just thought it might be nice to fly over Red Rock Canyon, maybe take some pictures from the air."

"Ooh, that does sound nice. You seem to know just the right things to say to a girl."

I smiled. "No, just one girl."

We stayed in the air for several hours before going back. That evening, we bought tickets to a minor-league ball game. We got back to the hotel pretty late. "Do you want to spend the night?" I asked, expecting another no.

"Yes, I think I do," she said.

I blinked. "Really?"

She nodded. "I have to warn you, though, I'm tired. I just want to fall asleep with you, not have sex. Do you think you can handle that?"

It was more than I had expected. "I'll behave. Promise."

Once we were in my room, Kayla slipped off her shoes and began to remove her clothes, until she wore nothing but a tee shirt and underpants. She took her bra off without removing her shirt, a talent I had witnessed several times in my life, but never quite understood.

I stripped down to my boxers and got into bed beside her. I turned on HBO and we sat in bed, watching some B-movie while Kay fell asleep on my shoulder. I sat there, watching her sleep, stroking her hair, and smelling the faint aroma of her perfume.

"I think I love you," I whispered, and drifted off to sleep.

***

Kay was gone when I awoke the next morning. There was a hastily-scrawled note on her pillow: "Went to get fresh clothes. Be right back."

I smiled. At least she hadn't changed her mind. I was a little sad that I didn't wake up with her still in my arms.

I went in and took a shower. I heard the door open. "It's just me," called Kay. "I had to go get my clothes."

"Yeah, I saw the note. Did you sleep well?"

"Yes, I did."

I got out of the shower and wrapped a towel around my waist. I held the towel securely before I emerged from the bathroom. "Uh, I would have brought my clothes in here if I had known you'd be back before I was done."

"It's okay," she said. "I'm not afraid to see you naked." Kayla's suitcase was leaning against the wall. She hadn't just gotten changed, she had packed.

"You're not leaving, are you? Going back to D.C., I mean?"

Kay looked puzzled. "What?" Following my gaze to her suitcase, she laughed and shook her head. "No, I'm not."

"You're quitting?"

"No, that's not what I meant. I'm going back to D.C., just not today. I just... I checked out of my room." She bit her lip shyly. "I... I'm ready, Tony."

"Ready?"

"God, you're thick, sometimes. I don't need my room anymore, because I want to stay here. With you."

"Seriously?"

"It's all right, isn't it? I guess I should have asked you, first, but you've been asking me every night."

"No, it's fine. I mean, yes, please stay with me."

Kay touched my still bare chest. "And I promise that tonight, I'll try not to be too tired."

Part of me wanted to take her to bed right then and there, but the voice inside my head, the one that's usually right, but I almost never listened to, said, *don't rush this. You want your first time with her to be special, not rushed.* I put my shirt on before I kissed her. "So will I. Let's get breakfast."

It was about a quarter to nine by the time we had finished breakfast and headed out to the car.

"What do you have planned for us today?" Kay asked.

I held up one of the brochures I had pulled from the rack in the hotel lobby. "How about the Myriad Botanical Gardens?"

She leafed through the brochure as I began navigating through the busy streets. "Good choice, Tony. It looks like there's a lot to see." She winked. "And it shouldn't tire us out too much, if you know what I mean."

I was pretty sure I did. "I'm looking forward to that, too. To tell you the truth, though, just lying in bed with you asleep in my arms was well worth the wait, all by itself."

"Wow, Tony," said Kay. "You really have done some growing up while we were apart, haven't you? I guess I misjudged you."

I laughed. "Nope. You were pretty much on the money. I've kind of been a jerk for most of the time you've known me."

***

We were stopped at a light when a scooter came zipping between the lanes of cars behind us. It pulled to a stop right beside us.

I rolled my window down. "Do you always drive like that? You're going to get yourself killed!"

"Don't act like you care about me," said a voice I recognized.

"Janet?" I said.

The woman on the scooter leaned on the window. "How do you know my name? Oh, I know you! You're Wayne's friends. You were at the wedding!"

"Look, I know it's none of my business how you drive, but what you're doing is dangerous."

Janet sighed. "I know, but I'm running late for a meeting." She grumbled. "I hate this light. It holds forever."

"At least it's not a train," I said. "I'll let you in front of me when the light changes. Just don't get yourself killed, all right? I know Wayne would be devastated."

"He'll probably kill me himself for being late," she said. "Thanks, though. I probably ought to—"

She didn't finish her thought. A loud blast shook the

ground and set off several car alarms from vehicles parked on the side of the street. A thick plume of black and gray smoke began to rise from somewhere only a few blocks from where we stood. The traffic light turned green, but no one moved forward. Many had gotten out of their cars and were looking in the direction of the smoke.

"What the hell was that?" said Kay. "A gas leak, maybe?"

"I wish I knew," said Janet. She started shaking. "That looks like it was right where I was headed!"

I started hearing sirens somewhere behind us. In my loudest voice, I called out, "Let's get these cars out of the road! Let the emergency vehicles through!"

People immediately followed my direction. By the time the first police cars began arriving, there was an open corridor for them.

The third or fourth police cruiser stopped in front of my car. "You from Tinker?"

"Andrews, actually," I said, showing him my ID. "We were in town for a wedding."

"DSS, huh? I'd love to chat about that, but we're a little busy."

"Anything we can do to help?"

"You the ones who cleared the road? You've already done a bunch, sir. Appreciate it."

"What's going on?"

"Explosion at the Murrah Federal Building," he said.

Janet nearly fainted. Kay caught her before she fell.

"You all right, Miss?"

"I was on my way there," she said. "I was late for a 9:00 meeting."

"Well, you're the luckiest woman in OKC, today," he said.

My phone began to ring. "Excuse me," I said. "This can't be good."

"Biggs?" asked Kay.

I nodded and answered. "Yeah, Boss?"

"I need you to head to Groom Lake ASAP," said Biggs. "Something big is going down, and Freed's off the grid."

"What do you mean?"

"His phone's off, so we can't track him. I'm already in the air. I want you in the air, too. Get to Tinker. There's an Import waiting for you there."

"Yes, Boss." I hung up the phone. "Shit. I have to go to

Tinker, like now."

"Now?" said Kayla. "What about me?"

"Biggs just said me. He might not have known you were with me. Even if he did know..."

"I know. I'm not on the team anymore."

I kissed her. "Sorry, Kay. I was really looking forward to tonight. But I have to go. Wayne's off the grid."

"What does Wayne have to do with this?" said Janet. "And why do you have a phone like his? He said it was a prototype."

"Sorry, Janet. No time to explain." I looked at the officer. "You've already seen my credentials. I need a Code 3 to Tinker."

The officer turned pale. "You got it, Captain! Hop in."

"I'll call you when I can," I said to Kay. "I wish I knew when that was."

Kay nodded. "Be careful."

"What does Wayne have to do with this?" I heard Janet ask Kay. "What's a DSS?"

I didn't envy Kay the task she was going to have containing Janet. I blamed myself. I shouldn't have used Wayne's name in front of her.

"I ain't never done anything like this before," said the officer, as we raced toward Tinker. "And I ain't never met a DSS agent before. I don't suppose you're allowed to tell me what's going on."

I shrugged. "I don't know what's going on," I said. "My boss tells me to get to Tinker yesterday, so I jump."

"You think it has something to do with the Federal building?"

"I never assume anything I haven't been told," I said. I chuckled, and added, "At least, I get in less trouble when I don't assume."

The officer snorted. "Ass, You, and Me. I get told that a lot."

I grinned. "That said, it wouldn't surprise me if it did. Thanks for the lift. You can drop me off there by the gatepost. They probably won't let you in with me."

"No problem." He stopped the car. As I got out, he said, "Can I ask you a question?"

"Shoot."

"Who's Wayne?"

"A damn nice guy," I said. "And quite possibly the single most important human being on the planet. Are you a praying man?"

"Yes, sir, I am."

"Then you'd better say a prayer that Wayne's still alive."

"I will. I'll pray for you, too, Captain."

"Thanks. I'm going to need all the help I can get."

The Import that Biggs mentioned was, as far as anyone looking at it from the outside could tell, a standard F-117, as if anything like the Nighthawk could be described as standard. Once it was in the air, though, I used its Denebian-made engines to their fullest extent, letting me get to Groom Lake faster than it would have taken Janet to get across town on her scooter. The way she drove, it might not have been much faster, but still.

I landed at Groom Lake and headed for my ship.

Biggs was already there. "What took you so long?"

"I was a couple of blocks from the Murrah Building when you called."

"Really?" he said. "Did you see anything?"

"Nothing but smoke," I said. "Why?"

Biggs sighed. The man was rattled, which made me all the more nervous. "The Murrah Building wasn't the only explosion. Reports are coming in from all over the galaxy. We have orders to bring Wayne to a special emergency Council Session on the Carrier *Enpressa*. Assuming we can find him, that is."

"He's still off the grid?"

Biggs nodded. "His phone must be off. I don't know why."

"C'mon, Boss," I said. "You're married. Did you have your phone turned on when you went on your honeymoon?" I smiled. "Did they even have phones back then? Or did you have to watch the horizon for signal fires?"

Biggs grunted. "Okay, so maybe he's got a good reason to shut off his phone. But our being out of contact with him does not bode well. For all we know, Deneb's already sending a fleet of orbital bombers."

"I didn't think of that. What do we do?"

"All we can do is wait," said Biggs. "As soon as he turns on his phone, we can pinpoint his location, but until he does, the Grand Canyon is way too big an area to search. It's bad enough we're going to have to go pick him up in this vessel."

"What if we're seen?" I said. "That could create a panic!"

Biggs nodded. "The Air Force will probably have to re-open Project Blue Book. If we're lucky, though, the worst that'll happen is an increase in UFO-themed television shows."

Waiting at high alert while nothing is going on can be pretty nerve-wracking. Looking around, I could tell that no one else was any less tense than I was. "Can I call Kay?" I asked Biggs. "She was with me when I took your call. She's going to want to know what's going on."

"How was that going?"

"Better than I would have hoped." I sighed. "We were almost there, too. I almost asked her to come with me. She still has clearance, doesn't she?"

Biggs nodded. "Yeah, but it's best that you didn't. You're going to need focus where we're going, and if 'there' is where I think it is, neither of you would have been bringing your 'A' game."

I sighed. "No, Kay would have gone back to being all business. I'm the only one whose focus would have suffered."

"You're focused now, I hope."

"Like I need focus, sitting on the tarmac," I said. "Screw it. I'm calling Kay, unless you specifically order me not to."

Biggs gave a half-smile. "Don't blame you a bit. Go, make the call. Tell her I said hi. Then get your head in the game."

Kay picked up right away. "Are you safe?"

"No one is safe, right now," I said. "We still can't raise Wayne, and we're stuck on the ground until he makes contact. If I had known how long we'd be stuck here, I wouldn't have left you so quickly. God knows I'd rather be walking the Gardens with you than strapped in a thrust seat. Uh, sorry about leaving you alone to handle Janet, too."

Kayla sighed. "Yeah, what, did you forget his ex-girlfriend was standing right next to us?"

I chuckled. "Actually, that's exactly what happened. I only had eyes for you, Babe."

"Tony, in light of the great week we were having, I'm not going to hold it against you, but if we're going to have any kind of future together, you'd better come up with a better pet name for me than 'Babe', all right?"

"Yeah, I was just trying it on for size. It doesn't fit. I'm not the sugar-and-spice type. What do you want me to call you?"

"Kay works," she said. "It is my name."

"As you wish," I said. "So, how did you handle Janet?"

"I just told her 'it's classified', and left it at that." Kayla chuckled. "I don't think Janet likes me very much, Tony. She called me worse things than 'Babe'."

"Don't take it too personally, Kay." I said. "I'm sorry we

didn't get that one more night."

"Me, too," she said. "Just so you know, I'm still ready. But I don't know if I'll feel right about sleeping with you once we're both back in DC."

"I understand," I said. "The whole District feels like a workplace, doesn't it?"

"You really do understand," she said.

"I told you, I'm trying."

"I appreciate it. Next time we get a vacation, I'm all yours."

"It's a deal. Call you when I can."

It was almost three hours before Wayne's phone switched on. We immediately strapped in and got ready to go get him. As soon as we were in the air, Biggs' phone made an alert tone I hadn't heard before.

"What's that, Boss?"

"A 9-1-1 operator just keyed in Wayne's ID code," said Biggs. He picked up his phone, checked the screen, and tapped a button.

"I'm calling in regard to the code you just typed in. It doesn't really matter how I know. All you need to know is that this is a national security matter. You are to tell the caller that we have picked up his signal, and we are coming to his aid. Our ETA is fifteen minutes. No, it doesn't matter. Tell him to hang up, but to leave his phone turned on. Then, you are to delete the call from the computer logs and destroy the tape reel. Yes, the whole tape. Then, you need to do your best to forget that the conversation ever happened. This one, too. Oh, and if you happen to receive any crank calls over the next few hours, you should probably delete them, too. What kind of crank calls? I'm not at liberty to say, but you'll know them when you hear them. Your country thanks you, Mrs. Evans. What? Just a lucky guess, I suppose."

"You enjoyed that far too much, Boss," I said when he had put his phone away.

"I've been waiting almost my entire career to do that," Biggs said, cracking the widest smile I'd ever seen on his face. It just as quickly vanished. "Lynne has a broken leg. They're near a washed-out trail. We won't likely be able to land very close to them. We're going to need a stretcher team ready to go as soon as we land!"

The medics had Lynne safely secured in the infirmary within minutes. Wayne had applied a well-constructed splint on Lynne's leg. He kissed Lynne, and ran straight to the launch seats and strapped in.

I knew that an emergency thrust was coming. As sturdy as the splint was, it wasn't going to be much comfort to Lynne during the thrust. I looked at Wayne and saw the anguish in his eyes. He knew it, too.

As soon as the thrust was completed, he threw off his straps and headed back to his wife. Biggs and I stopped to help a crewman who had gotten the wind knocked out of him. At least he hadn't broken his neck.

We helped the man slowly make his way to the infirmary, then went looking for Wayne and Lynne.

Dr. Howard was putting Lynne's leg in traction by the time we got there. "How bad is it?" asked Biggs.

Wayne showed us the video he had been recording when she fell. I felt sympathy pains in my own leg as I watched her leg collapsing under her.

"That had to totally suck," I said. "I'm sure the heavy-thrust launch didn't tickle, either."

Lynne nodded. "I'm pretty sure I passed out."

"Sorry about your honeymoon," I said. "How long do you have to stay shackled to this contraption?"

"It's already been too long," she said. "At least I don't need surgery. I'll get a cast in a few days, I hope."

"I just hope we don't have to endure anymore max-gees," said Wayne. "I never would have used my code if I knew this would happen."

"It wouldn't have mattered," said Biggs. "We've been on high alert since the bombs went off. We would have collected you sooner, but we couldn't track your phone while it was turned off."

"That reminds me," said Wayne. "I have lots of messages to go through. You all wouldn't mind excusing us, would you?"

"Not at all," said Biggs. "We'll be just outside if you need us."

Wayne laughed. "I'm pretty sure I'll be safe enough on this vessel, right?"

Biggs nodded. "I suppose. Old habits, Wayne."

"I understand. Go, take it easy. I shouldn't need you until we get to... where are we going, anyway?"

"Union Flagship *Enpresa*," said Biggs. "Biggest ship in the galaxy, I'm told."

Wayne grinned. "You know that means 'Enterprise' in Euskara, don't you?"

"Does it?" I said. "Small, uh, galaxy, eh?"

We headed down to the crew lounge and played cribbage while we waited for our ship to reach the rendezvous.

Chapter 14: *Enpresa*

"That's a big ship, all right," I said, as we made our final approach.

In the blackness of space, it's hard to gauge size from a distance, because there's nothing to compare a single object against. I remarked that *Enpresa* was a big ship while we were still quite a distance off. I had no idea how far from the ship we were, so I had no idea how colossal an understatement I had just made until we got a few kilometers closer.

"That's a really big ship."

I still hadn't fully comprehended its size. We approached even closer.

"That's not a ship at all, is it, Boss? It's got to be at least the size of, what, midtown Manhattan?"

Biggs nodded. "About that. It's almost like a city in space, from what Zeru says."

As we approached the docking pad, I began to feel tiny and insignificant. "I suppose we should go find Wayne, eh?"

"Won't be too hard," said Biggs. "He's with Lynne. She isn't going anywhere."

We got there just as they were getting ready to wheel Lynne's bed down to the docking bay. The orderlies were taking extreme care not to jostle the traction frame as they did so.

"Will there be any bumps?" Lynne asked, understandably fearful.

"The bed's rollers are equipped with dampers," said Wayne. "They're being super-careful."

Lynne gritted her teeth. "Have you ever broken anything, *Maiteakren*?"

"Sprained an ankle, once," said Wayne. "That was bad enough. But trust me when I say that I feel every spasm of pain you do." He grasped her hand. "Squeeze when you need to. I wish I could do more."

Once we were across the threshold and down the ramp, the floor became level and smooth, and Lynne's breathing came easier. "Okay, that wasn't so bad."

"I really wish I hadn't turned my phone off," said Wayne.

"We would have been picked up at least an hour or so before you fell."

Lynne smiled. "Considering what we were doing an hour or so before I fell, do you really think that would have been a better option?"

Wayne blushed and looked around. "No, now that you mention it. It still pains me to think I could have prevented this."

"Don't second-guess yourself, Boss," I said. "A man who shuts off the phone on his honeymoon sounds like he's got his priorities straight. Right, Biggs?"

"My rule is 'always be reachable'," said Biggs. "Especially if the lives of billions depend on assurances you're still alive."

Wayne looked stunned. "You're right, Biggs. What would you have done?"

"I would have turned off my phone," he said. "Sometimes, rules are meant to be broken. But it does expose a design flaw in the phone, or in our protocol, at least. In an emergency, there ought to be a way to remotely turn it on, or at least track it."

Wayne nodded. "Makes sense. Speaking of communication, though, Tony, why didn't you tell me Janet was with you guys when the bomb went off?"

Lynne nodded. "For a moment during the message playback, we thought she had been killed."

"My bad," I said. "I'm really sorry about that."

"No harm done," said Wayne. "Um, is there any way to make sure she stays safe? I mean, it's totally possible that this bombing was intended... I mean, what if I was the intended target? They might start going after people I care about."

Biggs nodded. "That's already being taken care of. Agent Moss is keeping watch over her, and there are agents tailing your family, as well. They'll stay active until we are reasonably certain the threat has passed."

Wayne sighed. "One less thing for me to worry about."

The hospital bed was taken to a corridor where many injured men, women, and gender-ambiguous beings were waiting for medical treatment. Several nurses and doctors were already performing triage, putting the most critically-injured patients at the head of the line.

As bad as Lynne's broken leg was, her injury was still relatively minor compared to some of the others still waiting for care. "Good thing you're already in traction, Lynne," I said. "You'd be in a world of hurt, otherwise."

"It's not too bad, is it?" said Wayne.

Lynne smiled. "I've had worse. Not much worse, but I'll manage. I've been in emergency wards often enough to understand how triage works."

Other people did not share Lynne's sentiment, and many people complained about the long wait whenever a doctor or nurse passed by. Occasionally, a person flashed a badge or an ID chit and got taken into the medical center sooner than I would have thought their conditions warranted. It disgusted me.

It had apparently disgusted Lynne even more. She became irate when an orderly tried to assist her ahead of the obviously more seriously injured patients in the corridor.

The orderly respectfully bowed. "You are truly a selfless person, Mrs. Freed. It is not necessary for you to receive treatment at this time, since your leg has already been set. I have been instructed to take you to a room so that we can clear the corridor for the more serious cases."

"Oh. Well that's different, then. I apologize."

"I wish more of these diplomats were like you, Ma'am. There is one pompous twit from Polaris who is making a big stink about his wife's sprained ankle. She wasn't even a bomb victim. She missed a step as she left their ship."

Lynne scoffed. "Good thing I didn't see that. I'd give him a piece of my mind."

Wayne leaned over to kiss Lynne. "I love you."

We followed as the orderly wheeled Lynne's bed up to her room. The room looked very comfortable and roomy, even if one did not take into account that we were on a large spaceship and not in a four-star hotel.

Lynne blinked. "Are all the hospital rooms this nice?"

"This is not a hospital room. This is your suite on the embassy level."

"I don't understand."

The orderly smiled. "I told you that you do not require further treatment at this time. There is no need for you to stay in a hospital room. Your ship's doctor will be in to check on you once his services are no longer required in triage."

"This is nice. Thank you. What was your name?"

"Otto, Ma'am. Thank you for asking. No one ever does."

"And they call themselves diplomats. Thank you, Otto."

Biggs and I followed Otto out to give the newlyweds some privacy. "Call if you need us," said Biggs.

Our own staterooms were not nearly as roomy as the one we had just left, but as crew quarters went, I had no complaints. Diplomats were often expected to host gatherings or informal meetings in their rooms, so it only made sense that they were given large rooms. Crew, on the other hand, generally only used their quarters for sleeping, or for study, so they tended to be sized appropriately.

My room, which was a mirror image of Biggs', had a desk with a swivel chair, a locker, and a bed. The bed was in a loft above the desk. A ladder provided access to the bed, or a control on the wall lowered the bed down to the desktop level if one did not wish to climb the ladder...or was unable to climb, due to an injury, I supposed.

I remembered the week that Tanya Orlov and I had shared our *maitalea*. I imagined her trying to navigate the ladder, all the while cursing at me for putting her on crutches. Why she ever had consented to sleep with me... but then, she hadn't consented, had she? She had invited me. Heck, she had practically ordered me to sleep with her. But she didn't love me, she just wanted me.

No, that wasn't really accurate, either, was it? She didn't want me, she wanted sex. It was a way to pass the time on a week-long voyage, nothing more. I was willing, not because I particularly cared for her, but because I felt responsible for her injury.

"She took advantage of me!" I said out loud, even though there was no one but me in the room. "The bitch!"

My oft-ignored inner voice came through loud and clear. *You didn't exactly turn the offer down, did you?*

"Saying no to a beautiful woman who wanted to have sex with me just wasn't in my repertoire, now, was it?"

But did you love her?

Where had that thought come from? "Of course not. I didn't even like her. She was just... available."

I realized that not only was I talking to myself, I was getting answers. I really needed to go find something to do, before I really started going crazy.

Coward.

***

I headed down a half-dozen levels to the recreation area. There were beings from just about every settled planet in the Union milling about, playing games, engaging in conversation, watching the news on holovideo, or arranging *maitalea* agreements. Of the latter, I received several offers as I made my way through the crowd. I politely turned them all down.

At least, I hoped I had done so politely. I was still not used to every race's standard of protocol. But, since no one offered to break my legs, I was reasonably certain I at least hadn't offended anyone.

I ran into a few people I recognized as Denebian DipSec agents, Ben Elan's team. Including, I noticed, Tanya Orlov.

"Well, well, Tony Diego. I am pleased to see you have survived this day. You are staying out of the way, I trust?"

I laughed. "Are the rules about running the same on a ship this size?"

Tanya shook her head. "Here, no. Too many civilians. Means too many idiots. But there are facilities. Dedicated running tracks, on the level below this one."

"You sound like you've been on this ship before."

Tanya smiled. "No, but I am a naval officer, or was. My first instinct is to learn the ship. I have explored every place that we are allowed to go. How did you spend your last few hours, Tony?"

"Medical center. Lynne Freed broke her leg in the Grand Canyon several hours ago."

"Not your fault, I trust?"

I smiled. "Not this time. I am a little better coordinated than I used to be."

"We shall see. Are you looking for *maitalea*? As I recall, you did not get the best of me last time."

"I had no complaints. It was my fault you were in a cast in the first place."

"This is true."

"Thanks, Tanya, but I must decline your offer."

"A pity. Ah, well, I will find another. Perhaps I can find that Ursan again." A smile came to her lips. "Now there was a body worth remembering."

I gasped. "You slept with an Ursan?"

"I have slept with several alien life forms. Do not be so prudish, Tony. Nearly all humanoid races share the same physiology."

"I knew that," I said, my face becoming hot. "I just thought Ursans tended to keep to their own kind. Never mind. It's none of my business, anyway. I guess I'll see you around."

Tanya smiled and returned to her comrades. I left the rec center with a sour taste in my mouth. How had I ever been attracted to such a woman, anyway?

Right. She had been naked. And breathing.

What an ass I had been. Kay had been right to dislike me. I was damn lucky she never hated me.

I suddenly felt a desire to call her, just to hear her voice.

I checked my watch and swore. It was almost midnight in Oklahoma City. Kay would be asleep by now, and she might kill me if I woke her up. In our line of work, a midnight phone call was almost never good news. I made a mental note to call her tomorrow, then headed back to my room. I seriously needed sleep. Once I was well rested, I might be better able to ignore my inner voice.

Chapter 15: In Council

The following morning, nearly every monitor on the vast carrier was tuned in to the emergency Council Session.

I watched as the camera panned around the Council room. Around a central dais were rows upon rows of pods. They reminded me of the luxury skyboxes in a football stadium, if the stadium was a mile wide and there were no bleachers. Each pod contained either a Council delegate and a party of aides or companions, or a holovideo projection of the delegate. I notice that only a small percentage of pods contained actual beings. The vast majority were communicating remotely from their individual quarters.

I supposed that many delegates had been injured or even killed by explosions. "What do you think this means, Boss?"

"I'm not big on making assumptions," said Biggs, "and I'm not a gambling man, but I would bet real money that whoever was behind this was targeting the delegates intentionally."

The briefing was mediated by Dok Fil. He stood at the dais, flanked by his security team and his chief of staff, Merv.

Most of the delegates appeared relieved to see him still alive.

"Sentient beings of the galaxy," he began. "I thank you for participating in this unprecedented event. As you all know, approximately twenty-four hours ago, many systems in the Galactic Union experienced terrorist bombings. There was no prior warning. Although several groups have claimed responsibility for the attacks, we have no credible evidence linking any of the bombings to any one group."

"The attacks had to have been coordinated by someone," someone shouted. The view screen identified the speaker as Ambassador Rrowlf Sharpfang of Merak.

"I am of that opinion also," said Dok Fil, nodding. "The Office of the Mediator has launched investigations in every system where we have a presence, and we are receiving intelligence from those systems where we do not."

"It seems rather unlikely a connection will ever be found," said the acting Polaran Ambassador, Stevis Solless.

"With such a large scale attack as this," said Dok Fil, "the likelihood of at least one perpetrator making a mistake is high. I am confident we will eventually find out who coordinated it."

"I only hope it is before they can strike again," said Solless. "My own system has been left in turmoil. I suddenly find myself the highest ranking government official left alive on Polaris. I am confident that I will be able to restore order, as soon as I may return to my system."

His tone of voice made it abundantly clear that he did not appreciate being summoned out to the emergency Session when he had work to do back home.

"We will attempt to end this session as soon as we can and send everyone on their way," said Dok Fil. He turned and whispered something to his aide, Merv.

Merv left the dais, and Dok Fil faced the microphone once more. "We will now hear reports from each system on the damage and loss of life."

There had been a cabinet meeting in progress on Polaris when a bomb destroyed High Chancellor Hans Conrad's office. All had perished, including his wife, Council Ambassador Angela Conrad. Stevis Solless, who had been one of her aides, was currently acting in both roles.

Council Ambassador Xanti, of Deneb, rose to report on Deneb, along with Sol, its protectorate. It took me a moment to realize he was referring to Earth.

"I am pleased to announce that neither of the *Umea Bakearen* of the Sol-Deneb Treaty were injured in the attack. We suspect that the attacks on our planets were intended to harm them in order to sever the Sol-Deneb Treaty."

As each system gave its report, a pattern began to emerge. Most of the attacks were against people who were the custodians of treaties between their system and another.

"I knew it," said Biggs. "It's a damn good thing that Wayne and Lynne wasted no time getting married. The abrupt change in their routine probably saved their lives."

The worst attack was against the underwater city of Subaquarius Alpha on Betelgeuse. The bomb had destroyed the embassy, but it had also created a breach in the city's outer wall. The city's emergency bulkheads had closed immediately, isolating the breached section, but it was the city's most populated area. None of the people trapped in the flooded section survived. The death toll was over half a million people. The rest of the planet was temporarily withdrawing from the Union to mourn.

"The withdrawal of Betelgeuse means that an alternate UnionCon host must be selected," said Dok Fil.

"With all respect," said Solless, "Since Polaris has just hosted the last one, our infrastructure is already equipped to handle UnionCon. We would be willing to host it again this year."

"The Union thanks you for the offer," said Dok Fil, "but you will have enough on your agenda reorganizing your government to take on the added responsibility of another UnionCon."

"Every system will face similar challenges," Solless retorted, "but I will respect the decision of the Council."

Ambassador Xanti rose again. "Union bylaws stipulate that the current seat of government is to host UnionCon when the chosen host must withdraw, and when no other system is able or willing to host. I move that Aldebaran host UnionCon this year."

Solless rose. "I will second that motion."

"Is there any discussion?" said Dok Fil.

"Just one thought," said Ambassador Sharpfang. "If Aldebaran is host, will that not spread thin the resources of the Office of the Mediator? What will become of the investigation?"

"Only the Aldebaran Office would be affected," said Dok Fil. "Each system that has a branch office would be unhindered in their investigations. But the point is valid. The Aldebaran Office of the Mediator facility was destroyed in the attack."

"It is generally the local government, and not the Office of the Mediator, that organizes UnionCon," said Xanti. "Dok Fil will be able to focus his attention on rebuilding his office, even if UnionCon is to be held there."

The vote went in favor of moving UnionCon to Aldebaran.

Dok Fil closed the briefing with a moment of silence for those lost.

"It will be months, maybe years, before we know exactly how many were lost," said Biggs. "Did you know anyone who worked at the Murrah Building?"

I shrugged. "I'll probably recognize names when the roll comes out, but I wasn't aware of anyone I knew working there."

Biggs nodded. "It usually works out that way. What bothers me is how did someone manage to coordinate the attacks? No one ought to be landing on Earth except through Groom Lake. There's going to be a shake-up at Immigration for sure."

"It would be even worse if the mole was in DSS," I said.

"I wish you hadn't said that," said Biggs. "I was hoping I was just being paranoid."

"Just because you're paranoid doesn't make you wrong."

"You got that one from me. Good. I didn't think any of you whelps were paying attention."

Chapter 16: The Waiting

I called Kay the following morning. "How's it going?"

"I was going to ask you the same thing. News from out there isn't exactly easy to come by, you know."

I told her everything that we had learned from the Council Session. "Over 500 planets reported explosions."

"How's Lynne?"

"She's supposed to get a cast on her leg today. I can't imagine how tedious it must be, lying in traction for days."

"Tedious is the word." Kay paused. "Do you have any idea when you're coming home? I mean, back to Earth?"

"I wish I knew. Delegates have begun leaving *Empresa* for their home systems, but Deneb still hasn't opened its airspace, which means Earth hasn't, either. Besides that, I suspect that Wayne and Lynne are going to spend at least a few days on Deneb with the Elans."

"That's going to amount to at least two weeks!"

I sighed. "I really wish you could have come with me. I haven't stopped thinking about you since I got here."

"Is... is Tanya there?"

"She is. You're not going to believe this, but she made me another offer."

"No kidding?" She paused. "Look, Tony, I understand if you want to..."

I laughed. "You don't seriously think I would take her up on it, do you?"

"You did, once."

"Once. Look, Kay, I was an idiot back then. Heck, I guess I still am, sometimes."

"You'll get no arguments from me."

"The point is, to her, I'm just another piece of meat. Right after I declined her offer, she started cataloging her other options. She was so... I don't know."

"Blasé?"

"Yeah, that's a good word. It was like she'd had so many conquests, I didn't even matter to her."

"So, how many partners have you had since then?" Kay

sighed. "No, never mind, Tony, I don't really want to know. It's none of my business."

"You wanna know the truth? Very nearly... one."

"Seriously? I would have been the first since then?"

"I didn't want anyone else. I still don't."

"I don't know what to say to that."

"You don't have to say anything."

"You know I'll have to report back in to DC within two weeks. Our window's closing, Tony."

"I know. And it's probably going to be almost a year before we get another chance. You think you can wait that long?"

"I've waited this long. What's another year?"

"We can at least spend some time together, can't we?"

"Sure," she said, "As long as we keep it platonic."

"What, you want me to drink hemlock?"

She laughed. "That's Socrates!"

"I know. I'll talk to you later."

"Bye."

I pocketed my phone and went looking for the gym.

***

Two Aldebarans were sparring on one of the mats. They were using a martial art technique I had never seen, which intrigued me. "I remember you two. You are Van Dam, and Far Polk, yes?"

The two bowed to each other, and then to me. "You are Tony Diego," said the man. "I pray you are well."

"I hope I'm nor interrupting. I was intrigued by your form."

"Are you a master?"

"Not yet. But I walk the path."

Van Dam nodded. "Would you care to spar? I will teach you what I know, if you will reciprocate."

I stepped onto the mat and bowed, then assumed a stance.

Van Dam took me down in less than a second.

I got up, grinning. "I would not have expected one so tall to move so fast. Again?"

This time, I dodged his sweep and countered with a throw. Van Dam went down.

He smiled. "You are indeed a quick study. We both shall learn much today."

Aldebaran martial arts are fundamentally similar to Terran styles, so we had no trouble at all learning each other's techniques. After several hours, I was exhausted. I took much comfort in knowing that the next time I faced Jack on the mat, I was so going to kick his ass. I might even be able to take Biggs down for once.

Van Dam extended his hand. "Thank you for a most enthralling afternoon, Tony Diego."

"My friends call me Tony," I said. "After this workout, I would be proud to count you both among them."

Van Dam nodded. "Agreed. Would you care to join us for dinner, or do you have plans?"

"Yes, I'd like to join you. I need to check in on the Freeds, but I will meet you at the commissary in an hour, say?"

No one answered at their suite, so I called Wayne's phone.

Wayne answered on the first ring. "Hi, Tony. Everything all right?"

"I was going to ask you the same thing, Boss."

Wayne laughed. "Apart from getting my butt kicked in cribbage, I'm fine."

"Since you're not in your room, I assume Lynne's out of bed."

"Yes, we're with Ben and Sonja. I guess I should have let you or Leroy know. Sorry."

"No big deal, Boss. I suppose this ship is the securest place in the galaxy, right?"

"Everyone I've met sure seems to think so."

"You don't sound convinced."

"I'm sure it's nothing, but whenever I hear 'unsinkable', I think 'Titanic'. The sooner we're off this ship, the safer I'll feel."

"Any idea when that'll be?"

"Ben expects Deneb to reopen its airspace in a day or two. We're probably going to spend a few days there before returning home. That's all right, isn't it?"

I smiled. "Wayne, I've told you before, we're at your service. You don't need our permission to go anywhere."

Wayne sighed. "I suppose you're right, but I'm not the one signing everybody's paychecks. It's not my ship, and you're not my crew."

"For all intents and purposes, we are. You're kind of like the President. Only, you're more important... and you don't wield any real political power."

Wayne's laughter was so loud that several passersby looked

at me quizzically. "You sure know just the right words to uplift and humble at the same time."

"Sorry, Boss. I didn't mean it as an insult."

"Oh, no, it's no insult. It is the truth, though. You, Biggs, and the crew of... what the heck is the name of the ship, anyway?"

I shrugged. "I'm not really sure it has a name. I've only ever heard serial numbers."

"Huh. Well, anyway, you all are the only ones who ever listen to anything I say."

"I'm sure that's going to change, one day."

"Thanks, Tony."

I grinned. "No, I meant we'll stop listening. Kidding. Call if you need me. I've got a dinner date."

"Oh? Is she pretty?"

"Not that kind of date, unfortunately. See you later."

"Bye, Tony."

After a shower, I headed to the Commissary.

Chapter 17: Another Crisis

The best part about Wayne and Lynne returning to Deneb was that I would get to fly the limo. Biggs usually claimed the driver's seat whenever we were in a ground-only vehicle, but he didn't like to fly.

The worst part about being on Deneb was that Kay and I weren't going to get the chance to finish what we had started.

By the time we got back to Earth, DSS had decided that there was no credible threat to Janet or the Freed family. Kay and the other agents on the ground were recalled to DC.

Back in DC, Kay went back to being Agent Moss, and I went back to being Diego. It wasn't exactly as though Oklahoma City hadn't happened, but neither did she give any indication that it had. The window had officially closed.

It wasn't as though it couldn't be reopened, of course. I just had no idea how. I wasn't entirely certain how I had managed to open the window this last time. Nor could I be sure the same method would work twice. I did resolve to try as soon as the opportunity arose.

I never got the chance. We hadn't been back in DC forty-eight hours when Biggs came in to the office with an odd expression on his face. "Grab your overnight bags, team. We're going back to Groom Lake, via Rock Creek Park."

"Aw, Boss, we just came from there!"

"Your point, Diego?"

"Not valid. Getting my gear."

"Good." Biggs tossed me the keys. "You're driving."

"Yes, Boss."

We all piled into the van. Biggs rode shotgun, while Jack and Rita climbed in the back.

Once everyone was strapped in, I started the engine and drove out of the parking garage. "I was supposed to have dinner with Kayla this evening."

Biggs shook his head. "My daughter has a piano recital tonight."

"This job sucks, sometimes."

No one said anything for the entire ride to Rock Creek

Park. Once we were relatively sure no one could see us, I took us vertical. "On the other hand, this kind of makes it all worth it."

"Kind of," said Biggs.

"Now that we're in the air, what's the crisis?"

"I got a call from the White House Chief. The President was talking to the Mediator earlier this afternoon, when the Res Net connection went dead."

Rita gasped. "I thought that wasn't possible."

"It's not supposed to be possible. I don't have to tell you that without it, we're deaf and blind to the rest of the galaxy. Our Res Net phones won't work, either. If that's not bad enough, Wayne thinks there might be trouble brewing on Deneb. The Chief didn't have details, but he did say that Wayne's heading back out, and he needs backup. That's us."

***

We maxed out the van's engines, reaching Groom Lake in just under twenty-eight minutes. We had the van and the limo loaded into the cargo bay when another car landed in the lot.

Biggs opened Wayne's door and saluted him.

Jack and Rita looked at me. I shrugged. "I've never seen Biggs act that formal, either. Even at the wedding, but he was definitely off duty at the time."

Janet and Lynne got out of the car with Wayne. Jack glanced at Janet, then leaned toward me to whisper in my ear. "So... which one is his wife, again?"

"The one with crutches and the huge cast. Haven't you been paying attention?"

"Then what is Janet to him?"

"She's a friend of his, and she works for him. I'm surprised to see her here, though. She was definitely not in the loop April Nineteenth."

Rita smiled. "I guess she's more than just a friend, then, huh?"

Jack glared at Rita before getting into the car. He pulled it up the ramp into the cargo bay as the rest of us filed into the crew lounge. The doors closed and we strapped in. An announcement came over the speakers. "All hands, prepare for emergency launch in thirty seconds."

"What does that mean?" Janet asked.

"It means I hope you haven't eaten in the last two hours," said Wayne. "Better move quickly."

"I hate emergency launches!" said Lynne, struggling to get strapped in. "My leg is starting to hurt just remembering that last one."

Wayne helped Lynne cushion her leg. "I'm sorry, love. This is another emergency."

I got my own straps fastened as we were all pressed into our seats.

Lynne screamed as the gee forces multiplied. I could not even imagine the pain she had to be going through during the ten minutes of the thrust. Wayne held her hand, tears in his own eyes. "I'm sorry, *Maiteakren*. I'm so sorry!"

Gradually, the gee forces began to subside. Lynne's screaming gave way to sobbing.

"That totally sucked!" said Janet when the all clear was given. "Are you okay, Lynne?"

Between sobs, Lynne said, "I'll take that wheelchair, now. I think I broke my leg."

Biggs and Wayne carefully helped her into the wheelchair and quickly wheeled her down to the sickbay.

"Launches aren't always like that, are they?" asked Janet. "Because if they are, I'm not liking this whole 'space travel' thing."

"Most of the time, they're nice and leisurely. Of course, this is the second emergency launch for us in the last few weeks." I looked back toward the corridor to the infirmary. "I feel sorry for Lynne. At least this time her leg was protected in a cast. Last time... well, I didn't see her during the launch, but that one had to be even worse."

"That was the day of the bombing, wasn't it? Lynne mentioned some things that didn't make sense until just now. She must really be suffering. Is there anything I can do for her?"

"Doc Howard is looking after her, and Wayne's with her. If worse comes to worst, he'll probably put her in traction again. The best thing you can do now is get comfortable and settle in."

"Stay out of the way, you mean, right?"

I smiled. "Speaking of that, if you're in the outer perimeter corridor, stay to the inside, no matter which direction you're going. Runners use the corridor. They're always going counter-clockwise, and they'll always be on the outside."

Jack laughed. "Tony knows of what he speaks. Our first time out, he actually broke a girl's leg tripping her up!"

"No! Really?"

I shrugged. "No one had ever told me. That's the other thing. Veteran spacers always assume everyone knows what they know, so they never volunteer information. At least, not until after you've pissed them off. There really ought to be a handbook, or something."

Jack grinned. "I didn't know you could read."

I made like I was going to punch him, but Biggs was coming around the corridor. "I didn't see that."

"Sorry, Boss. How's Lynne?"

Biggs shrugged. "It doesn't look too bad. The Doc prescribed bed rest and elevation until the swelling goes down again. We probably won't see much of Lynne, or Wayne, for that matter, until we get to Deneb."

"What do we actually do once we get there?"

Biggs shrugged. "I honestly hope there is nothing to do. The reason we're taking this trip is because Res Net went down."

"What's Res Net?" asked Janet. "I mean, if it isn't classified, or anything."

Biggs smiled. "Miss Clarke, your being on this ship means that you have been taken into Wayne's confidence. For better or worse, you have just become a citizen of the greater Galactic Union."

"So, what's Res Net?"

"It's short for Resonator Network. I couldn't begin to tell you how it works. I'm not even sure the folks who build the transceiver beacons know. But it allows for instant communication between distances that radio waves would take hours—or years—to cross."

"You mean it's actually faster than light?"

"Someone tried to explain it to me once," said Biggs. He made a gesture with his arm in which his hand flew over and past his head.

Jack smiled. "You're just not geeky enough, Biggs. It's not faster, because that would imply speed. It's truly instantaneous. The resonators stay in tune with each other, no matter how far apart they are. It's like they're always connected."

"Ah, like being in love?"

Jack blushed. "Uh, I hadn't thought about it that way, but if the analogy helps, sure. I could go for you... um, that. I could go for that, if the analogy helps you understand."

Janet nodded. "So one of these beacons went down?"

"Our system has three," I said. "They all went down."

"Oh. That can't be good."

"They're supposed to have all kinds of fail-safes," said Jack. "One going down is not good."

"All three is suspicious. Plus, the creepy guy that came into the office. He said he was someone named Merv, but Lynne said he was lying."

"If Lynne said that, I'd believe her," I said.

"That's why Wayne called for help," said Janet. "But his phone wouldn't work. Probably because of the Res Net."

I pulled out my phone. "Our phones are useless without it."

"That's why your phone is like Wayne's! You're not aliens, too, are you?"

I laughed. "Not all of us. Biggs, Rita, Jack, and me, We're all human. Well, everyone on the ship is human, really, but we're Terran. Everybody else on the ship is Denebian."

"There are a half-dozen or so systems settled by humans," said Biggs. "I've only ever been to two of them. Three, if you include Earth. Cygnus is the other system I've been to."

I put my useless phone away. "What's that planet like, Boss?"

"It's pretty much like Earth. Or Deneb. That's probably why humans settled it."

Janet sat down. "Whoa. It's really real, isn't it? There's life on other planets?"

Jack sat down beside her, a steadying hand on her shoulder. "I know it can be a bit much to take."

"A bit much? Do you have any idea how many things I 'knew' when I woke up this morning have just crapped on my windshield and flown away?"

"That's... that's an odd metaphor."

Janet looked at Jack. "You know, like if ideas were birds."

"Oh, I'm not saying I don't understand it, it's just... crapped on your windshield?"

"Well, that's what birds do, right?"

"But, do ideas do that?"

"Let me get this straight. We're flying through space with a crew of Denebians. Wayne and his wife are aliens. Her sister and brother-in-law are possibly in danger. We can't call for backup because Res Net is down, even though Res Net never goes down. And you're critiquing my metaphor?"

Jack blushed. "I didn't say it wasn't a cute metaphor. For all

I know, it's a totally accurate picture of how your day is going. It just seemed... Ah, hell. I'm sorry, Janet. Can we start over? I'm Jack. Pleased to meet you."

Janet shook his outstretched hand. "Nice to meet you, Jack. It's a pleasure. And confidentially, I don't even own a windshield. I drive a Vespa."

Jack laughed. "You still have a cute... metaphor."

Janet smiled. "You just keep your hands off my metaphor, buddy."

Jack put up his hands. "I'll be the perfect gentleman."

"About time I found one of those. I mean, besides Wayne, but he's taken."

"That doesn't bother you, does it?"

Janet sighed. "You know, it really doesn't? Wayne and I have known each other for, like, ever. I'm his sister's best friend, you know. I always hoped he'd fall in love with me, someday." Her eyes got wide. "This is where he used to go when he went away, isn't it? I mean, that's why he left for weeks at a time. That's why he was always so secretive."

I nodded. "For what it's worth, he used to tell me how he wished he could let you in on the whole thing."

Janet sighed. "Yeah. Well, as much as I wanted Wayne, I really never understood why he was so focused on his studies. I mean, love is more important than a career, right?"

Try telling that to Kay. "Yeah, I've heard that. But I guess it's not as simple as that. You know what would happen to Earth if Wayne dies, right?"

Janet nodded soberly. "That has to be a pretty heavy burden. Lynne understands it more than I ever could. I think that's why I don't feel jealous. I could never help ease that burden. In fact, I think I made it worse on him, throwing myself at him." She blushed. "I guess that's TMI, huh?"

Jack gave her a one-armed hug. "It's your story. Tell it any way you want. I'm all ears."

Janet returned the gesture. "There seems to be more to you than ears, Jack. Have we met before? There's something familiar about you."

Jack shrugged. "I wish we had. Uh, are you hungry? Thirsty? I can get you something."

"That would be great," she said. "I'll have whatever you're having."

"Be right back."

Once Jack left, Janet turned back to Rita and me. "So, what do people do for entertainment on flights like these, anyway?"

"Whatever it takes," said Rita. "There are various games, music, videos, and books. People run around the perimeter corridor. I've even known people to pair off for short-term relationships. Right, Diego?"

"I'm not proud."

Janet smiled. "It wasn't with a certain Agent Kayla Moss, was it?"

"I don't really feel comfortable with how this conversation is going."

Rita laughed. "No, it wasn't Kayla. But I'm willing to bet a week's pay Tony wishes it had been."

I blushed. "No, really. New subject, please."

Janet and Rita laughed.

I was about to seek refuge when Jack came back with a plate of sandwiches from the kitchen and several sodas. "I figured everyone could use something, too."

"Thanks, Jack," I said.

Janet selected a sandwich. "Very thoughtful of you. Does anyone know how to play Spades?

We were a few hands in when Wayne came back out. "Glad to see you're settling in."

Janet smiled and nodded. "Is Lynne okay? It looked like she was in a lot of pain after that launch."

"She's resting in our room. Doc said to put it up to keep it from swelling too bad. Emergency launches are hard enough without having to endure one with a broken limb. Lynne has already had to endure two. The first one was less than an hour after she broke it in the first place. This same ship was our airlift out of the Grand Canyon."

"Is there anything I can do for her?"

"No, but thanks. I'm going to go back to her as soon as I meet with the pilot. So, what do you think of space travel so far?"

"It's not such a big deal, really. I mean, the emergency launch sucked, but now we're just here. I thought we might at least fly past Saturn or something."

"I know what you mean. My first deep-space flight was kind of tedious. When there is no emergency, it takes three days or more just to get out of the solar system."

"Where are we now?"

"No idea. That's why I need to see the pilot. Want to

come?"

"Why not? I'm losing my shirt right now, anyway."

Wayne smiled. "Now, there's a mental image."

Janet punched Wayne's arm. "Not literally, you pervert!" She tossed her cards on the table and thanked Jack for feeding her. "I'll talk to you later. Jack, was it?"

"That's me. I'll be here."

Biggs strode in and took a sandwich off the plate. "Looks like you have an open seat. What's the game?"

Jack shuffled the deck. "Janet and Rita were whipping me and Tony in Spades. Anyone mind if we change games? Or partners?"

I tossed a candy at Jack. "I hope you're not blaming me, bro. You were the distracted one."

Jack sighed. "It wasn't that obvious, was it?"

"I've seen that look before."

Rita smiled. "Jack's got a thing for the lady, eh?"

"Since college."

"She was always with Wayne," said Jack. "I figured I never had a chance, you know? Biggs, you gotta let me be her bodyguard. Please?"

Biggs grunted. "It's against my better judgment, Forbes. I'll agree to it, for now. But if you two start getting too close, I'm reassigning you. Got it?"

"Got it. I promise not to compromise the mission."

"I'm still not sure there is a mission."

"Boss," I said, "with all respect, if Lynne thinks there's trouble, we'd better assume she's right. She's got a talent for reading people."

Biggs nodded. "Trust your gut, I always say. You heard the man. We're going to plan for the worst."

After a while, Janet came back. "Wayne's gone back to take care of his wife. Res Net is still down and the pilot thinks someone may have been trying to abduct or assassinate Wayne. This isn't a typical day for you guys, is it?"

Jack laughed. "No, honest. Apart from the bombing a few weeks ago, nothing ever happens."

"We're three hours from the jump, whatever that means. What does it mean, Jack?"

"Hyperspace jump. Not exactly sure how it works, but it's like a shortcut from one star system to another. Without it, it would take years to get where we're going."

Janet smiled. "You're my new favorite geek."

"Uh, thanks, I think."

"I mean it in a good way."

Jack smiled. "If you say so. In my experience, when a pretty girl says I'm a geek, it means we're not likely to be going out for coffee any time soon, so I should just move on."

Janet smiled and sat next to Jack. "So you think I'm pretty, then?"

Once Jack and Janet started flirting with each other, the rest of us scattered to our rooms. I tried to call Kay, then realized that with no Res Net, that wasn't happening, so I just went to sleep.

Chapter 18: Deneb's Southern Continent

When I awoke the next morning, I was pleased to see that my phone was operational. My joy gave way to frustration when I tried to call Kay. There was still no Res Net in the Sol system.

When I got to the lounge, I found Jack having breakfast, with Janet leaned against him, fast asleep. Wayne was comforting Lynne, who was silently weeping. Biggs and Rita were clearing their plates.

"Whoa, what'd I miss?"

Jack whispered, "We got Res Net as soon as we entered Deneb space, and I guess she stayed up all night reading the news. She fell asleep on me as soon as I sat down. Ben and Sonja are confirmed missing, and so is Dok Fil. Also, we just found out that the guy who visited Wayne's office was definitely an imposter, since the real Merv's body was found in the rubble of the Aldebaran OM."

"Damn,"

"We're going to have to reverse thrusters to land," said Wayne. "That's going to hurt Lynne as bad as the thrust did."

"You should probably go to the infirmary then. Maybe if Lynne's in a bed with her leg well cushioned, it won't be so bad."

"Good thinking," said Wayne. "Isn't there a girl on the ship with a broken arm? She ought to go there, too."

"That's Molly," said Biggs. "Separated shoulder. I'll go fetch her. The rest of you, get ready. I figure we'll be braking in less than thirty minutes."

Jack nudged Janet awake. She stirred and yawned. "Did I fall asleep? I hope no one pranked me."

"Not with Jack watching out for you," said Rita. "He's way too soft. Me, I would have painted your nose red, or something."

Janet smiled at Jack. "Thanks for that."

Everyone got into their seats even before the warning announcement, so that no one went flying when thrusters began firing.

After we landed at Deneb City Spaceport, Jack drove Janet, Wayne and Lynne to her parents' home, while the rest of us coordinated with the Denebian DipSec.

Ben Elan's ship had gone down over the Southern Continent, which, from all accounts I had read, made Australia look like Disneyland. DipSec had been unable to send search and rescue teams in, because whatever storms had caused the ship to go down were also playing havoc with flight controls. The effects had dwindled over the last few hours, so they were finally able to safely send drop ships in.

No one wanted to tell Lynne she couldn't come. Wayne tried, but Lynne wielded one of her crutches like a mace. "I am going to find my sister!"

We finally decided that Lynne would be less likely to hurt herself if we let her stay on the lead drop ship. We helped her strap into one of the medical evacuation seats, her cast properly supported and cushioned against most shocks from rough weather or landings. Wayne sat beside her. Jack and Janet sat on the other side of the aisle. Janet was so tired that she was asleep before we were even over the ocean.

I got to take the copilot's seat, while Zeru flew. "Flying one of these babies isn't much different from the van. The controls are pretty much the same, though the beast is ten times the size."

I nodded. "I bet flying the spaceships isn't that different from airplanes, either."

"Except for VTOL, you're right. And to tell you the truth, the VTOL system is a lot easier to master than landing a Terran airplane."

"Can I give it a shot when we get there?"

Zeru shook his head. "If it were up to me, I'd say sure. But we're flying in formation, so protocols must be followed to the letter."

"I understand."

"Sooner or later Terran pilots are going to earn the respect you deserve, Tony."

"Sooner or later," I agreed. "I guess I'll just watch, for now."

"We're about a half an hour from the coast. Why don't you gently wake anyone who's sleeping? We're going to need all eyes if we're going to spot anything."

"What do you say our chances are?"

"I'd rather not say. It's already been almost twenty-four hours since contact was lost. Their engines will be cold by now, so predators will start getting braver. But don't tell anyone back there that."

"I wouldn't dream of it."

Janet was asleep on Jack's shoulder. Jack was smiling, running his fingers through her pink hair. There was a gleam in his eye as I approached, and I had been his friend long enough to know what was going through his mind. He loved the woman, and he hoped she remained asleep for just a while longer so as not to destroy the illusion that they were a couple.

I couldn't blame him. I'd felt the same way when I held Kay asleep in my arms. The poor guy. Janet was way out of his league.

But, then again, Kay was way out of my league, and I seemed to have at least a slim chance with her. Maybe it wasn't such an impossible goal, after all.

Jack looked at me. I pointed to my watch and gave him the signal for half. He nodded, and began to whisper Janet's name.

Wayne was already beginning to wake his wife. She yawned and looked out the window. "Where are we?"

"About twenty-five minutes from the coast," I said. "Zeru says we need everyone's eyes."

Janet stirred and opened her eyes. She looked up, saw Jack, and smiled back at him.

I shrugged as I went back to rouse Biggs and Rita. Maybe it really was possible.

As we crossed the beach and began to fan out to explore the jungle below, Lynne sighed. "We're never going to find them, are we?"

Wayne kissed her. "Never say never."

We began a parallel sweep of the forest. Each swath of the search path was about two kilometers wide. If something in the distance caught someone's attention, the pilot circled the area in widening circles until we were certain the lead had been false.

At that rate, it would take weeks to search the entire continent.

From time to time, we would see one of the other rescue shuttles scanning for debris. Occasionally, a report would come in that a debris field had been located, but over the years there had been many vessels lost over the continent. Salvage was too dangerous, so most wrecks were left behind. Survivors were rarely ever found. Thanks to scavengers, the dead never were.

At night, we would set up a camp near the shore. The large predators rarely came out of the deep jungle, so we were safe, mostly. Even so, no one wanted to be in a flimsy tent, so people took turns sleeping on the seats and gurneys, while those who were awake stood watch for the apex predators.

On the second night, something got into one of the search vehicles. It looked like someone had taken it apart with a can opener. Not a trace of the crew could be found.

On the afternoon of our third day into the search, Janet saw something on the distant horizon. "Wow. That thing looks like Mothra!"

Wayne looked confused. "What's Mothra?"

"Oh come on," she replied. "Didn't you ever watch those Japanese monster movies? There was Godzilla, Mothra, Rodan…"

"Godzilla, I've heard of, but what was Mothra?"

"I used to love *daikaiju* movies. That's Japanese for 'giant monster'."

Lynne nodded. "I knew that. My neighbors in Aix-en-Provence were Japanese. We watched some of the classics together. Mothra was supposed to be, what, a giant moth?"

"Yeah," said Janet. "This one is not as colorful as the movie version. It's kind of brown and white. The wings almost look like birch bark."

Wayne shrugged. "That sounds more like an Aldebaran barkmoth."

"Aldebaran? Then what's it doing on Deneb?"

Lynne got excited and tried to undo her straps. "There's only one barkmoth on Deneb, as far as I know!"

Wayne jumped up to look out Janet's window.

"You're right! By the One, that's Little Hank! It's got to be! He's circling!"

"What's little Hank?"

"Remember that caterpillar that carried Sonja down to the ranger station? It imprinted on Ben."

"How did it get to Deneb?"

"Barkmoths can teleport. And they're telepathic, too! If it's circling, then it's tracking Ben!"

The remaining rescue ships created a protective perimeter around the downed ship. Our ship landed, ripping a few branches from surrounding trees in the process. The landing was a little rough.

We all looked at Lynne.

"I'm okay," she said. "That only hurt a little. Help me out of this harness!"

Wayne shook his head. "No, *Maiteakren*, you are staying right there."

"I want to see my sister!"

"You'll see her when she's safe. Remember your promise."

"Help me!"

Wayne looked sternly at Biggs. "Watch her, Leroy. If she tries to remove her harness, shoot her."

Lynne looked daggers at Wayne, who simply strode toward the hatch. Jack held Janet back, as well. Rita and I followed Wayne out to the wreckage.

The barkmoth had perched itself above the crashed ship's lifeboat. It somehow must have let Ben know help had arrived, because the reinforced door began to whir and groan. After a short silence, it opened with a slight hiss as the pressure equalized.

Ben looked rather pale as he staggered out of the hatch. He held his arm against his side. He blinked in the bright sunlight and looked around until he saw who he was looking for. "Ah, Wayne! I am so glad that you are not dead!"

Rita and I caught him as he passed out, lowering him safely to the ground. I signaled to the medics to come collect Ben, then I entered the hatch.

Sonja's left ankle and right arm were splinted, and she was lying on a cushion. She recognized my face and began to cry. "Tony! You came with my sister? Wayne?"

I nodded and she tried to get up. I bent down. "Stay there, Sonja. You're hurt."

"It's not as bad as it looks. Ben's in worse shape than me, but he won't admit it. He spent all his energy caring for me." Sonja started to cry again.

I held her as she sobbed, while Rita called for another stretcher.

My phone finally began to ring as Sonja and Ben were being loaded into the Med-Evac transport. "Kay? Oh, thank God. Res Net must be working again."

"Where are you?"

"Right now? Deneb's Southern Continent. It's a dreadful place, but I wouldn't want to live here. Or die here. Look, Kay, I'm sorry about our date. I've been trying to call you for... Christ, what day is it, anyway?"

"It's Wednesday. I haven't heard anything from you since Friday. I waited at the cafe for three hours, Tony. When you didn't show, I thought you'd changed your mind! I tried to call you, but my phone was dead."

"Yeah, mine too, or I would have called." I heard a rather

loud and menacing roar from the jungle beyond the crash site.

"What the hell was that noise?"

"Uh, look, Kay, can I call you back? We're losing daylight, and I really want to be in the air before whatever the hell that was decides I'm edible."

There was another roar, and I didn't wait for Kay to answer. Folding up the phone, I shouted, "Let's get out of here!"

By the time I got aboard, Lynne appeared to have forgiven Wayne, who was holding her as she sobbed.

"Everyone's accounted for," I said.

Wayne nodded and shouted out to Zeru, "Take us out of here. And go easy on the throttle, or I swear I'll kill you myself!"

Once we were safely in the air on our way back to the mainland, I decided to call Kay back.

Her phone went straight to voicemail.

I sighed. "Hi, Kay, it's me. Sorry for hanging up on you, but that... thing was getting way too close for comfort. I don't blame you for being upset. I'll talk to you when I get home, I guess."

Zeru gave me a sympathetic look. "Trouble with your lady friend?"

"At this point, I'm not even sure she is still my lady friend. No matter how hard we try, something keeps getting in the way. Maybe we just weren't meant to be."

"Perhaps. It is also possible that it is not yet time for you and her to be together. A wise teacher once wrote that there is a time for every purpose under the One."

"I never would have taken you for a theologian, Zeru."

"How can one see all the wonders of the universe and not give credit to the Creator?"

"There are terrible things, too. Maybe it's all just random coincidence."

"Ah, but you do not believe that, yourself, do you? Did you not just say that maybe you and Kayla were not meant to be?"

I paused to think that over. "I could be wrong."

Zeru smiled broadly. "Then there is no reason not to pursue the relationship, is there? Do the potential rewards of succeeding not outweigh the consequences of failure?"

"But what if pursuing one relationship costs me the chance at another somewhere down the line?"

"Another wise teacher once wrote, 'It is better to aim at the quarry you can see than the one you cannot; for a miss means to lose them both'."

"Where do you get all these sayings, anyway?"

Zeru shrugged. "Fortune cookies, mostly."

"You're kidding, right?"

"That is what I usually tell people. The truth is that I like to read. I do not mean simply reading text on a screen, mind you. I have in my home a library full of real books, with pages; scrolls and codices made of vellum; and ostraca from ancient civilizations most people have never even heard of."

"Wow. Seriously?"

Zeru cocked his head and grinned. "No. I just say that to impress the ladies. I do have a few ancient codices, which I treasure, but most of my reading is from the tablet. And fortune cookies."

I laughed. "Does it work?"

"You would be surprised. But only when I am looking for a *maitalea*. For some reason, the ladies become angry when they learn I have... exaggerated my assets. I would only tell truth to a woman I love."

"How many women have you loved?"

"There was one," he said, wistfully. "I did not realize it of course, until after I had aimed at the quarry I could not see."

"What happened to her?"

"She married another, wiser man. I still hope that I might find another like her, but finding one is rare enough."

I tried calling Kay back several times during the voyage home, but all I ever got was her voice mail.

Chapter 19: Relocation and Redemption

Several weeks went by before I saw Kay again. I called her at least once a week, but all I ever got was her voice mail. I left messages asking her to call me, but she never did.

Finally, I decided to try going over her head. There was one person at the DSS office who knew where any agent would be at any given time.

Jess looked at me over the top of her horn-rimmed reading glasses. "Can I help you, Agent Diego?"

"I certainly hope so. I'm having trouble reaching Agent Moss. You haven't seen her recently, have you?"

"Didn't you know? She's been assigned to protect Ambassador Albrecht on his fact-finding tour of Darfur."

"Darfur? When did she leave?"

Jess checked her file. "It's been at least a few weeks. There it is. Yep. She left four weeks ago. Should be back in another day or two."

"Would you mind asking her to give me a call?"

"You could leave her a voice mail."

I gave Jess one of my best sad puppy faces.

She rolled her eyes. "Fine, consider it done. Nobody ever does anything for themselves anymore."

"Thanks, Jess."

"You don't have to thank me. Chocolate is all I require. You know from where."

I grinned. "I promise to bring some back from UnionCon."

"Now, that's the way to win a girl's heart, Diego."

"If only it were that easy."

"Don't give up hope. You mean more to her than you think." Jess laughed. "More than she thinks, too, I'd wager."

I got a call from Kay a few days later. "Fifteen messages, Diego? Do you have any idea how desperate you sound?"

"You could have called me back."

"I didn't even know you called!"

"What?"

"Didn't anyone tell you where I was?"

"Not 'til I asked," I said. "What difference does it make?"

I heard Kay sigh. "Can you come over? We need to talk."

"Uh, okay. If you're breaking up with me, shouldn't we at least have a date first?"

"What?" After a moment, she laughed. "No, it's not that. Come over, please?"

On the way to Kay's apartment, I stopped to pick up a box of Godiva. Sure, it wasn't Sjokolade, but it was the best I could do on Earth.

I held out the box as she opened the door. "Me make peace with pretty lady?"

Kay laughed. "Come on in." She was wearing a pair of blue jeans and a pink tee shirt, both of which hugged her body tightly.

I had never been so jealous of clothing.

We sat on the sofa. "I didn't mean to scare you, Tony." Kay reached for a truffle from the box. "All the same, chocolate is better than flowers in my book."

"Why didn't you return my calls?"

"I was in Darfur, Tony. Don't you know what that entails?"

"Uh, pretend that I don't."

"'Certain alien technologies may not be taken into hostile territory'. Didn't you read the DSS handbook?"

"Uh, pretend that I didn't."

Kay rolled her eyes, but she was smiling. "Darfur is a bad place, Tony. I had to leave this"—she held up her phone— "at home."

"You could have told me you were going."

"You hung up on me, remember?"

"I called you right back! It wasn't even fifteen minutes later!"

"I had to catch a plane. That was why I called you in the first place."

"Oh."

"Don't get me wrong—I was pissed that you stood me up. I waited for three hours!"

"What was I supposed to do? I tried to call you, but my phone was dead."

"You couldn't get to another phone?"

"Even if I had, your phone wouldn't have worked."

"You could have left a message on my land line."

"I... didn't think of that. Even so, by the time I realized I couldn't call you on my phone, we were at Groom Lake, preparing for launch. I had to fly the van at Mach 10 to get there in time."

"You got to fly the van?"

"I'm sorry for not finding a way."

"I forgive you. I'm sorry, too. I was so mad at you after you hung up on me, I just put the phone away and left. I should have left you a message first."

"I didn't want to hang up. But you didn't see what those things did to one of the other drop ships."

Kay looked at me. "What happened?"

"In the middle of the night, predators ripped it apart like it was made of foil. We didn't even recover any remains to bury."

"How many?"

"I don't know. Our drop ship had eight people, so it was probably about that."

Kay hugged me. "I'm sorry. I had no idea."

I don't know how long we sat together, holding each other. "I missed you, Kay."

"I missed you, too. Once I got home and started checking my voicemail, I started feeling like an ass."

"Do you have plans? I still owe you a dinner."

Kay blinked. "You still want to take me out?"

"Or we could eat in. I'm a pretty good cook. What do you have in your cupboard?"

"I just got back from four weeks in Darfur, remember? If there is anything in the fridge, it's probably got legs by now."

I offered Kay my arm. "Let me treat you to dinner, then."

"Should I put something a little nicer on?"

"I've got my motorcycle. What you're wearing is perfect."

As we drove down the street, Kay leaned forward and wrapped her arms around my chest. Her body pressed against mine reminded me why I had bought a motorcycle in the first place. I hadn't planned on going as far as Chinatown, but I was enjoying the ride. Neither did Kay complain.

We parked in front of an open-air hibachi stand. As we watched the chef prepare our pork fried rice, I put my arm around Kay and she rested her head on my shoulder.

"So, what's Deneb's Southern Continent like?"

"Jungle, mostly. Or maybe it's rainforest. I'm not really sure what's the difference."

"Did you see any of the big predators?"

I shook my head. "No, and I can't say I'm disappointed. I don't really want to see the thing that did... what it did... to the other drop ship. From what I hear, very few people have seen one up close."

"And even fewer lived to tell about it, right? Aren't there at least some blurry photos of it? Like Bigfoot, or something like that?"

"Do you want me to tell the story, or not?"

"I'm sorry." Kay squeezed my hand. "For what it's worth, I'm glad you weren't on that drop ship."

The chef rang a bell. "Number eighty-four! Pork fried rice for two!"

I looked around. "We're the only ones here. What do you need to call out the number for?"

The little old man smiled. "Habit. Lots of people here in daytime. Ticket?"

I held up my ticket. "Eighty-four. What do I owe you?"

"Eleven dollars. You want drinks?"

I nodded. "Ginger ale, and a diet Coke."

"Thirteen dollars. Bad luck. You should order something else."

I picked up a couple bags of crunchy chow mein noodles. "That better?"

"Fifteen Dollars. Better."

I handed him a twenty. "Keep the change."

"Thank you. Enjoy."

"This is delicious," said Kay. "I wondered why we were going so far. This was definitely worth the ride."

I brushed my hand against her arm. "I was kind of enjoying the ride on its own."

She shivered at my touch. "That, too."

"So, how was Darfur?"

"About like you'd expect," she said. She shuddered. "Lots of very hungry people, and its government buys guns instead of food. Not sure why they picked me for the assignment. I felt like every Janjaweed soldier there was trying to decide if I'd be good sport. I slept with a knife under my pillow."

"You weren't the only security, were you?"

"No, my whole team was there, too. But Albrecht wanted me near him. I started wondering if he was trying to decide the same thing."

"I'll kill him."

"Nah, I decided he's a good man, just a little chauvinistic." She sipped her drink. "Or chivalrous, depending on your point of view. I was there to protect him, and he wanted me to be safe. Go figure."

"I'd want you to be safe."

"I know. You don't think I could handle myself in a fight."

"No, it's not that, at all. I just... I'd rather not see you hurt. It's not because you're a woman. Well, actually, I guess it is, but it's not because I think you're weak. It's because... It's because I think you're special."

Kay's eyes sparkled. "Why, Tony, I think you just shared your feelings. It didn't hurt, did it?"

I held my fingers close together. "A little bit."

Kay leaned forward. "I'm really glad you're not dead."

"Me too. I mean, not that I'm not dead. Well, I am glad I'm not dead, but I'm really glad you're not..."

Our lips touched, and for what felt like an eternity wrapped up in an instant, nothing else mattered.

"Um, can we do that again?"

The second kiss was every bit as pleasurable as the first.

Kay was starting to shiver as we walked back to my motorcycle, so I gave her my jacket. "The ride back might be a little chilly."

She put the jacket on. "Won't you be cold?"

"Not a problem." I opened up one of my saddlebags and pulled out a sweatshirt. "See?"

"You could have just given me the sweatshirt."

I paused. "I suppose, but my jacket looks better on you than this old thing would."

I pulled on the sweatshirt. "See? Totally unflattering."

Kay's voice was barely a whisper. "Take me home, Tony."

"Did I do something wrong?"

Kay smiled. "Not this time."

Back at her apartment, we walked hand-in-hand up the walk to her door. "I'll call you," I said. I kissed her and turned to go.

"You don't have to go, do you?"

"Not if you want me to stay," I said. "But you once said that wasn't going to happen in DC."

"I did say that, didn't I?" Kay took my hand. "I changed my mind. Please, stay."

I followed her into her apartment. Kay took off my jacket and carefully hung it up on an empty hook. She sat on her sofa and gestured for me to join her. I removed my sweatshirt and put it on the same hook as my jacket, then I sat beside her. We kissed again and slowly began to help each other remove clothing. When there was almost nothing left to remove, Kay led me to her bedroom...where the contents of her suitcase were still strewn about the bed. "Dammit! I forgot I was in the middle of unpacking when I started to check messages. I'm really sorry, Tony."

"It's okay, really. Do you want help?"

"What, in our underwear?"

I looked at her and smiled. "Okay, I admit that would be a bit distracting. Should I go, then?"

Kay held on to me. "I don't want you to go."

I kissed her. "We have time, Kay. How about tomorrow I'll bring in some groceries and make you dinner?"

Kay sat on the edge of the bed and nodded. "I'd like that. I promise this room will be tidy tomorrow. Nothing is going to stop us. You can count on it!"

Kay watched me as I put my clothes back on. When I reached for my sweatshirt, she stopped me. "Do you think I could borrow that?"

"This old thing? Don't see why not. What are you going to do with it?"

"Wear it, of course." She took it at pulled it over her head. "What do you think?" It was way too big for her, since I was almost a foot taller than she was, but it somehow made it look like she was wearing even less than she had been seconds ago.

My jaw dropped. "I think there is something very sexy about a gorgeous woman wearing my clothes. Even an old, ratty sweatshirt like that one. Why don't you just keep it?"

She inhaled deeply. "It even smells a bit like you. I'm going to sleep in it, I think."

I smiled. "There's an image that'll make it hard for me to get to sleep tonight."

She kissed me goodnight. "See you tomorrow, Diego."

As I drove home I made a mental note to bring a change of clothing tomorrow. I had a feeling that many of my clothes were soon going to become hers. Not that I minded. Seeing her in my sweatshirt made me feel...like I was a part of her, now, and she was a part of me.

Another thought occurred to me as I was driving home. As much as we were both willing, we would not be sleeping together tomorrow night, either. Sure, I had no rational reason to think so, but she had used a phrase that my vast experience of watching low-budget action movies had caused me to dread: "You can count on it."

I know, it's silly and superstitious nonsense. Words really don't have power to affect destiny, right? But in the kind of movies I watch, "You can count on me" is almost as deadly a phrase as "I'll be right back." It's not just my private superstition, either. There are alien cultures, according to Wayne, that have taboos against saying anything is a sure thing, unless it is obviously not going to happen.

By the time I got home, I had almost convinced myself that everything was going to be fine.

The next morning, I arose much later than I intended. I wasn't too worried about it, since our hours were pretty flexible. I called Biggs and told him I'd be in around ten. I showered, ate breakfast, then started a grocery list of the ingredients I'd need to make Kay a dinner she wouldn't forget.

When I got to the office, I noticed two things right away. First, Jack wasn't at his desk. That didn't concern me too badly, since I knew he had vacation time coming.

The second thing I noticed was that Kay was sitting at her old desk. She looked up as I passed and gave me a half-smile that was as apologetic as it was regretful. "Good morning, Diego."

"Hi, Kay." I almost bent down to kiss her, but I stopped myself before it was too late. "What are you doing here?"

Kay smiled and nodded. Her facial expression said *I know what you were about to do, and I'm as thankful as I am sorry that you didn't do it.* "Biggs called me about an hour ago. It looks like I'm back on the team."

"Forbes is taking a couple of weeks off," said Biggs. "About time you got here."

"I, uh, overslept, Boss. Won't happen again."

"We didn't get called in, so no harm done. I hope you and Moss aren't going to have any issues about working together. If you do, you'd better resolve them ASAP."

"What's going on?"

"Lynne Freed got the UN job she applied for. They're going to be moving to the East Coast. And Wayne doesn't know it yet, but his security detail is being stepped up."

"Why?"

"That whole abduction attempt about a month or so ago has got the higher-ups biting their nails. Wayne was pretty well anonymous while he was in college, but now that he runs a law firm, and his wife's going to be a UN interpreter, he's a lot more high-profile than he used to be. Even if no one here knows about Sol-Deneb, we still can't afford to have him get killed in some random robbery attempt now, can we?"

I nodded. "Makes sense. Where does Kay fit in?"

"I don't know if you've noticed that Forbes and Janet Clarke have taken an interest in each other. He can't be her bodyguard anymore, so I'm assigning Kayla. You're Wayne's bodyguard. Rita's going to be Lynne's. I'll be in charge of household security, and Jack's going to be my assistant."

"Jack's going to be my boss?" I shook my head. "He's never going to let me hear the end of that. This day just keeps getting better and better."

"Cheer up," said Rita. "It can't be as bad as all that."

Kay tilted her head. "Are we going to need to relocate? How long is this assignment going to last?"

"The assignment is permanent. And yes, we're all going to have to relocate."

"I guess I can live with that. When do we move?"

"Probably won't be for a week or so. Ms. Clarke is scouting out homes for Wayne and Lynne. It's probably a good thing that Jack and Janet have gotten friendly. I don't think it even occurred to Wayne to let us know about their move ahead of time."

"Is that what Jack's doing on his vacation?"

Biggs nodded. "Janet called Jack. They're scouting out locations in Freehold, New Jersey. It's a good location. About 45 minutes from the UN, and maybe three hours from here."

I nodded. "I know the region. Grew up around Monmouth."

"That's it, folks. Start packing."

At the end of the workday, Kay and I walked out to the parking lot together. "I'm sorry, Tony."

"It's not your fault, Kay."

"I could have turned down the assignment."

"No, you couldn't. You want to travel out to space again. I don't blame you. And at least it means we'll get to see more of each other, right? I mean, we just spent almost six weeks apart because our assignments took us away from each other. If it's a choice between sleeping with you between separate assignments and at least getting to see you every day, I'll take having you around any day."

"I think you mean that," Kay said.

"I promise to try really hard not to touch your ass the next time we dance together at someone's wedding, no matter how badly I want to."

Kay laughed and touched my cheek. "I'll promise to try really hard not to get mad at you when you do it anyway. And I won't get mad at you if someone offers you a *maitalea*."

I scoffed. "After you, what other woman could possibly have anything else to offer me?"

Kay gave me a half smile, though there were tears in her eyes. "Technically speaking, you never have had me."

"No, but I've come close. And just because we can't, doesn't mean I wouldn't."

"How long are you willing to wait, Tony?"

"As long as you are. Deal?"

Kay put her arms around me and kissed my cheek. "Deal."

"I promised to make you dinner tonight," I said. "Are we still on for that?"

"I was hoping you'd ask."

Chapter 20: Freehold

Wayne gave us no argument when Biggs told him that DSS would provide Lynne with a bodyguard. He heartily approved of Biggs' choice of Rita for the job.

When Biggs announced that I was to be Wayne's bodyguard, it was a different story. He didn't think he needed one.

Lynne, however, was solidly on our side. "If I need a driver and bodyguard as the wife of an ambassador, how much more so does my ambassador husband?"

"I'm not going into the city every day. I'm just going to be going between here and my office!"

Biggs intervened. "It's a routine. You're going to the same location at the same time every day. A terrorist could exploit it. Tony has the same qualifications as Rita. He's also a veteran fighter pilot. I'd bet that with a little training, he could even handle one of those Denebian spaceships. You're the boss, of course, but I would strongly urge you to consider my recommendation."

Lynne was firm. "If I need Rita, you need Tony."

Wayne sighed and threw up his hands in defeat. "Okay, okay. You win."

Biggs addressed Janet, next. "Jack Forbes has asked to be your bodyguard, but it's clear to me that you both have feelings for each other. That'll make it harder for him to concentrate on your safety."

"Do I even need a bodyguard? I'm just an assistant."

"You are more than just an assistant," said Lynne. "You're family."

Wayne agreed. "You are as important to me as my wife, Janet. That means you're a potential target. I think you'll like Kayla."

Janet brightened up when Kay stepped forward. "Oh, I remember you! You were Ms. Information after the Murrah bombing!"

Kay nodded. "I'd hoped you would have forgiven me for that by now."

"Of course I do. I understand a lot more now than I did then." Janet stuck out her hand. "Friends?"

"Friends," said Kay.

"Janet's living on the grounds, so we'll probably carpool most of the time." Wayne looked back and forth between Kay and me. "That means that you two will be together a lot. Are you okay with that?"

Kay nodded. "We're professionals, Wayne. Your safety will always be our first priority. Right, Tony?"

"Absolutely. There is no one I'd rather be paired with. Uh, professionally, I mean."

Kay let me see the slightest smile before putting on her poker face. "I've become an expert at resisting Diego's charms."

Lynne caught Kay's smile and grinned herself. "I have every trust in these two, Wayne."

"That's good enough for me."

"So, what do I do?" asked Jack.

Biggs pointed to the small security office building. "We're going to assemble grounds security. There may well eventually be E.T. VIPs visiting here, so we need thorough background checks on every candidate. You up to the challenge?"

"You mean I'm second-in-command?" Jack eyed me ruthlessly. "Won't that be fun?"

"Don't get too high-and-mighty," said Biggs. "Moss, Cruz, and Diego answer directly to Wayne, now, same as us. We'll be focused on grounds staff."

"Oh, man, we dodged a bullet, there," I said.

Biggs stifled a grin. "This property is like a fortress. Whoever built it had a strong desire for security, and privacy."

Janet nodded. "It was built for a movie star whose career unfortunately didn't meet his budget expectations. It had been sitting vacant for several years when I found it. The realtor was glad to finally sell it."

"It's a beautiful house," said Lynne. "It'll be perfect for raising our family."

***

The best part of the whole arrangement was that Kay and I were partners again. During the day, while Wayne and Janet did lawyer things, Kay and I wandered around the office park, keeping an eye out for anything suspicious. The other offices belonged to doctors, accountants, and other professionals.

The office park had its own security team. By the third day, one of the guards had become suspicious of our wanderings. He got out of his van and asked us for some identification. We showed him our DSS badges.

"What the hell is DSS?"

"Diplomatic Security Service," I said, putting my badge back into my jacket pocket. "We guard and protect foreign dignitaries."

"Well, there aren't any foreign dignitaries here, Agent Diego. What are you doing here?"

"We're not really at liberty to say," said Kay. "It's classified."

"Right. Let me see your badges, again. I'm going to call this in."

Kay and I handed him our badges once more and sat on a park bench as he stepped out of earshot. After about five minutes, the rent-a-cop looked back at us, his face pale.

Kay leaned into my shoulder. "I'm guessing he just got our verification back."

I chuckled. "I wish this sort of thing happened more often. I love that look of panic on their faces."

The man's voice shook as he handed back our badges. "W-who are you people? My dispatcher just shit a brick."

Kay raised her eyebrow. "Excuse me?"

"Uh, sorry ma'am. It's just that I've never heard him sound so nervous before. He said that he's been ordered to destroy any record of the inquiry, and he quoted a protocol neither of us have ever heard of before."

"Yeah," I said, "we get that a lot."

"S-so w-who are you, anyway?"

Kay's face remained expressionless. "If we told you, your memory would have to be erased. I'd hate to have to do that to you, again, Stanley."

"How do you know my name? And what do you mean, again?"

His name was on his ID badge, plain as day, but I couldn't resist. "We had this conversation yesterday." I shook my head. "Every time it happens, we run the risk of wiping, well, too much. Remember that poor guy down in Trenton, Kay? Forgot where he lived?"

She shuddered. "I'd rather not."

"Oh? That can be arranged."

The guard slowly backed away. "You two have a nice day,

now. I'll put the word out to leave you alone. No! No, I won't! I mean, I won't say a thing to anyone."

After he got back into his van and drove off, Kay and I looked at each other and started laughing.

Kay shrugged. "Do you think we should tell Biggs?"

"He's probably who the dispatcher spoke to, but yeah, better let him know when we get back to the villa."

***

I fully expected Biggs to give us a lecture about not riling the locals. I did not expect him to be even remotely amused.

So when he threw back his head and guffawed, I thought for sure something was wrong with him. "Uh, you okay, Boss?"

"Yeah," said Kay. "You're usually a lot more stoic."

"I guess you caught me at a good time. I'll bet the rent-a-cops won't give you any more trouble after that. But what really makes it funny is that a thing like that happened to me about ten years ago."

"You don't say?"

"It was right after I joined DSS. My partner at the time— you probably know Fowler, right?"

"Dirk Fowler?" Kay nodded. "I didn't even know he was read into the program. He was my team leader."

"Well, we were escorting Robert to UnionCon, when this uppity Ursan started giving us a hard time. Dirk warned him to be nice, because we didn't want a repeat of 'last year'. Well, of course, the Ursan had no recollection of ever meeting us before, so Dirk asked me how much Lethe I had used on him."

Kay laughed. "I think I see where this is going."

Biggs nodded. "Exactly. I said that we might have used too much, but we had to do it in order to save his life. Then Dirk explained that after I had knocked him unconscious, he had gone into convulsions and almost died. Since I hadn't wanted to kill him, I revived him with Lethe, which has remarkable healing properties, but in too-large doses, it completely erases any memory of the traumatic event."

"You both thought all that up on the fly?"

"Yep. Of course, he asked where one could find Lethe, and I told him I couldn't remember—it was a side-effect of the drug, and I wasn't sure if was ever going to get my hands on it again. The

Ursan believed me. He actually thought that I had saved his life after defeating him in combat! He swore a life-debt to us both, and said that if he ever found the supplier of Lethe, he would be sure to send us some."

I laughed. "Oh, that took balls. Did he ever find out you had lied to him?"

Biggs smiled. "I don't remember."

"I'll have to ask Fowler about that the next time I see him." said Kay. "See you tomorrow, Biggs. Tony."

After she left, Biggs turned to me. "How are you and Kayla getting along?"

"We're behaving ourselves, if that's what you mean. We haven't killed each other, yet. Or slept together. I don't know if you were trying to be nice partnering us up again, or cruel."

Biggs grunted.

"No, really, Boss. Did it even occur to you just how much time Kay and I would be alone together during the day?"

"I sure as hell wasn't going to partner you up with Forbes."

"Why not?"

"You act like frat boys when it's just the two of you. You've been friends for, what? Twenty years? You don't take anything seriously when you team up. Dirk and I were the same way, and it almost got us killed, once. Do you have any idea how seriously Ursans take life-debt oaths? If the one we pranked ever did find out, he might destroy half a dozen scout cruisers just to track us down. Why do you think Dirk and I don't go into space much anymore? I sure as hell won't go to UnionCon again."

"Jeez, Boss, I had no idea."

"You and Kayla are a better team than you think you are. I'd trust you both to fight tooth and nail to protect your charges, and each other, even if—and don't for one damn minute think I'm giving you permission—even if you do end up sleeping together."

"If you don't think it would affect our performance, why forbid it?"

"It's not my rule, Diego. It's the Department's. I personally don't care what you do, but you'd better make sure it's what you both want, because it will cost one or both of you your careers if anyone finds out. And it will be my ass for looking the other way."

"No pressure, though?"

Biggs laughed. "Don't think I'll blame you when it happens. My career isn't as important to me as it used to be. My girls are growing up. That's the other reason I don't go into space much anymore. They're going to start having moments I don't want to miss because I'm somewhere they can't even imagine exists."

"You sound like a man ready to retire, Boss."

"I am, Tony. As soon as I decide which one of you four is the most responsible, I'm tendering my resignation. Keep that to yourself."

I nodded. "No one would believe me, anyway. What should I do about Kay?"

"Trust your instincts. It's only half your decision, anyway, you know. She'll have a say, too."

"I hadn't thought of that."

"Then maybe I was wrong about trusting your instincts. Trust hers, instead. At least until you grow up."

I wanted to get angry with Biggs, but my gut told me he was right. "I hear you, Boss."

"One more thing you ought to know. Wayne's building a launch pad. By the end of the year, he's probably going to have his own spaceship. I've already recommended two pilots to train on it."

"I don't know what to say, Boss."

"Oh, did you think I meant you?"

"What?"

"I'm kidding! You and Kayla are my tops. Jack and Rita can probably learn, but neither of them have half the experience. But don't forget that Wayne's a pilot, too."

"Still, I've been waiting for years to get to fly a spaceship. Thanks, Boss. See you tomorrow."

***

I wasn't sure what to do with the information. Biggs seemed to be giving his blessing to Kay and me, even though he wasn't granting permission to break the rules. "Of course not," I said to the wind. "He's Biggs. The man won't go to the bathroom unless it's in accordance with Section IV, Rule 42, Paragraph 2a of the handbook."

I laughed to myself, imagining what such a regulation would sound like, particularly as read by Biggs in his Drill Sergeant voice.

Chapter 21: Some Guys Get All The Luck

Wayne wasted no time building the launch pad, and a hangar large enough to house three or four helicopters. I had mentioned to Kay what Biggs had said about our training as space pilots, and so we spent lots of our working hours discussing what piloting one of the bigger vessels would feel like.

"The drop ship had controls that were a lot like an Apache. The limo is like that, too. Zeru says spaceship controls are pretty much the same, except for the astrogation console. But using that isn't that much different than using any other computer."

"Sure, except for the whole crashing-into-the-sun-if-you-make-a-bad-calculation thing."

"I'm sure it doesn't happen that often." I grinned. "I mean, no pilot I've ever talked to has done it."

"Yeah, that's reassuring."

"You don't sound that enthusiastic."

Kay looked at the ground. "Don't get me wrong, I've always loved flying. But I'm just a cargo pilot."

"You once got mad at me for calling you 'just a cargo pilot.' Don't go using it on yourself. You know as well as I do that out there, there are nearly as many female pilots as men."

"I know. But we're still here. On Earth. In the good-old patriarchal U.S.A. They've only just started letting women fly combat. Too late for me, but still."

"You're not over-the-hill, you know. You're only a couple years older than me. And it's not the U.S. Government's decision. Wayne will let us fly his ship. I know he will."

"You know I love Wayne. He's a sweet guy, but he seems to have old-fashioned views about things. His father and mother certainly do."

"Kay, you haven't spent as much time with him as I have. He's chivalrous, but he's not narrow-minded. You should give him a chance."

"I will. It's just that experience has taught me caution "

I gave her a hug. "You'll get a shot. And if you don't, I'll back you up all the way."

"Still trying to come to my rescue, eh, Diego?"

"It's not because you're a woman. It's because you're my partner."

Kay looked at me quizzically. "I believe you mean that."

"Just because I think you're sexy doesn't mean I wouldn't trust you with my life."

"You really shouldn't say things like that. We can't be partners if we're lovers. Rules are rules."

"Rules suck," I said, grumpily.

Kay looked around to make sure no one was watching us before kissing me. "They sure do."

***

Wayne's birth father, Kurtis Elan, delivered a spaceship to the villa soon after the completion of the launch pad. Wayne showed it to us when we arrived to take him and Janet to work.

"Kurtis and I are going to be working on the interior together after hours. You're welcome to participate, if you want to. It's only fair, since you'll be training with me on it."

"Nice lines," said Kay, running her hands along the hull. "I love how it feels, too. Do we have time to check out the inside?"

The inside wasn't that much to look at, at least not yet. The cockpit was the only part that was fully finished. Of course, that was what we most wanted to see, anyway.

"This cockpit is huge," said Kay. "Why four seats?"

"This is an Explorer, Class 7," said Wayne. "The extra seats were originally designed for sciences and mapping. But don't you just love the panoramic view? Well, I mean, all you can see right now is the hangar interior, but imagine once we're out in space."

"How did you get it here without attracting attention?"

"Stealth package. It's got silent engines and an invisibility cloak. Of course, with the stealth mode on it doesn't accelerate so fast it'll throw people into bulkheads, but with it off, it rivals military ships in acceleration and maneuverability."

"I think I'm in love," I said. "When do we get to take her up?"

"A few weeks. Once the interior work is done, we're going on a shakedown cruise."

***

When at last the ship was finished, Wayne called all of us together to christen it.

"Lynne and I have decided to name it *Lasaitasuna*, which is Euskara for 'Peace' or 'Serenity.' Kurtis is a certified trainer. He's going to bring us all up to speed on how to fly it. Tony and Kayla are the most experienced pilots on the team, so I'm putting them, and myself, at the top of the training roster for now. My goal is to get us all flight-certified in time for UnionCon. As grateful as I am to the DSS and Denebian DipSec for the use of the cruisers at Area 51, I really like the idea of flying my own ship to Aldebaran."

"Can't say I blame you," said Rita. "This looks like a much more comfortable ride. When do we leave?"

"Just after sunset tomorrow evening. I'm confident that the stealth package works, but the darkness will give us a bit of extra cover."

As we prepared for launch, Kurtis went over the controls with us. "I think you will find that the controls are not that different from one of your military helicopters."

"What does it take to be legal to fly one of these babies?" I asked.

"You need an atmospheric aircraft pilot's license from your planet of origin. Wayne assures me that you have that already."

"Yeah. Kay and I both have military flight experience."

Kurtis nodded. "Good. You'll also need 120 hours of training from an experienced star-pilot and astrogator. That's me. This time counts. To complete your training, you take your hyperspace jump test. If you make a successful jump, you receive your certificate."

"What counts as a successful jump?"

"Surviving the jump, for one. But accuracy counts, too. You need to have jumped to within two light-hours of the edge of the system you were aiming at. Jump too close in and you risk crashing into an asteroid. Jump too far and it can take days or weeks to make the outer edge of the system."

"That sounds a little challenging," said Kayla. "I'd think people fail all the time."

"Not as many as you might think. The ship's computer handles the most difficult computations, including the exact time to jump. The hard part is waiting for the computer to make the jump.

All thrusters must be offline. The ship needs to maintain a constant inertial frame for the entire twenty-five seconds it takes to calculate and activate the jump. Any change in trajectory requires another twenty-five seconds or you get an inaccurate jump. You have to ensure that you are out of the influence of any gravity well strong enough to catch the ship in orbit. This is where most jump errors occur."

I grinned. "I guess traveling through hyperspace really isn't like dusting crops."

Kay slapped the back of my head. "This isn't funny, Tony. Keep your head in the game."

"My head's in the game," I said. "It was just a joke."

"I was kind of thinking the same thing," said Jack.

I began to think Biggs had been right. "I'll be good."

Kay just rolled her eyes. "Anything else we need to know?"

"No, that's all for now. Quiz time: At our current velocity, how long until it will be safe to begin hyper-jump calculations?"

I did the math in my head. "Wow, I get eighty-two to eighty three hours, right?"

"Eighty-two hours, twenty-seven minutes, eleven seconds," said Kay, looking up from her pocket calculator. "I win!"

I snorted. "Hardly. You used a calculator. That's cheating."

Kurtis laughed and shook his head. "It is better to be accurate than quick with these calculations."

"Relax, guys," said Wayne. "It's not a competition."

"Easy for you to say," said Kay. "You're the boss. You don't have to earn a pilot seat."

"Neither do you, Kay. You and Tony are already my first two choices to fly *Lasaitasuna*. I thought I had made that clear."

"Sure, Boss, but which one of us gets top billing?"

Wayne stood. "Oh, no. I'm not getting involved in that spat. If it comes down to it, I'll flip a coin." He winked. "Of course, if it does come down to a coin flip, the winner of the toss only gets co-pilot. It is my ship, right?"

Kayla scowled at me and followed Wayne down the ramp out of the cockpit.

I looked at Kurtis. "Uh, did I say something wrong?"

Kurtis shook his head. "I seem to be the wrong one to ask. Take my advice, though. Ask nicely."

Kay was sitting in the lounge sipping a cup of coffee. I poured myself a cup and sat beside her. "Are you okay? You seemed uptight."

"I'm sorry. It's just that I had flashbacks of my Air Force Academy days. You have no idea what it was like. There were three women in my avionics class, and twenty-three men. I was the only woman to pass. The other students were hostile, and the instructors weren't much better. Especially after the accident."

"No one was treating you any different than anyone else."

"You were."

"Was I? I didn't think I was."

Kay sighed. "I don't know. Maybe I imagined that, too."

"Well, if I did, I'm sorry. Would it help if I did make sexist remarks every now and then? You could yell at me or something. Just to get the tension out. But remember what Wayne said. You and I are at the top of the roster. You can be my co-pilot."

Kay smiled. "Why should you get to be the pilot? I'm older, and more experienced."

"Yeah, but you never flew combat, remember? Your experience doesn't count as much. You're a woman."

Kay fumed and punched my arm. "Pig!"

"Feel better?"

Kay laughed. "Yeah, actually. Thanks Tony."

"Can I kiss you?"

"Better not. This ship is too small. Someone might walk in on us."

"These next couple of weeks are going to be hell if I can't kiss you at least some of the time."

"I'd invite you to my stateroom, but someone might see you there, too."

"We can always go make out in the limo."

"Not happening, Tony. I'm sorry."

I sighed. "Someday, the rules aren't going to matter."

Kay winked. "In your dreams, Diego."

Janet and Jack came into the lounge. "I smell coffee," said Janet. "Thank you, whoever made it."

"Wayne did," said Kay. "Just before he went up into his room."

Janet sat down. "How is he taking being away from Lynne?"

Kay shrugged. "Tony's a better judge of Wayne's mood than I am. He's spent more time with him than I have."

"He seems to be all right," I said. "But we've all been focused on the pilot training. For all I know, if he's alone in his room, he's either talking on the phone, crying his eyes out, or reading. That's what I'd do in his place."

"Is that what you do alone in your room?" asked Jack. "I always thought you—"

"Thanks, Jack," I said. "Don't you have anything better to do than torment me?"

Jack grinned. "It's gotten me this far."

"I find it hard to believe you two never killed each other," said Janet.

"The secret is that we never, ever went after the same girl. There were the twins that one time."

I laughed. "We double-dated for three weeks before we figured out who was dating who."

Kay shook her head. "I'll bet that ended well."

"They broke it off with us when they realized that neither of us could tell them apart."

Jack laughed. "You were the one who couldn't tell them apart. Teri had more freckles on her left cheek than her right, and Tiffany had more on the right. You never noticed their faces because you couldn't take your eyes off their—"

"This conversation is going nowhere," I said. "I'm heading up to my room."

"Are you going to read, cry, or use the phone?"

Janet smacked the back of his head. "Be nice, Jack. I really don't want to watch best friends start duking it out."

"Aw, Tony knows I don't mean anything by it. Right, Tony?"

"Jack and I have been dissing each other since before you were born."

Now it was Kay's turn to scoff. "Before Janet was born you were what, three?"

"It's an expression," I said. "Besides, we probably were dissing each other at three."

"Whatever."

Jack kissed Janet. "I'm heading off to bed. See you in the morning."

"Hey, don't I get a kiss?" I said.

"Sure," said Jack. "Where do you want it?"

"On second thought, I'll pass."

Janet bent down and kissed my cheek. "Goodnight, Tony."

Once we were alone, Kay smiled. "I think we should probably go to bed, too."

"I'm all for that. Your room or mine?"

Kay's face went pink. "You know that would be a bad idea."

"I know. I don't really care, but I know."

Kay kissed me. "Well, I do care. I'm sorry, Tony."

"Yeah, well, so am I."

***

We assembled in the cockpit when it came time to begin the hyper-jump calculations. Kurtis led us through the steps, explaining as he went along.

"We're traveling to the Deneb system, so that's what I'm entering into the astrogation computer. Notice that as I type, the names of known systems appear in a drop-down list. Make sure that you read the coordinates as well as the name of the system, because if you jump to the wrong system, you'll have to reverse thrusters and head back out of that system's gravity well before you can calculate another jump. It can take as long as half a day to reverse thrust, because your velocity after a jump is the same as before the jump. Understand?"

Rita raised her hand. "Does a missed jump happen often?"

Kurtis shook his head. "Not very. The program calculates projected trajectories based on which systems the ship is travelling toward at the time, so you won't accidentally select a system in the opposite direction. Good thing, too, because a hyper-jump back the way we came might throw us through one of the planets, or even the sun itself. That's as bad as it sounds. You will never know what hit you, and your body will never be recovered."

"Has that ever happened?"

"Not in my lifetime, but in the earliest days of hyperspace travel, the odds were one in ten."

We all shuddered.

"Once I've made sure I've punched in the correct system, then I hit the AUTOLAUNCH button. That starts the calculations. As soon as the course is plotted, it will engage automatically. At this point, the controls are dead. If an emergency arises and you have to maneuver, hit the ABORT button. Then you'll have to start all over again from the beginning. Everyone ready?"

"Will we feel anything?"

"No. The hyper-jump does not affect inertia or momentum, it just happens."

Most of us were looking out the canopy when the jump

occurred. Most of us got physically ill. I don't want to go into detail, but it's a good idea to close your eyes before the jump, or at least not be looking out the window. Kurtis neglected to mention that. When he came out of hyperspace, most of us wanted to kill Wayne's birth father.

"You are an evil man," I said.

"Many pardons. I should have mentioned that. Most pilots either put their visors down or wear darkened glasses during a hyper-jump. That is a reflex action for me. I don't even think about it anymore."

"I would rather never think of it again," said Rita. "I'm not so sure I want to be a pilot anymore."

"It does get better, I promise you. I'm really sorry."

***

The rest of the flight to Deneb went without any more unpleasantness. When it came time to land the ship, we drew straws for the pilot seat. I drew the pilot straw, while Kay drew co-pilot.

Wayne looked at his straw, the shortest. "I should have pulled rank."

"You still can," said Kay. "I'll understand if I get bumped."

"No, we agreed on the rules beforehand. It wouldn't be fair to you. I'll take the third seat this time around. We'll all get a turn, eventually."

"That's the spirit," said Kurtis.

Landing the ship was a lot like landing an Apache, except I couldn't see the ground. I had to rely solely on the view screens. "This is a little unnerving."

"You're doing fine," said Kay. "All instruments read well within safe parameters."

"Yes," said Kurtis. "You two are doing quite well. I think you'll earn your spacers' wings in no time. You make a good team."

After the landing, Kay and I remained behind to review our landing footage while everyone else went out to greet Ben and Sonja.

"I've been wanting to hold you all morning," I said.

"Aren't you afraid someone might walk in on us?"

"Not particularly. You know how Ben can talk. I figure we've got at least an hour." I flipped a switch. "And no one will be able to board without us knowing about it."

Kay sat on my lap and put her arms around me. "I suppose it couldn't hurt."

I kissed her neck. "Come to my room?"

"You have no idea how badly I want to."

"But you won't."

"Tony, we can't! We can't. We'd lose our jobs if DSS found out. And then they'd can Biggs."

I stopped kissing her neck. "Did Biggs talk to you, too?"

"Yes. He probably talked to each of us. He knows we've come close to crossing the line, Tony."

I nodded. "Yeah. He's no fool."

"Do you know what would happen to Biggs if he lost his job because of us? He'd lose his pension, too. I can't do that to him."

I sighed. "I hate it when you're right."

"If it was just you and me at risk, it would probably be different."

"Oh?"

"Well, maybe. We're a good team, Tony. I'm afraid of what would happen if we lost that. You can't team up with Jack. You'd revert back to frat boys and get yourselves killed or something."

"Funny, Biggs said the same thing. You're right. We probably would."

"You can't team up with Rita, either. Your personalities would clash too much."

"So what do we do, wait for Biggs to retire? Kay, I've been waiting for years."

"I don't know, Tony. I still need time."

I kissed her. "This is frustrating, you know."

"I know. I appreciate you putting up with me."

I smiled. "I think you're worth it."

"Keep saying things like that, and I'm going to start believing you mean it."

We were about to kiss again when the boarding alert beeped. Kay jumped up and sat back in the co-pilot seat. "That was nowhere near an hour, Tony."

I shut off the alarm. "Yeah. Guess it's a good thing we kept our clothes on."

Jack entered the cockpit. "Have you been in here this whole time?"

Kay nodded. "We've been talking."

"What's up, bro? Did we miss something?"

Jack threw his hands up in the air. "I'll say you did. I'm getting married!"

"What? To Janet?"

"Yeah, to Janet. Who else?"

"When did that happen?"

"Just now. Sonja took Janet into town to buy a wedding dress. I hope you packed your Class As, because I need a best man. Oh, and Kay, can you stand in as Janet's maid of honor? Thanks! I have stuff to do, like now."

Jack disappeared back down the corridor.

Kay watched him go. "Well, that was interesting."

"Do you think there will dancing? I'll try not to grab your ass."

Kay laughed. "Let's go get dressed."

I raised my head. "Together?"

"No."

***

When Janet and Sonja returned from shopping, she and Jack had a short, private conversation. Janet must have given Jack the option to back out, because the next thing I knew, he was on one knee, offering her his grandmother's engagement ring.

Kay whispered in my ear, "Where did he get that?"

"From his grandmother, I presume."

"No, I mean, he's been carrying an engagement ring around? That's kind of romantic. I never would have expected that from him. Do you carry your grandmother's engagement ring around?"

"Nah, my grandmother is still alive. Also, she hates me."

"That's awful."

"Oh, it's okay. She hates everybody."

We all took our places in the ship's lounge. I stood beside Jack, while Kay waited on the other side of the aisle.

Janet came down the corridor on Wayne's arm. She did make a beautiful bride.

Wayne kissed her and put her hand in Jack's, then went to stand by Rita, who was holding a camera phone. Lynne was watching from Earth, I supposed.

Ben began the ceremony. "I guess a long speech would be kind of inappropriate under the circumstances, so I'll just get straight to the point. Jack, do you know what you're getting yourself into? From what Wayne tells me, Janet is kind of a handful. Are you prepared to take her as your wife, and never give up, and never surrender?"

"I am."

"And you, Janet, are you planning to give up some of your independence? Are you prepared to take Jack as your husband, et cetera, et cetera?"

Janet looked at him suspiciously. "You don't do weddings much, do you?"

"Nope. This is a first for me. Well, are you?"

"I am."

"What's next? Oh! Do you have rings?"

Jack produced a small box. "Here you go. I've had these awhile, too."

"Good man. Put them on each other. They go on your fingers."

"Yeah, we've got this." Jack held Janet's trembling hand and slipped the ring on her finger. He then gave her his ring and she put it on his finger.

"All right, this is it. Are you both sure? Last chance to back out."

"Would you please get on with it, already?" said Jack and Janet together. They looked at each other and started to laugh.

"Sorry," said Ben. "Where was I? Oh, yes, it's time to exchange vows. Jack, you know what to do."

"According to the custom of this world, I, Jack Forbes, in front of these witnesses, do name thee, Janet Clarke, my *Maiteakren*."

Janet looked over at Sonja, who nodded. She turned back toward Jack. "I, Janet Clarke, I mean, Forbes, in front of these witnesses, do name thee, Jack Forbes, my *Maiteakren*." She threw her arms around Jack and kissed him.

Ben looked hurt. "Hey, you were supposed to wait for me to tell you you're married! Oh, what the heck. Congratulations, Mr. and Mrs. Forbes. Be excellent to each other!"

Janet and Jack kissed, and we all applauded. Mr. and Mrs. Forbes walked hand-in-hand up the steps to the staterooms, then Jack swept up his bride and carried her into their stateroom.

Kay and I followed them down the aisle. "Tony, if we ever..."

"I know. We're not letting Ben do the ceremony."

After Ben and Sonja said their farewells, we prepared the ship for launch.

Kurtis looked toward the newlyweds' stateroom. "I don't think we'll see much of those two on the trip back. Don't forget to secure all loose items and equipment. This is going to be a max-gee launch test. We don't want anything to go flying. Or anyone."

Wayne switched on the ship's intercom. "Everybody strap in for emergency launch. Report once you're strapped in."

"Honeymoon suite, strapped in," Janet's slightly-out-of-breath voice came back over the speaker. "Make it quick, will you please?"

I cocked my head. "Uh, Boss? Besides the newlyweds, we're the only ones on the ship. Everyone is strapped in but you."

"I'm just establishing launch protocols. I do not want anyone flying through the air on my ship. I hate full-power launches, and I really hate how military ships just go without making sure the ship is secure. Lynne's right on that point. It seems to me that a bunch of casualties could be avoided."

"That makes perfect sense," said Kurtis. "That's probably why they don't do it that way."

Wayne sat in one of the conference room couches and strapped in. "Okay, Kurtis. Let's do this!"

As soon as the ship was clear of the spaceport, Kurtis initiated the emergency burn. Within a few seconds, the blue sky was replaced by black. Kurtis applied full thrust for about ten minutes, then called the all clear. "You can now move freely about the ship."

Wayne came back up to the cockpit. "You know, full-power thrust isn't so bad when it's your ship."

"You might make a pilot yet," said Kurtis. "We've got about six hours before the hyper jump."

"We're that far out already?" said Rita. "It took days before."

"That's emergency thrust," said Kurtis. "If it were a real emergency, we would have kept up the burn for about an hour and a half. That would take us right out to the jump point."

"Why don't we always do that?" I said. "Seems like that would save lots of time."

Kay shook her head. "Who wants to be plastered to their seats for an hour and a half?"

"Ten minutes is fine with me," said Wayne.

This time, we all remembered to lower our blast-shields for

the hyper-jump. "That wasn't half bad with the visor down," I said. "Why can't the cockpit window have shutters like the passenger windows do?"

Kurtis shrugged. "I'm really not sure. That's just the way we've always done it."

"That's a bad reason, Mr. Elan. My mother used to always cut the end off of a roast before she put it in the oven. The piece she cut off would get put in a different pan and roasted separately. One day us kids asked why. Do you know what she told us? She said it was the way her mother always did it. So we asked grandma."

"The one who hates everybody?" asked Kay.

"No, that's my dad's side. Do you know why grandma used to do it? It had nothing to do with proper cooking technique. It was because she had small pans! She couldn't fit the whole roast in the pan, so she cut off one end, and stuck it in another small pan. I always got stuck cleaning two pans instead of one, because my mother never thought to ask why. She just assumed it was the proper way to do it. So don't tell me I had to endure a cage match between my eyes and my stomach because that's the way it's always been done!"

Wayne looked at me oddly. "Are you feeling okay, Tony?"

"Just had to blow off some steam, Boss."

When the ship returned to normal space, Kurtis frowned. "This is no good. No good at all."

Wayne looked at the panel. "What's wrong?"

"These readings are all wrong. We are supposed to be on the edge of the Sol planetary system, but we are not."

"So where are we, then?"

Kurtis checked the astrogator program. His face went white.

"Kurtis, where are we?"

"We're lost."

Chapter 22: Lost... And Found

We all sat around the large conference table as Kurtis explained the situation. "The ship's astrogator program is offline. Without it, we can't calculate another hyperspace jump."

Janet held up her phone. "Couldn't we call for a tow or something?"

Kurtis nodded. "Yes, thanks to Wayne's insistence that we install Res Net access. I can send out a distress call, but with our astrogator computer off line, we couldn't tell anyone where to look for us. It might take up to a week for rescuers to triangulate our position and then send a ship out to us."

Wayne shrugged. "We should send it out right away, then. Is there anything else can we do?"

Kurtis nodded. "There are always two backup computers kept in storage. It will take about eight hours to remove a damaged computer core and put in a new one, but I would advise that we scan them fully before do so."

"Why?"

"It is fairly common for a computer to burn out after years of service, but for a system to fail on the third hyper-jump? That's almost unheard of. And in every failure I've ever seen, the system fails during calculations, not after a jump."

I tilted my head. "Sabotage, then?"

Again, he nodded. "That is my suspicion. Whatever was done to the main computer might have been done to the backups as well. There would have been no way to know which of the three systems would get installed first."

"You don't think it could have been sabotaged after installation?"

Kurtis shook his head. "I supervised the installation myself. It was the last thing to go in before I left for Earth. It had to have been done prior."

Jack raised his hand. "I'm a forensic computer specialist. I've been into computers since I was ten years old. If Denebian computers are anything at all like Terran computers, I may be able to help you find the sabotage. If they're not, I still want to try."

"You are such a nerd," said Janet, putting her arms around

his chest and resting her head on his shoulder. "I love that about you."

About an hour later, Kurtis and Jack called us back into the conference room.

"Jack found a nasty piece of code in the jump program. Jack, why don't you tell them what you told me?"

"The astrogator program was programmed to fail the second time the Sol system was entered as a destination with Deneb as the starting point. Whoever did it knew that we'd take the ship to Deneb and back on its shakedown."

Wayne gasped. "So this isn't a random bit of mischief, is it?"

Jack shook his head. "I doubt it. But there's more. It didn't just send us to the wrong place and burn out the system. It was also programmed to send a burst transmission to some location. Whoever placed the code knows we're here. They also know that we're stuck. If we had just put a backup in without testing it first, we would have wasted eight hours, and the backup would have fried, too, as soon as we tried to jump away from here."

"Can you at least figure out exactly where we are from the code?"

"I thought it might be possible, but the program randomly selects destination coordinates. That information was probably in the burst transmission, but only the burned-out system contains the data. I could probably pull the data off, if I had enough time, but it would take less time to just wait for rescue."

Kurtis checked his pad. "We're already reformatting the backup systems. Once that's done, it will take about eighteen hours to download and install a new OS, and another day to make sure the new OS is devoid of any further malicious code. Only then can we triangulate our current position and jump on out of here. We're looking at two, maybe three days of sitting here."

"We're also working against the clock," said Jack. "The computer sent out a burst transmission before it fried its own circuits. Whoever set the trap may already be on their way to intercept."

Wayne nodded. "We must assume the trap was meant for us. Where did the computers come from? Who installed the OS?"

Kurtis sighed. "They came from my own company. I have already called the VP in charge of production and told him to launch an investigation. I also ordered diagnostics on every computer built in the last four months."

"Do you trust your VP?"

"He is my oldest and dearest friend. If I cannot trust him, I cannot trust anybody. If there is a traitor in my company, he will find the person. It won't help with the current situation, though."

Wayne nodded. "We need a plan. What are our liabilities?"

Kayla spoke up first. "We don't know the enemy's intentions. Is this an assassination attempt, or a kidnapping?"

"We're dead in space," I said. "We can't jump."

"Good. What else?"

"The enemy has resources," said Kurtis. "No one could have planted the code remotely. They had to have planted someone in my company, or bribed someone."

"Or they could have used a stolen ID," said Janet. "Don't blame your people without solid evidence."

Wayne nodded. "Hold that thought. Assets?"

"We've got weapons," I said. "There's a locker in the hold. If someone attempts to board us, we can put up a fight."

"We have a skilled programmer," said Janet, her arms around Jack. "The enemy might not be in a big hurry if they think we're stuck here indefinitely."

"Call your security chief," said Kurtis, suddenly. "Have him get our wives to a safe house."

"Why?"

"There is a chance that you are not the culprit's immediate target."

Wayne gasped. "Oh, no. Tony, call Leroy. Tell him to get everyone to Groom Lake immediately. Jack, call DSS, and tell them to secure the airspace over the villa."

Biggs went into action immediately. "Good thing we've got the limo. I'll call as soon as we're secure. Is DSS aware?"

"Jack's contacting them."

Once we made the calls, anyone who wasn't busy with the reformatting began securing the ship, in case we might need to take evasive action. I double-checked my key to the weapons locker, and ensured all the guns were ready to go, should we need them.

Our position, out in the open, meant we were sitting ducks. Cloaking the ship would serve little purpose, since any vessel looking for us would use active radar scans. Cloaks only helped to prevent being noticed. If someone was actively look for you, the cloak almost wouldn't matter.

On the other hand, being out in the open meant no one could sneak up on us either. We could at least run. Maybe.

Kay and I took a turn watching the blackness as Kurtis watched the computers install. I wasn't sure which was more tedious.

"How's it going?" I finally asked.

"We're about five percent. At this rate, we ought to be on our way by 1500 tomorrow."

Kay groaned irritably. "Are we supposed to keep watch the whole time?"

Kurtis shrugged. "The ship is equipped with long range scanners. We can engage a proximity alarm."

"Oh, yes, let's! How do you do that?"

Kurtis pointed to a panel. "Set it to max proximity."

"Done." I nodded to Kay. "Want some coffee?"

Kay smirked. "Like I really need caffeine right now. A diet Coke would be nice, though."

"Uh, that has caffeine, too."

Kay gave me a look that told me all I needed to know. She was stressed, and it wouldn't take that much to set her off. Any other time, I would have wisely trodden lightly, but I was stressed, too.

When we got to the lounge, Jack and Wayne were immobilizing Janet's foot. "What the hell happened to you?"

Jack blushed. "She tickled me."

I nodded. "Ooh, you should have warned her."

"He tried," said Janet. "I didn't listen. He didn't mean to throw me, but when I landed, my ankle rolled and popped. These two think it's broken. I think they're being overprotective."

Kay smiled. "Unless we have an x-ray machine available, you're better off treating the worst-case scenario."

"Ugh. You're as bad as them."

"It's military training," I said. "We've all had it. Well, except Wayne."

"I've always been a first-aid enthusiast, myself," said Wayne. "Did you ever watch that paramedics show back in the seventies?"

"Oh, yeah," I said. "I remember that."

Jack finished wrapping the splint. "I'm really sorry, Janet."

"You're going to need to stay in bed," said Wayne. "I really hope we don't need to use evasive maneuvers."

"With the splint and all, it doesn't even hurt." Janet moved and winced. "Much."

Wayne's phone rang. "It's Lynne. Are you safe, *Maiteakren?*"

She was. After a short conversation, Wayne closed the

phone and sighed. "She's safe. Sara, too."

Janet got up from her seat and hopped over to sit beside him.

"Janet, I told you to stay off that ankle."

"I'm not on it," she said. "Besides, you look like you need a hug. At least we know we're on scenario one, Wayne."

Wayne began to weep. Janet held him until he was finished. The rest of us minded our own business.

Finally, Wayne said, "Thanks, Janet. I needed that."

Janet smiled. "You would have done the same for me, *Maitearen*. Are you going to be okay?"

Wayne nodded and looked at her sternly. "I'm fine now. You need to rest that ankle. That is your top priority."

"Fine," she said. "But I am going to do it my way. Jack, my husband, please take me to bed."

"That doesn't really sound like rest," said Jack.

"Take me to bed, Jack. I won't need my ankle for what I'm planning."

Jack smiled, his face turning red. "By your command, my lady." He walked up to his wife, effortlessly took her up in his arms, nodded to the rest of us, and gently carried her up the steps to the honeymoon suite.

"Now there's a happy couple," said Kayla, watching them leave. "They sure are well suited to each other. I wonder where I might find a guy like that."

That was more than I could take. "I'm still available. Once you go Latino, you'll never go back."

"If you weren't such a pain in the ass, I might consider it, Diego. But that's a pretty big if."

"And that's a pretty nice ass."

Kayla snapped. "That's sexual harassment, buddy! Can I space him, Wayne?"

"If that's what you really want to do. Out here we're not under any particular jurisdiction."

I'd had enough. "Now, let's not be too hasty. I take it back. That's not a nice ass at all."

"You are not exactly getting back on my good side," said Kayla.

"I didn't know you had one, sweetie."

"That does it!" she said. "Defend yourself, Diego!"

Wayne stood between us. "Stop it, both of you! Someone's going to get hurt."

"Yeah," said Kayla. "Him."

"This is not a good place to fight," said Rita. "I'll bet we can set up a ring in the cargo hold."

Wayne looked at Rita as if she had lost her mind. "You aren't seriously suggesting I let these two duke it out?"

"Trust me, Boss," said Rita. "It will work out all right. Besides, it will give us something to do while we are waiting."

"Fine, but if anyone gets hurt, you both will be confined to your quarters. That means no more pilot training for either of you."

I didn't care at that point. Kay had pissed me off. I managed to calm down enough to find materials that might make a suitable mat.

"It's crude, but it will work, for now."

"Good," said Kayla. "The sooner I beat the crap out of you, the sooner I might start getting some respect."

Wayne shook his head. "I'm still opposed to this."

"You don't have to watch," said Rita. "I promise I'll keep them from killing each other."

We stepped out onto the mat, tested our footing, and bowed to each other. I almost didn't expect Kay to attack as furiously as she did. She aimed a kick at my chest, which would have had enough power behind it to knock the wind out of me, even crack my ribs. I dodged the kick.

I blinked. Kay was seriously trying to hurt me. She must have been pissed.

I tried to figure out what I had said. We had said ruder things to each other, in the past.

Kay came at me again. I dodged her attack and countered, which she also dodged. Damn, but she was good.

For the first forty minutes or so, I let her be the aggressor. I was pretty sure she'd keep attacking until she tired herself out. Then I would go on the attack, and I would beat her. She would learn not to mess with me.

Sure enough, she was tiring faster than I was. I began to attack more, making her dodge me. Being on the offensive gave me more time to think. From the first moment I laid eyes on her, I had wanted her. What had I wanted to do? Take her to bed? Yes, but not right away.

I aimed a kick at her chest, which she dodged, but she was slowing down.

I had wanted to get to know her. She was beautiful. I had

even told her so, but that always just made her mad.

Kay tried another kick, but her form was getting sloppy. I almost had her. I threw a punch, which barely missed.

She had complained that all I saw was her beauty, as if that was all she was, something to look at. She had said if I ever figured out any other way to measure beauty, we could talk.

I attempted a take-down, which she evaded. She wasn't tired enough, or slow enough, yet. Soon, I would be able to make my move.

Then there was Biggs. Why the hell did he keep putting us together, even though he knew we'd either end up killing each other, or... or what?

He had as much as said Kay was way out of my league. Maybe that was why I always wanted her. She was a trophy. I had wanted to conquer her. And I had made progress. Twice, she had offered to sleep with me. And twice, circumstances got in our way.

I threw another punch. She dodged again, but my fist brushed against her hair. She was definitely slowing down.

She had told me to grow up. Why? Had she been trying to insult me, or had she been trying to change me? Why couldn't she have just accepted me the way I was?

I aimed a kick. She jumped and dodged. If I had connected, I would have knocked her legs out from under her, then I'd have her pinned. Next time for sure.

I looked back at some of the things I had said to her in the past. If she had been my girlfriend, and some punk talked to her that way, I would have punched him out. Come to think of it, if Kay had decided to punch me out, I didn't think I would have blamed her. I'd been an ass.

Another swing, another miss. Kay struck at me, breathing heavier.

Why hadn't she punched me out? Maybe it was because she was attracted to me, too. Maybe that was why she had agreed on dances and dates, even though it was a bad idea. She always had liked something about me. But I wasn't perfect. Hell, nobody was perfect.

Except for Kay.

I dodged another blow. I countered, almost making contact.

No, Kay wasn't perfect. She had flaws just like anyone else. Her biggest flaw was that she thought I could be reformed.

Biggs had told me that understanding women was next to impossible. It was enough to understand one woman. I had assumed that understanding Kay would give me an advantage over her, make her love me. But I was wrong.

Kay finally made the mistake I had been waiting for. She had left an opening. I knew exactly what I needed to do. I could take her down. I'd win the fight.

Suddenly, I saw Kay. I saw beyond her beauty. I saw her strengths, her weaknesses, her flaws. I understood her.

And I loved her. I didn't care about winning or losing anymore. All I cared about was her. I had hurt her feelings. I had been wrong.

I loved her.

"Hold! I yield."

"Really?" said Kay, panting. "I don't get it. You were winning."

I heard Wayne's voice. "How can you tell?"

Rita laughed. "At the beginning of the fight, Kay was on the offensive. But as things progressed, Tony became more aggressive. Kayla was pretty much just defending by the end, and she was tiring out. If they had kept at it for much longer, she would have either had to yield, or Tony would have succeeded in taking her down."

"So Tony won?"

Kay shook her head. "No, by yielding, he conceded defeat." Kay looked at me sharply. "Dammit, Diego, you just might be a gentleman, after all."

I scoffed. "You go spreading slander like that around the DSS, and next time I will take you down." I bent down so only she could hear me. "You do have a nice ass, you know."

"Don't think you'll get to see it any time soon."

"I don't blame you for being angry with me. I've been an ass. I'm sorry. We'll talk later. I hope."

I hit the shower, then I went to bed.

An alarm woke me up early the next morning. I rolled out of bed, got dressed, and opened the door and headed to the conference room. I figured everyone would be gathering there.

Kurtis came down from the cockpit when he heard me. "That's the proximity alarm. We've got company!"

Wayne ran up, tucking in his shirt as he went. "Can we jump yet?"

Kurtis shook his head. "The installation is finished, even on the backup, but I'm still running the virus scan on the main. I don't want to jump until I know the program's clean. Even so, we can't jump while pulling evasive maneuvers."

Wayne turned to me. "Prepare to defend the ship."

"Right, Boss." I began to head toward the cargo area. I grabbed Kay along the way. "Come with me!"

"What's going on?"

"Proximity alarm. We're going to hand out weapons."

In the cargo hold, Kay and I handed everyone a rifle and a sidearm. "These guns are safe for use on the ship. They've got hollow-point anti-personnel rounds. They can bring down an elephant, but they won't pierce the ship's hull. Of course, that means we're screwed if they're wearing body armor. Sorry, I should have thought of that, before now."

"So we aim for the seams," said Kayla. "If they have armor, go for the neck, arms, and legs. Keep shooting until they stop coming at you."

We all conned flak jackets and helmets. "Rita and Kayla, guard the forward hatch. The rest of us will try to hold the cargo bay."

We were ready to defend the ship when Janet's voice came over the loudspeakers. "Wayne, please come to the cockpit. Someone wants to talk to you. The rest of you can relax. We're not being attacked."

"Well, that's a relief." Wayne removed his armor and handed the guns back to me. I put them all back into the locker, then locked the door once more.

The incoming ship was *Enpresa*. They had received our distress call and were standing by to render aid.

Our ship was taken into its hold, and we were all given physical examinations. Everyone was found to be in top shape, except for Janet, whose ankle was not broken, but badly sprained. She was given crutches and orders to use them until it healed.

***

Our first destination on Earth was Groom Lake. Wayne was too eager to see Lynne to be any use in the cockpit, and he knew it, so he gave up his turn at co-pilot. I sat in the co-pilot seat as Kay guided the ship in. "I could so get used to this," she said, once we were on the ground. "That was fun."

"Just remember we have to take turns."

"You really hate second fiddle, don't you?"

I grinned. "Not when my pilot's got seniority."

Kay blushed. "I believe you actually mean that."

Lynne and Wayne shared a tearful hug as Biggs pulled the limo into the ship's hold. Kurtis hugged his wife, then came back up to the cockpit.

"You've both done quite well. Why don't you fly us home?"

The flight to Freehold took minutes. Kurtis praised us both for being such fast learners and left us to shut down and secure the ship while the rest of the team checked the villa to ensure it was safe.

Biggs gave the all clear, and everyone filed out of the ship.

Kayla held me back when we were the last ones left on the ship. "Something's been bugging me since that fight, Tony. Why did you yield? You had me beat, and you knew it. You seemed just as pissed as I was."

I sighed. "I was. I'd said worse things to you before, and I thought you were overreacting this time. I wanted to take you down, too, at first."

"Why didn't you? I was overreacting. I see that, now."

"The more I thought about things, the less beating you mattered. I was an ass, Kay. I'm sorry."

"I forgive you."

"I mean, I'm sorry about being such a jerk from the beginning. You're way out of my league."

Kay smiled. "Maybe once. I'm not so sure, now."

"For what it's worth, Kay, I... I love you."

Kay didn't say anything for several minutes. When she did speak, her voice was barely a whisper. "I love you, too, Tony. I have for a long time."

I held her close and our lips met. We kissed for what could have been a minute or two, or it could have been several lifetimes. All that mattered to me was Kay.

"So what do we do now, Tony?"

I kissed her again. "We wait. For as long as it takes, we wait. I don't think it will be for much longer. Things are changing. Wayne's secret isn't going to be a secret for much longer, I think. The next few months are going to be hard on everyone. I imagine we'll get on each other's nerves. We might even duke it out in the ring again. But no matter what, I love you. That's never going to change."

"It's going to be hard to hide our love from the others."

"I don't think we have to. Biggs himself said we answer to

Wayne, now. As long as Wayne and Lynne are okay with it, and I'm pretty sure they will be, it's not going to get back to DSS."

Kay looked admiringly up at me. "You've grown up, Diego."

I grinned. "No one's more surprised than me."

As we walked down the ramp, Kay stopped me. "One more thing. Where did you learn some of those moves?"

"I did some training with a couple of Dok Fil's bodyguards a while back. I'll introduce you next time we meet. I think you'll like them."

Chapter 23: Learning To Fly

Kay and I were sent to Aldebaran on one of the DSS ships to complete our star-pilot training. The Aldebarans had been among the first civilizations to develop space flight, so there were many colonies scattered among the eleven planets and fifty or so moons that made up the star system. This made it an excellent place to train pilots in launches, interplanetary navigation, and landings.

Launches were fairly straightforward. You throttled up until the ship left the ground. As long as the sky was in front, and the ground was behind, you were in good shape.

Interplanetary navigation was also fairly straightforward. Whenever two ships were on a collision course, the smaller and more maneuverable ship was required to yield the right of way to the larger vessel. Of course, this meant that the smaller the vessel you were piloting, the more course corrections and evasive maneuvers you routinely had to perform. The training vessels we flew were about a fifth the size of *Lasaitasuna*, which meant we always had to stay alert. I suppose that was the point.

Landings were the most critical part of flying. It required a very precise hand on the controls. Coming down much too hard and fast was called crashing, and it was generally frowned upon. We witnessed a crash during our second week of flight training, which resulted in the deaths of both the student, a young Ursan, and her instructor, a well-respected Aldebaran. The student had apparently panicked, and the instructor had not been able to override the pilot controls in time.

The flight school shut down during the ensuing investigation, leaving Kay and me an extended period of leisure time.

Remembering the promise I had made to Jess, Kay and I headed to Sjokolade, the galaxy's finest chocolate shop. I picked up a five-pound box for Jess, and a small block of fudge to share.

Kay closed her eyes, savoring the fudge as it melted on her tongue. "We could make a fortune selling this on Earth."

"Maybe whenever Earth becomes a member of the Galactic Union, we can become Earth's exclusive distributor of

Sjokolade. We'll be able to buy our own ship."

"You never struck me as the businessman type."

"I guess I'm not, really. I'd be happy just flying, even if it paid squat."

"I think that's one of the reasons I love you," said Kay. "You enjoy what you do. It probably helps that I love it, too."

"I don't know if I've ever said this, but you've never been just a cargo pilot to me. I've seen you fly the trainers, and I think you would have made a decent fighter pilot. I'll deny it if you tell anyone, but I think you might even be better than me."

"Coming from you, that means something." We walked for a little while before she said, "Tony, can I ask you something personal?"

"Shoot."

"Since that time in the cockpit, when you first said you love me, you haven't tried to get me to go to bed with you."

"That's not a question."

"I was getting to it. Why don't you want to sleep with me anymore?"

I paused to think. Why, indeed? I knew that she would say yes if I asked. "It's not that I don't want to, because I do. I want you more than ever. But it's not so urgent, now. I don't want to force it. Also, I don't want to jeopardize our jobs, just when it's starting to get fun. I mean, we're learning to pilot spaceships!"

"Oh, so you'd rather be in space than in bed?"

I smiled. "In bed in space would be good, too."

Kay laughed. "There's naughty Tony. I like naughty Tony. I always did, you know, even when it frustrated me."

"I thought I had to change before you would love me."

"It was never about change, it was about balance. You have a fun-loving, not-very-mature side, and a serious, dutiful and loyal side. But when both sides come together, you're downright irresistible."

I smiled. "I can't believe it took you that long to figure me out."

"It didn't take me long at all. I just waited for you to figure out how to be both. I think it's interesting that it all clicked during a fight."

"Speaking of which, I still need to introduce you to Van Dam and Far Polk. They live in Union City. I bet you'll like them."

***

Their apartment was above a martial arts dojo in the Capitol District of Union City. Van Dam and Far Polk were teaching a class of youths when we arrived.

Van Dam spoke up as we entered. "Ah, students. Today you are in for a special treat. The man who has just entered the Dojo is Tony Diego, a master of many Terran forms, and a bodyguard of the Terran *Umea Bakearen*. Greet him and his lady friend with honor."

He, Far Polk, and the entire class bowed.

Kay and I bowed back.

"It is a pleasure and an honor to see you again," said Far Polk. "Is this Kayla Moss? She is as attractive as you described."

Kay smiled. "You told them I was attractive?"

"Beautiful was the term I used."

"Have you come to spar with us?" Van Dam sounded eager. "The demonstration would be most enlightening to our students."

I nodded. "It would be an honor. Give us a minute to change."

Once we were dressed, Kay and I stepped out onto the mat. "Kay, why don't you and Far Polk go first? The match will be three falls, or ten minutes and a decision."

Kay and Far Polk bowed and began to fight. Kay was on the ground within five seconds.

"Wow," said Kay, bowing to Far Polk. "I had no idea Aldebarans could move so quickly."

"Anyone can learn," said Far Polk. "Again?"

This time, Kay succeeded in taking Far Polk down. The students looked on in shock. That apparently did not happen often.

"You are as quick a study as your partner," said Far Polk. "Well done."

They bowed again, and once more began to fight. Time expired before either of them scored another throw.

Far Polk and Kay bowed to each other, then to the class.

Van Dam and I were next. We had fought before, so I was confident that I could match him this time. He took me down quickly, the first time, but I took him down twice, with two minutes still on the clock.

Van Dam bowed. "You have surpassed me, my friend."

"I had a fine teacher," I said, bowing in return.

Kay and I faced each other for the third match. We bowed to each other, then began to fight. Time expired before either of us had managed a throw.

We bowed to one another, then to the class, who applauded.

Later, we all sat in their apartment. Far Polk gestured toward us. "Your dance was beautiful to behold. How long have you been in love?"

Kay grinned. "There are multiple ways to answer that. I've been in love with Tony for at least a couple of years, but we only just declared our love a few weeks ago."

"A couple of years?"

Kay winked. "I told you I'd loved you for a long time, didn't I?"

"I had no idea it was that long."

"I wasn't going to make it easy for you. You needed to grow up, first."

"You are well matched," said Van Dam. "And I do not merely mean on the mat. You appear to be soul mates."

"So what brings you to Aldebaran? You are not here with the *Umea Bakearen*."

"No, but we are here in his service. We're in pilot training. At least, we were, before the accident."

"A tragic incident," said Far Polk. "Lee Post was a legendary flier. He instructed both my husband and me."

"We are very close to certification. Then we'll return to Sol. We'll be back again for UnionCon."

"Visit us when you can. Our dojo is forever open to you." Van Dam smiled. "Before this day, my last defeat on the mat was before either of you were born. It is an honor to call you my friend, Tony. And you, Kayla."

***

The flight school reopened after two weeks. For the rest of our training, we spent much of our off time with Van Dam and Far Polk. By the time we departed Aldebaran, they were as dear to us as any of our human friends.

Kay and I grew closer together, as well. We avoided displaying our affection publicly, since we didn't want to create trouble for Biggs so close to his retirement. We treasured those moments when we could be together, alone and unobserved, brief though they were.

Once we had completed our training, Van Dam and Far Polk took us both out to dinner to celebrate. "You are the first Terrans, to my knowledge, to graduate from the Union Flight School of Aldebaran. You may well be the first Terran star-pilots ever."

"There are several space programs on Earth," said Kay. "Both the US and Russia have been in competition for years."

Far Polk's face darkened in the Aldebaran equivalence of a blush. "I meant no offense, Kayla."

Kay laughed. "I'm not offended, Far Polk. Truth is, any of Earth's programs are extremely primitive, compared to the training we've just been through. But I can't help but wonder how our astronauts are going to feel once the reality of interstellar travel becomes known to them."

I nodded. "Kay's right. What we're doing right now, having dinner on an alien planet—or maybe I ought to say on a planet where we are aliens—most of the agents we work with couldn't even begin to imagine this. Earth's most advanced technology would probably seem like toys to most of the Union."

"Do not be so certain. Have you never seen an intricate piece of clockwork that was hundreds of years old?" Van Dam produced from his pocket a fob watch. "This timepiece once belonged to my grandfather. It was built—no, crafted—on Apus, an even more primitive world than Earth. It keeps near perfect time, but contains no circuitry. It is all cogwheels and springs. If it were to break, I would have to take it back to Apus to be repaired, because there are no craftsman anywhere else in the galaxy with the skill to repair it."

"It is my husband's most prized possession." Far Polk put her arms around his neck. "I sometimes think he loves it more than me."

"It would grieve me to part with it, but I would trade it as a ransom for you, my love. It is a treasured thing, but it is still a mere thing."

Far Polk kissed him. "That is one more reason why I love you."

***

As we headed back to our hotel, Kay laid her head on my shoulder. "Do you think our love will be like that?"

"I'd like to think it already is."

"What if it came to a choice between being together or continuing to be DSS agents?"

"I'd miss you."

Kay slapped the back of my head. "I'm serious!"

"Sorry. I guess that wasn't very funny. I love you, Kay. If it came down to it, I'd resign from DSS to be with you, even if it meant never going into space again."

"You'd do that for me?"

"If I stayed on and you left, I'd have to break in a new partner. I don't want another partner."

"I don't think I'd want another partner, either."

I smiled. "That gives us a bit of leverage. The DSS will have to work with us, or they'll lose us both. I'm sure they're not going to want to lose the only Terran star-pilots in the galaxy, especially after all the money they just paid Aldebaran to train us."

"What if you're wrong?"

I shrugged. "I don't think I am, but even so, you're worth more to me than flying the galaxy."

"You've no idea what it means to me to hear you say that." Kay laid her head on my shoulder. "I love you."

I smiled. "I never get tired of hearing that."

"Tony? Before we go back to Earth, I want to share a... what's the word? *Maitalea?*"

"I'm not sure we can."

"What, don't you want to sleep with me?"

I smiled. "Don't get me wrong. I've wanted you from pretty much the first time I laid eyes on you. But I don't want a *Maitalea*. Not with you, or anybody else. The Denebians can have their word back, for all I care. I don't just want sex anymore."

"Who are you, and what have you done to Diego?"

"I know. I bet you never expected to hear that from me, right? I don't want a temporary fling. I want a real relationship." I grinned. "And sex, too, but mostly that other stuff."

Kay laughed. Her eyes glistened in the light of the dashboard. "We're finally on the same page, then."

I parked the car in the hotel lot and walked with Kay back

to the elevator. "Um, whose room do you want to go to?"

Kay bit her lip. "Yours, but first I want to pack an overnight bag. I don't want to have to leave you."

"You're beautiful when you do that, you know."

"Do what?"

"You bite your lip when you're being shy."

"Like this?"

"Well, no. I mean, yes, but when you do it intentionally, it doesn't have the same effect on me. Hmm. Maybe I shouldn't have told you about it." I kissed her. "You're prettiest when you don't know you're beautiful."

I sat in a chair and watched Kay pack her bag. "Aha. You're doing it again."

"Biting my lip? I don't think I was."

"No. Being beautiful."

Kay beamed. "We're never getting to your room at this rate."

I placed my room key on the table. "I'll wait for you there."

A few minutes later, Kay arrived at my door. "Why are you sitting in the hallway?"

"Once I got here, I realized that you've got my key."

***

I put on an Aldebaran jazz station and asked Kay to dance with me. As we moved in time to the music, we slowly undressed each other, until there was nothing between us. I ran my fingers down the small of her back and she shivered as I ventured into previously forbidden territory. This time, there was no fabric.

I took her by the hand and led her to the bed. She lay down and smiled at me. "What are you waiting for?"

"I just wanted to take you in. You're beautiful."

Kay bit her lip, unconsciously, and therefore irresistibly. "I'm ready, Tony. Please come to bed."

I'd slept with a number of women before Kay, but each time it had been casual, for fun. I'd never been with someone I truly loved before, and who loved me. Somehow, it made a difference. Every movement sent shivers up and down my spine, and I could tell Kay was feeling it, too.

I kissed her beautiful bottom lip. "I am sorry, my love."

Kay looked at me. "Sorry? What for?"

"I'm sorry that I ever gave my body to less worthy women. Kay, you're the only woman I've ever really loved. I'm sorry that you're not the only one I've ever slept with."

Tears came to her eyes. "You really mean that, don't you, Tony?"

I nodded, tears coming to my own eyes. "You are so out of my league."

Kay wiped her tears, as well as mine. "Not anymore. I'm all yours, now and always." She laughed. "We must look silly, laying here crying."

"I love you, Kay."

She looked into my eyes. "I love you. I don't think I'm going to need my own room anymore."

"It's going to suck, going home."

"Yeah." Kay played with the hair on my chest. "I'm not sorry we did it, though."

"Me neither. I'm already looking forward to the next time."

Kay smiled. "I'm definitely not going to need my room anymore."

We fell asleep in each other's arms.

Chapter 24: Preparations

The population of Wayne's villa had increased by the time we got back. Ben Elan and Dok Fil were staying for the time being in guest houses. Jack and Janet had moved in together, which, I remembered, was perfectly reasonable, since they were married. Professor Remington was also a guest, and Ada Stein. Robert and Doris Freed were also staying there, which surprised me.

"Jeez, Boss, what did we miss?"

"Let's go to my office," said Biggs. "I'll fill you in. I'm guessing you've got stories to tell, too."

We followed Biggs into the control room, where an agent was watching rows of monitors.

"Watson, why don't you patrol the grounds before your dinner break, all right?"

"Yes, Agent Biggs. Hey, Diego, Moss. Good to see you guys back in one piece. How was flight school?"

"Well, we survived it."

After Watson left, Biggs had us all sit down. "So, was it worth the trip?"

I showed Biggs my wings. "We're certified star-pilots. First Terrans to graduate from flight school on Aldebaran. With honors, even."

"Figured you would. I take it you've resolved your personal issues, am I right?"

Kay grinned. "You could say that."

"We're keeping it on the down-low, Boss."

"See that you do. Off the record, I figured you would. It's about time."

Kay smiled and hugged Biggs. "Sure was."

"So, what's been going on around here?"

"What do you know?"

"There's a crap-load of guests about. I've seen Remington, Dok Fil, Ada Stein, Elan, and Wayne's parents. I'm guessing Doris is back in the loop?"

Biggs nodded. "She knows everything again. Wayne and Ben know they're cousins, and Vader is Luke's father."

"How did Dok Fil get here? We heard he was missing."

"Not missing. Turns out he's been in secret negotiations with the Vegans."

"There's been a lot of bad blood where the Vegans are involved. Kay and I have seen reports of serious brutality against them. Claims that they were behind the bombings, I hear."

"It's all bull." Biggs sipped his coffee. "We still don't know who was behind it, but it wasn't them. The guys who spooked Wayne and Ben were Vegans, but they were working for Dok Fil. They were actually trying to save both *Umea Bakearen*, believe it or not."

"So, have we gotten anything right?"

"Someone wants to keep Earth out of the Union, apparently."

"So, why is the gang all here?"

Biggs rubbed his temples. "Wayne's getting ready to reveal himself to the UN General Assembly. He's going to ask the world leaders to vote to petition the Union for admission. There's a big meeting in the great hall tonight. I hope you both are ready to get back to work."

***

The huge dining room known as the great hall was arranged like a miniature version of the Galactic Council Chambers.

Wayne hugged Kay and shook my hand. "I'm glad you two are back. Things are about to become a little crazy, but with you here, I feel a lot better about it."

"Thanks for the vote of confidence," said Kay. "We'll do our best."

After the meal was cleared, Wayne called the meeting to order. "Tomorrow, Ben and I are going to address the United Nations General Assembly. The meeting is going to change the world, but I have no idea exactly how."

"What do you intend to say, exactly?" The question came from Professor Remington.

"I am preparing a statement. I will reveal myself as a Denebian ambassador and deliver an invitation to join the galactic community. If this invitation is accepted, I will sponsor a petition at UnionCon for Earth, officially designated Sol III, to be admitted into the Galactic Union."

"That sounds reckless, Mr. Freed. Do you have any idea

how people will react?"

"No, I do not. That is why I am issuing a warning to everyone present. There are several possible scenarios, and I want everyone to be prepared for the worst."

"What are the scenarios?"

"The best case is that the UN will accept my statement and vote to petition the Galactic Union to admit Earth as a member world. The worst case is that they react with fear and hostility and put all our lives in danger. If that is the case, we will have no choice but to evacuate the planet. There is enough space on board all three ships docked here that everyone here who wishes to may leave with us. We'll be given political asylum on Deneb."

"You're sure of this?"

"I have a personal invitation from President Walker of Deneb."

The professor began cleaning his glasses.

I leaned to whisper to Kay. "Wayne once told me that Remington always does that when he knows his position is weak, and isn't sure how to proceed."

Wayne held out his hands. "I offer this as a worst case scenario only. I don't think it will come to that."

"It is still a possibility," said the Professor, pointing his glasses at Wayne.

"The most likely scenario lies somewhere in between. What I expect will happen is that they will hear me out, and then ask for some sort of proof. When I provide the proof, I expect that there will be a period of debate that will take several weeks, or months, to become a resolution. I am hoping that by then, the member nations will decide to join the union unanimously. If they do not, then I will negotiate with each nation individually. Eventually, the other nations will come around."

"And if they don't?"

"The upcoming war will result in far more death and destruction than if the Earth joins."

"How can a planet cause more death by being isolated than by being a member of the Galactic Union? That sounds illogical to me."

"Earth is the only planet in the galaxy that has the capability to manufacture nuclear weapons. If they join the Union, they will fall under the protection of the entire Galactic Union. Deneb and other worlds will help Earth to become a productive member of a larger community. If they do not, they will be on their own. Deneb has been Earth's suzerain for years, but a negative UN vote will end that relationship, as well as effectively nullify the Sol-Deneb Treaty. Deneb will no longer be bound to prevent Earth's being undermined and exploited by unscrupulous entities outside of the influence of the Galactic Council."

"What do you mean?"

"The governments of Earth live under the constant threat of nuclear war. The Cold War resulted in huge stockpiles of weapons designed to ensure that nuclear war would result in the extinction of all life-forms on the planet. Since no one wants to be destroyed, no one initiates a war. Since the end of the Cold War, the stockpiles are being decommissioned. If an entity started sowing seeds of distrust, governments may begin to increase their stockpiles again. Without any agencies watching the system, stockpiles of weapons could be smuggled off-planet. The consequences of such an event are unthinkable."

"How do you know that Earth would not be exploited by the Galactic Union itself?"

"My dear Professor," said Dok Fil. "You have been to several of the worlds in the Union. When have you seen anything but a spirit of cooperation and mutual respect between member worlds? What is the purpose of UnionCon, if it is not to foster this spirit?"

Wayne nodded approvingly to Dok Fil. "Your point is well made, Mediator. The Galactic Union exists to prevent exploitation of any of its member worlds. Earth can only benefit from admission."

"I still have reservations," said Remington.

"They are noted, Professor, but this is not a matter to be voted for or against. I alone bear the responsibility for this decision. The potential benefits of admission far outweigh any risks, and the price of isolation is too dear. My responsibility is clear. I will go before the United Nations General Assembly tomorrow."

The mood in the dining hall was upbeat. Most of the people in the room were excited by the prospect of Earth expanding its horizons.

***

The ride into New York the next morning was tense. The limo had been provided by Deneb, which meant it had the ability to fly, though Wayne had made it clear that we were to stay on the ground, unless conditions became too dangerous.

Wayne and Lynne sat closest to the front, near Dok Fil and Ben. A couple of Vegans sat beside him, talking to Jack and Janet. Kay and Rita sat in the back by the door, along with Ben's guards, Kat Jericho and Tanya Orlov.

I smiled. I was pretty sure that Ben was ever faithful to his wife, but it amused me that he still surrounded himself with pretty women.

Next to me sat Othgar, one of Dok Fil's Vegan aides. His other aide, Theodore, sat in the back, looking out at landmarks.

There was a secure diplomatic entrance at the UN complex, but this was the first time Wayne had chosen to use it. He had always maintained a low profile, but not today.

I parked near the entrance and opened the back door. Rita and Kay got out first, followed by Kat and Tanya. Tanya winked at me as she got out. Kay's face was almost expressionless, but I saw her give Tanya a look of mild amusement. She knew Tanya was a flirt, but that she was no longer a credible threat. Kay looked back to me and smiled, almost imperceptibly.

I led Wayne and party to the assembly hall, where he was already being introduced by the Secretary-General.

Wayne looked out at the assembly, and the video cameras in the press area, cleared his throat, then walked to the microphone.

"Ladies and Gentlemen, I bring you greetings from President Horace Walker of Deneb, and the Galactic Union of Star Systems, headquartered on Aldebaran. My name is Ambassador Wayne Ross Freed of Deneb, *Umea Bakearen* of the Sol-Deneb Treaty of April 19, 1968. With me is Ben Elan, *Umea Bakearen* of Earth, and Union Mediator Dok Fil of Aldebaran."

Wayne told the assembly about the colony that had been established ten thousand years ago, and how contact had been lost. He told them how the "War That Almost Was" had nearly led to the destruction of all life on the planet.

He told them of the Exchange, which was the heart of the Sol-Deneb Treaty of April 19, 1968.

Finally, he told them of the April 19 bombings across the entire galaxy. The events following the bombings were plunging the galaxy into unrest, such as had not been seen for almost two thousand years.

"The Galactic Union is under a great deal of stress, and an entire race of beings is being blamed and persecuted. The scale of the persecution is similar to what occurred in Europe between 1938 and 1945, except that it is happening on a galactic scale.

"This planet will most certainly be affected by the coming galactic war, because you maintain a stockpile of weapons that are no longer available anywhere else in the galaxy. Even now, it is suspected that unknown parties are attempting to secure these weapons for their own use.

"This world has, since 1968, been under the protection of Deneb. My world has insulated yours from exploitation until you were capable of defending yourselves. When war comes, our resources will be stretched to the point that we will be unable to maintain the same level of protection.

"We stand ready to sponsor your petition to the council. If you align with the Galactic Union, your status will be changed from a quarantined protectorate to a full member world, with all of the rights and privileges that come with that status. Deneb will no longer be your only protector, but the entire Union will stand in your defense.

"Should you decline, Deneb will honor your decision, but under galactic law, the Sol-Deneb treaty will be rendered null and void, and relations between our worlds will be severed. The quarantine would be broken, and Deneb will no longer be allowed to prevent potentially hostile worlds from exploiting this planet's resources or its people.

"I will tell you the truth. With Galactic war coming, entry into the Union will in no way guarantee one hundred percent safety for all of the citizens of this world. I can tell you that we will do what we can to protect you from the enemies of peace.

"We also stand ready to share technology that will accelerate your Aerospace industry. We will help you to build infrastructure that will enable you all to travel around the galaxy within the next ten to fifteen years.

"Nor is the technological exchange one-sided. Your scientists have achieved, in just the last two hundred years, innovations that took the rest of the galaxy over a thousand years to achieve. You will not be a welfare planet, but a contributing member of the galactic community, such as it is during the present crisis.

"Now, I leave it to you, the leaders of the united nations of Earth, to decide. You are not merely deciding your own fate, but the fate of the galaxy as well."

Wayne bowed at the end of his speech, stepped back and

was joined by his wife, Ben, Dok Fil, and the others. We began to hear the sound of hands clapping. Gradually, the volume increased as more and more representatives joined in the applause. Eventually, the sound reached a climax as every person in the chamber rose to their feet.

***

As everyone climbed back into the limo, I took Wayne aside. "Boss, now that the world knows you're an alien and all, you think it might be all right to, uh, use all the features of this fine automobile?"

Wayne laughed. "You'd like to take to the air, is that it? I don't blame you. Be careful, okay? You know how busy the skies over the Eastern Seaboard are."

"The first rule of flying: smaller, more agile craft must stay out of the paths of larger, less maneuverable ones. We'll be home before we get into any serious trouble."

"I'm riding shotgun, then," said Kay. "I can help keep an eye out for other aircraft."

Biggs was waiting for us when I touched the limo down at the villa.

Kay whistled. "Biggs looks pissed, Tony."

"He probably got an earful from DSS brass. I'll handle this."

"What the hell are you thinking, Diego? Never fly the imports in front of witnesses!"

Wayne popped his head up out of the limo's sunroof. "It's okay, Leroy. I authorized the flight. The need for secrecy is past."

Biggs rolled his eyes. "Just because you're *Umea Bekearen* doesn't give you the right to disrupt air traffic, Wayne."

Dok Fil smiled at Biggs. "My apologies, Leroy. I did not see the harm in showing the world a little taste of what entry into the Galactic Union might mean for Earth."

"Are you saying you authorized this?"

"I did not counsel against it. I will apologize to the NTSB, or the FAA, or whoever it was that complained to your superiors."

Biggs sighed, but he cracked a smile. "Aliens. Think you own the galaxy."

A few thousand people witnessed the car flying, and a few dozen took pictures. Before long, news had reached almost everywhere that alien technology could finally give us flying cars. It seemed that that alone was enough to bring popular opinion on board.

Within days, Wayne received a call from the Sec. Gen. that the UN had almost unanimously voted to petition the Council for admission. There was a lot of celebrating at the villa after that, but Wayne, already preparing his UnionCon speech, was subdued. "Getting Earth on board was the easy part. Now we actually have to convince the Union that this is a good thing."

"We're behind you all the way, Boss."

Chapter 25: The Way to UnionCon

Lasaitasuna was packed for the trip to UnionCon. I don't just mean that we had ample supplies. I mean that all the staterooms were full. Besides Wayne, Jack and Janet were coming, along with Robert and Doris. For every civilian on the ship, there was also a bodyguard.

Janet had informed Kay that as much as she liked her, she wanted Jack to be her bodyguard, no matter what Biggs' rules were. Kay would guard Doris Freed, instead. Wayne was still my responsibility. Dirk Fowler came along as Robert's bodyguard, as the two had been friends a long time.

Rita stayed home to keep Lynne and Ada Stein safe. Biggs stayed, too. There were a few extra guards on hand to keep the property safe, especially after the shakedown flight incident.

Wayne invited Professor Remington to come along, but he declined. "Your ship appears quite crowded, already. I shall stay here and enjoy your hospitality for a while longer, I think. I do hope you know what you are in for, Mr. Freed."

"Trust, me, Professor, I have put a lot of thought into this."

As we loaded luggage and people into the ship, Janet supervised, balancing on the pair of crutches she had received from *Empresa* after her honeymoon ankle sprain.

I looked at her with concern. "Jack didn't throw you out of bed again, did he?"

Janet laughed. "Oh, no, I'm fine."

"When she needed them, she refused to use them," Jack said, carrying a suitcase up the ramp. "Now that she doesn't need them, she won't put them away."

"After the last trip, it seemed like a good idea to store these in the new infirmary. You know, just in case."

I nodded. "Sounds sensible. You want me to put them away for you?"

Janet grinned impishly. "I'll do it, after I'm done playing."

Kay and I stashed our bags in the stateroom we were going to share for the trip. Someone had to pair up, and I much preferred sharing living quarters with Kay than with Dirk Fowler.

Wayne looked surprised. "So, I guess you've ironed out

your differences, huh?"

I wasn't quite ready to let Wayne know we were lovers, so I shrugged. "We're partners. Besides, if we pilot in shifts, it's unlikely we'll both be using the bed at the same time, anyway. Right, Kay?"

"Oh, absolutely. Besides, he knows if he tries anything, I can beat him up."

"Speaking of which, you'll note that there are actual athletic mats in the cargo hold, so hopefully you can work out aggression more constructively. But please don't let things come to blows again. I like you both, and I'd hate to have to let either of you go."

Kay kissed Wayne on the cheek. "We'll be fine, Wayne. I promise."

"Good. I'm glad we've straightened that out. You'll be glad to know that you're taking us up. I'd love to do it myself, but I'm entertaining guests."

"We'll treat *Lasaitasuna* like it was our very own baby, Boss."

"That's what I like to hear."

Kay and I climbed the ramp up to the cockpit to do the pre-flight. "So, how do we decide on the left chair, Tony? I know you want it as much as I do."

"I figure one of us gets it going, and the other one gets it on the way home, right?"

"Sure, unless Wayne decides he wants to fly. Coin flip, then?"

I won the toss and settled into the pilot's seat. "Hey, Kay, fifty bucks says I can lift off without anyone but you and me knowing it."

Kay kissed my cheek before taking the copilot's seat. "I know better than to take that bet. I've seen you do it."

"By the way, I just wanted to say that even though I'm going to try my best to behave, I can't guarantee I won't be thinking about sex."

Kay winked. "As long as it's only me you're thinking about when you do. Poker faces in public, though, agreed?"

"I'll try my best. Just try not to be so beautiful. I can't resist."

"Actually, I guess it's okay if you make passes at me. People have come to expect that from you."

"Are you sure you'll be able to resist me?"

Kay smiled. "Don't forget, lover, I've been resisting you for years. And that I was already in love with you for most of that time."

I winked. "Yeah, but now I know it."

"We might have to spend some time on the mats, I think."

"Fowler's really the only one on the ship we have to be wary of. Wayne probably wouldn't have a problem with it. Jack and Janet definitely wouldn't. Robert and Doris seem to be more focused on getting caught up with each other than meddling."

Wayne's voice came over the intercom. "All the gear is secured, cockpit. You can begin the launch sequence."

"Sure thing, Boss. Hey, Boss, are we in any kind of a hurry?"

"Why do you ask, Tony?"

"Well... I was just wondering, since we don't have to use stealth, what launch protocol can we use?"

"Tony, if you pull an emergency full-power launch, what do you suppose your chances of ever sitting in that pilot's seat again are?"

"Gotcha, Boss. Just asking. Ready for launch. Everybody check in. Just use that button on your launch seat to let me know you're not still standing and going to go flying through the air."

"Tony, we are going to have to have a little chat about professional behavior," said Jack. "Secure."

Once everyone had reported they were secure, I began to gently throttle up. I winked at Kay.

"Okay... Here we go folks... Uh, does anyone know how to turn off the windshield wipers? Oh, never mind. There they are. Okay, we're ready to go... I'm dying to see what happens when I hit this button here."

Kay was getting red in the face, trying not to laugh out loud.

Wayne seemed a bit less amused. "TONY!"

"Right. Sorry, Boss, just trying to ease the tension. You know how first-timers can get the jitters."

"How about just getting us off the ground?"

"Um, Boss, have you looked out the window, recently?"

We were already above the clouds. The sky darkened as blue gave way to black, and the stars became visible.

"Nice launch, Tony." Wayne switched off his com panel.

Kay smiled. "So, how many bets did you win?"

"About fifteen hundred bucks worth. I intend to spend most of that on you, by the way."

"That'll buy a lot of Sjokolade."

I grinned. "Yep."

Kay kissed me. "What would you have done if you'd lost?"

"Cried like a baby."

"I'm going to head downstairs, now. I'll grab a bite to eat, then try to get some sleep so I can relieve you for the night watch. Maybe, if we're lucky, the rest of the ship will be asleep by then."

I sighed. "Looking forward to it. Goodnight, Kay."

I was about to leave the ship on autopilot and get something to eat when Wayne's voice came over the intercom once more. "Uh, Tony, are you seeing anything outside?"

"No, Boss."

Suddenly, the ship's proximity alarm started going off.

"Uh, scratch that. Something is moving alongside us, about 400 miles away."

I used maximum magnification to get a closer look. It was definitely another spaceship, and it was definitely on a collision course.

"Uh, it might be a good idea to strap in, everybody. Boss, can you come up here?"

Within seconds, Wayne, Jack, and Janet entered the cockpit. Wayne slid into the copilot's seat. "What's going on?"

I pointed to the viewscreen. "We've got company. Ever seen a ship like that?"

Wayne shook his head. "It's definitely not of Denebian or Aldebaran make. Radio contact?"

"Not so far. I'm getting the idea they don't want to talk."

Another alarm sounded, and Janet jumped. "What's that?"

I checked my scan panel. "They're firing at us. Missiles, by the radar signature. I guess taking us alive is not a priority."

"Don't we have countermeasures?"

Wayne shook his head. "This is not a military ship, Janet."

"Then why the hell does it have an 'incoming missile' alarm?"

I silenced the alarm. "That's a great question. I'd love to discuss the issue at length at some point when NO ONE IS SHOOTING AT US!"

Janet stuck her tongue out at me. "Yelling at me isn't going to make the missiles go away."

"Crap," said Wayne. "Tony, you wanted an emergency thrust, right?"

I smiled. "Yes, sir, Boss!"

"Wait for it. Jack, read off the distance."

"Three fifty. Three. Two fifty. Two. One fifty. One. Fifty,

forty, thirty, twenty,"

"NOW!"

The ship lurched as the thrusters pushed us to the outer limits of the solar system.

Jack yelled, "Missiles no longer closing. Detonation. That was good thinking, Wayne."

The alarm went off again. "Hostile is firing again."

"I don't think that trick will work twice."

"What do we do?"

"We could head into the asteroid belt," said Jack.

Janet looked at Jack like he was insane. "Are you kidding?"

"They'd be crazy to follow us."

"Do you think it would work?"

"No."

I guided the ship toward the asteroid belt. "I'll try it, anyway. May I remind you that we need to be traveling in an inertial frame to make a jump? That's going to be hard to do while dodging missiles!"

"Can we just keep dodging until they're out of missiles?"

"Don't know. How many missiles do they have?"

"I don't even know who 'they' are!"

Janet started speaking into her comm panel. "This is *Lasaitasuna*, to the vessel trying to blow us up. Please identify yourselves, so we might be able to more effectively form an escape plan!"

Jack looked at his wife. "Do you really think that's going to help?"

"It couldn't hurt!"

Suddenly, I had an idea. "I'm going to brake and try to get closer."

"Are you nuts?" said Janet. "Get closer?"

Wayne nodded vigorously. "Do it. We'll keep an eye on the missiles."

"We're in space," said Jack. "Airspeed and altitude will be irrelevant. Don't forget that."

"What are you people talking about?" said Janet.

"Haven't you ever seen Top Gun?" Wayne said. "It's like the ultimate date movie!"

"Well, thank you, Gene Siskel! And just who was I going to go see a date movie with, if not you? Wait a minute, who did you see it with? It sure as hell wasn't me! Don't tell me you kept another girl hanging, too!"

Wayne sighed. "I fell for this girl on Betelgeuse, once. A mermaid, actually. Do we really need to bring this up now? We've got more important issues!"

I spun the ship around and started heading straight for the unknown enemy.

The second volley of missiles zipped past us.

"Detonation," said Jack. "I can't believe that worked!"

I used my best Sean Connery. "Hunt for Red October."

More alarms sounded. "Are they firing again?"

I shook my head. "No, that's the collision warning. Hang on!" We barely missed the other vessel. "That's a big ship. Any idea who they are, yet?"

Wayne looked behind us. "They're turning!"

I spun the ship around again. "The good news is that we can outmaneuver them. We've got pretty good engines. It'll take them a while to match us, and then we can change course again."

"As long as they don't have smaller fighters," said Jack. "We don't know if this ship is a carrier, or—"

As if on cue, a huge hatch opened on the side of the hostile ship. A dozen or more small, single-passenger fighters poured out of the hold.

"Okay, it's a carrier."

I glared at Jack. "I hate you, right now, bro."

"I hate me, too."

I spun the ship around again. "I'm open to suggestions!"

"Get close to the big one," said Wayne. "Maybe if we stay close to the big one, the smaller ones won't shoot at us."

"Unless they have deck guns," said Jack.

More hatches started opening on the large ship.

"I've got to stop doing that."

I began to put the ship into a series of barrel rolls. "Maybe that will confuse them."

Jack began to speak again, but both Janet and Wayne glared at him. "Right. Shutting up."

I don't know how long we kept it up, but what happened next surprised all of us.

At least, it surprised all of us but Janet.

A second huge ship approached from the outer edge of the system, and began firing at the other ship. Several shots damaged the carrier's hull. The smaller fighters broke off their attack and entered the open hatch. The hostile ship fired its thrusters and left the area. The new ship gave pursuit until the hostile jumped, then it slowed and returned to our position.

We all stared at the huge new vessel, unsure of what had just happened, until Janet's voice broke the silence.

"Thank you, *Leviathan*. This is *Lasaitasuna*, requesting a dock. That's okay with you, Wayne, isn't it?" Janet looked up from the Comm panel. "What, you never saw Star Wars? Say hello to the *Millennium Falcon*!"

I winked at Janet. "Last-minute rescues. Cinema gold."

"I love you," said Jack.

Janet nodded. "I know."

Wayne activated the intercom panel. "Check in. Is anyone hurt or dead down there?"

"We're fine," said Kayla. "You tell Tony he had better have a good excuse for all those twists and turns, or I'm killing him in his sleep!"

I gulped. "Bunking with Kay on this trip might have been a tactical error on my part."

"I'm sure she's kidding," said Janet. "Just to be on the safe side, though, you'd better keep a bat under your pillow."

Leviathan was a large carrier from the Vega system. Once we had landed in its large hangar, we learned that it carried Vegan Ambassador Izaga Zimov. He had heard Janet's distress call, and ordered an immediate hyper-jump to our location. It was a dangerous move, considering our proximity to the asteroid belt, but they had realized that our ship would not stand a chance for very long against our attackers.

We remained on *Leviathan* for the duration of the flight to Aldebaran. Wayne spent most of his time in the company of the Ambassador. That gave Kay and me plenty of private time, and we took full advantage of it.

Chapter 26: Admission Day Crisis

Kay and I sat with Wayne's family as Wayne shared his annual slide presentation. Doris was nearly in tears as she watched the reactions of people in the crowd.

"Does Wayne present slides every year?"

I nodded. "Dok Fil told me it was once necessary, because Robert couldn't bring Wayne himself."

"Because I had no memory of the exchange."

"Yes. Now, it's one of the most popular presentations. Wayne and Ben are both minor celebrities around the galaxy. I wonder if he'll have to keep sharing slides once Earth, that is, the Sol system, becomes a member of the Union and the Sol-Deneo Treaty officially ends."

Doris shook her head and smiled. "I regret that I never knew any of this. Look at him. I couldn't be more proud. Does Ben also do a slideshow?"

I chuckled. "Something like that. His presentation often feels more like a stand-up comic routine. You'll see. He's up after Wayne."

About halfway through Ben's routine, his mood suddenly changed, and he began hurrying through his monologue. He apologized to the audience and promised a more polished presentation next year. As soon as he had left the dais, he began walking hurriedly toward the nearest exit.

Wayne tapped my shoulder. "Come with me, please. Something's up."

"You got it, Boss."

We intercepted Ben and followed him outside.

"What's wrong, Ben?"

"Little Hank is agitated. Someone just tried to harm Sonja!"

I started. "How do you know that?"

"Ben and Little Hank share a telepathic connection," said Wayne.

Ben sighed and wiped sweat off his forehead. "A well-cloaked ship just tried to enter the airspace around my home. It was getting past the sensors and everything. It might have managed to land, but Little Hank detected hostile intent and started to attack the ship. Once he damaged their cloak, DipSec caught up with them. Wayne, I need to go home."

Little Hank teleported right next to where I was standing. "Jeez, Little Hank! You startled me!"

Little Hank looked at me. *Sorry, Diego man. Important.*

I stared. "Uh, okay. I forgive you."

Ben jumped on Little Hank's back, and they popped away.

Robert and Dirk came running up to where we were standing. "Was that a real live barkmoth?"

Wayne nodded. "That's Little Hank."

"Little?"

"I know, he gets that a lot."

Doris and Kay caught up to Robert. "What happened?"

"Someone tried to hurt Sonja."

"No! Is she all right?"

Ben and Little Hank popped back. "Oh, hi, Robert, Doris. Well, that was a close one. Sonja's a little shaken up, but they never got close to the house. DipSec is beefing up security."

"That's good."

Robert looked at Wayne. "Have you spoken to Lynne recently?"

"Yeah, I called her just before we left the hotel this morning." Wayne pulled out his phone and tried her number. "No answer. Tony, call Leroy, please."

"You got it." Biggs' phone rang, but no one picked up. "That's not good. I'm calling for backup."

It took at least half an hour for a DSS team to reach the villa. We waited impatiently for them to call me back.

"The villa's deserted, Diego. No sign of a struggle of any kind. All the alarms and sensors have been deactivated. We found a bowl in the main hall containing a bunch of phones and radios."

I relayed the information to Wayne, who sat down on the bench. "They knew we could track the phones. They could have taken her anywhere."

"They couldn't have left the planet," said the agent on the phone. "After the attack on the Ambassador's ship, Deneb has effectively blockaded the system. No hostile ships are going to be able to get in or out."

"A ship with a nearly undetectable cloak attempted to infiltrate the Elans' home on Deneb," I said. "Are you certain the system is airtight?"

"Yes, sir. The Denebians say they're using full sweeps. Even if a ship was totally invisible to scanners, their thrusts would still be detectable. Whoever did this, they are stuck on Earth. Of course, it's still a big planet. They're sniffing Res Net, too. Any communications will be traced."

"Good. Keep us posted."

"Will do, sir."

***

We all sat in Wayne's lounge, trying to determine how they could have breached security. I told the others what I knew. "There was no sign of struggle. That would mean that they were all taken without a fight."

Fowler scowled. "No one could have taken them by surprise. They would have set off the proximity alarms."

"The alarms were deactivated," I said. "Either they were never set, or they were turned off from the control office. The only people who have keys to disable the alarms are Wayne, Lynne, Jack, and Biggs."

Jack held up his control room key. "I have mine. I'm ninety percent sure Wayne has his."

Wayne nodded. "It's right here. Lynne usually keeps her keys in her handbag. It's possible that someone could have swiped it. I seriously doubt Leroy would let his key out of his sight."

"We screened the security staff thoroughly," said Jack. "There's no way one of them was a mole."

Fowler wrote names down on his notepad. The man actually carried a notepad. "What about one of the guests?"

"Ada Stein isn't about to put her great-grandbaby in danger," I said. "And I doubt she's a security risk. Dok Fil told me she used to be one of the best Envoys in the OM."

"Professor Remington, then?"

I shrugged. "I've never really liked the guy, but I'm biased. He has been off-planet, though. And he was opposed to Wayne's plan to reveal the Union to the U.N."

"It gives him motive."

"I'll give you that. And opportunity, too, since he could have ET connections, but so could Lynne, or Ada, or Biggs." I smiled. "And Biggs does have an Ursan with a life-debt owed him."

Fowler cringed. "It's been a long time since I've thought of that incident. Biggs told you about that, did he?"

I nodded. "It's why he says he won't go into space anymore, if he can avoid it."

Fowler nodded. "I don't blame him. That Ursan is here. I don't know if he'd recognize me, but there's no mistaking him."

"Who is he?"

"The Meraki Ambassador, Rrowlf Sharpfang. Granted, he wasn't ambassador at the time."

"You sure know how to pick your enemies. Do you think he could have planned this?"

Kay shook her head. "Ursans have a deep sense of honor. If Sharpfang had anything against Wayne, he'd come after him personally."

"I guess all we can do is wait, then. There will probably be demands."

***

The call finally came the following morning. Wayne got a call from an unknown or scrambled number. As soon as the call was over, he let me know. "They wanted me to stay out of council, but once I told them that my presence wouldn't change anything, they relented. They're using Remington as the contact. Tony, I think Remington is in on it."

"Why do you think that?"

"It's subtle. I'm not sure I can make you understand. But I've learned some things about telling when people are lying."

"If you learned it from Lynne, then I trust your gut. We were pretty sure there was a bad guy on the inside. Wish I could say I'm surprised it's him."

"You suspected him?"

"It had to be an inside job. The alarms were off. I knew it couldn't be Ada, Lynne, Rita, or Biggs."

Wayne laughed. "Okay, I guess that makes sense. But why?"

"Maybe you can get Remington to tell you."

"Should I let him know that I know?"

"You're the boss. It's your call. Also, you should try to keep him on the line as long as you can. I've no idea how long it takes to trace a Res Net call."

Wayne nodded. "I'll do what I can. Right now, I need to go introduce Ben to the council."

Kay and I waited outside the chamber, but we watched the

speech on one of hall monitors. "He sure can give a speech, can't he?"

I put an arm around her waist. "I'm not sure I could be as calm as he is, if the woman I loved was in danger."

"He trusts us. DSS. He believes we can save her."

"I hope we can. I really don't want to have to be the one to tell him his wife is dead. And his grandmother."

"Leroy and Rita are with them. They'll protect her."

"If they can. They got themselves taken right along with the rest of them. I would like to think we would have been less easily entrapped."

"Maybe. Then again, we might have been paying more attention to each other than a potential security breech. Maybe we shouldn't be partners, after all."

"Don't say that, Kay. I don't think I could tolerate not seeing you for weeks or months at a time."

"We've done it before."

"I hated it. And I didn't even realize I was in love with you at the time. Either we stay partners, or I quit the DSS."

"I'd quit, too." Kay smiled at me. "We've got interstellar pilot's licenses, now. We could probably get a job flying together."

"I love you, Kay."

Wayne suddenly burst out of the chamber. "He's calling me again. I'll put him on speaker."

"That was quite a stirring speech," said Remington. "Our hosts wanted me to remind you of our agreement."

"May I speak to my wife?"

"Wayne, I'm here. I watched your speech. You were wonderful."

"How are you watching?"

"It's on television," said Lynne. "All the networks are carrying it."

"I miss you, Lynne. I wish I could see your face."

"I'm sorry, Ambassador," said Remington. "Our hosts don't want to give you any clues to our location."

"I don't see how it would," said Lynne. "There are curtains in all the windows."

Wayne glanced at me before he continued. "If you want me to continue to cooperate, I want to see Lynne. I want to see all of my people, Professor. Tell your hosts that unless I see my people, I'm finished."

"You are risking the lives of your people by making

demands. I don't want to see anyone killed!"

"Professor Remington, I am not making a demand. I am humbly requesting that I be allowed to see my wife, my grandmother, and my people. You have known me long enough that you should know that I always keep my word. So listen now to this. Grant me this request. Allow me to see them, so that I may know they are unharmed, and in return, I give you my word that I will spare your life."

"I beg your pardon?" gasped the professor.

"You can drop the charade, Remington. You might be a brilliant debater, sir, but you are a terrible actor. You don't even know how to stay in character. Allow me to see all of my people, alive and well, and you will survive. But if any of my friends and family so much as gets a paper cut, I will see you hanged. Or spaced."

"Spaced?"

"You know, tossed out an open airlock. That is, I believe, the penalty for attempting to influence a Council vote by kidnapping a delegate's family. But, then, I don't really care. It is what I will see happen to you if I don't get a chance to see my people. Hmm. Now that I think of it, I guess I am making a demand, aren't I?"

There was silence on the other end for a long while. When the professor finally spoke again, his voice had a tone of resignation. "Very well. I will make arrangements, and call you back in a few minutes."

Wayne closed the connection. "I hope I did the right thing."

My phone rang. "Give me good news."

"Agent Diego, please tell the Ambassador that we have located them. We have special forces preparing to move in at your command."

"Hold a moment. Wayne, they found them. They're waiting for a signal."

"I want to see Lynne first."

I nodded. "I'll wait. DSS, when I hang up, that will be the signal to move in."

A few minutes later, Janet came out of the chamber. "They're taking a vote now. Ben gave a great speech. He's almost as good an orator as you are. What's wrong? You look pissed."

Wayne held up his phone. "Thanks for the update. I'm pissed because I have just learned that our Professor Remington is in league with the kidnappers."

Janet gasped. "I never would have guessed that the professor was a traitor. Manipulative, maybe. Intimidating, I suppose. I thought he liked you and Lynne."

"He respected us. It's not the same thing. I never would have suspected him, either. But over the last few weeks, he got a lot of information just by behaving the way he always has. Remember how curious he always was about everything."

"He had questions about you and me, you and Lynne, and Jack and me. He even once asked about Jack and Lynne."

"We had many conversations while he stayed with us. He probably got information about our security arrangements just by acting curious about everything. Not to mention just a little bit absentminded. I guess I haven't learned all of his tells, yet."

Wayne's phone rang again. He held it up so that he'd be the only one visible on the other end. "Show me my family, or I hang up."

"There, you see? No one has been harmed." Remington's voice sounded shaky, like he wasn't happy having to change plans.

"How did you do it, Professor? How did you manage to overcome all my security?"

"I drugged them," he said. "We were all in a festive mood after learning that the attack on your ship was unsuccessful. I mixed up a batch of eggnog. It's an old family recipe, actually, apart from the drug. I think almost everyone had a second glass."

"You drugged my wife? You ass, she's pregnant!"

"No, I did not drug Mrs. Freed. Not that I wouldn't have, but she refused to drink an alcoholic beverage. It didn't matter. When my colleagues arrived, she and I were the only ones conscious. She was easy to persuade, under the circumstances. Though she did say you would kill me. I told her that I doubted the *Umea Bakearen*, the Peace Child, would be a cold-blooded murderer."

"Did you have anything to do with the attack on my ship?"

"I was personally surprised that you survived, but pleased. I told them that it wasn't necessary to kill you."

"Who did you tell?"

"I'm not a fool, Ambassador. You know I don't want to hang for treason. It should not surprise you that I also don't want to be marked for death by turning on my friends, either. You are an intelligent man, Ambassador. I am sure you will eventually figure it out on your own without me endangering my own life."

"Why did you do it?"

"I assure you, it wasn't personal. I have always been quite fond of both of you. But I am fearful that you have allied with the wrong people. Your association with the Vegans will destroy the Union, and Earth along with it."

"How can you be sure?"

"Are you aware that the Vegans were once known by a different name, and that they came from a galaxy other than this one?"

"Where did you get this information?"

"They were once called Jhelin."

"Professor, please tell me. I need to know."

"They are hiding knowledge from you."

"Professor, do you know who attacked my ship? Because it wasn't the Jhelin. I have never seen them do anything aggressive, except in defense. You are wrong. Your information is bad."

"I see there is no convincing you. This conversation is over."

"Wait! Can I talk to my wife?"

"You can see your wife. That was our agreement. Now you will uphold your end of it."

"Indeed I will." Wayne nodded to me, and I hung up my phone. "Leroy, don't kill the professor."

I heard noises, gunshots, and women screaming before the call disconnected. Wayne dropped his phone and dropped into the seat behind him.

Jack picked it up. "This thing's pretty sturdy. The touchscreen didn't break."

Janet shrugged. "It's a polymer coating that makes the glass shatter-resistant. Wayne, I'm sure Lynne and Ada are safe."

"Someone is hurt. There was blood on the lens before we were disconnected."

A minute passed.

Two minutes passed.

Ben came out of the chamber, beaming. "The vote is finished. It was 397-104 in favor of admission. Earth is now a Union member. What's wrong?"

Janet shushed him.

Still, we waited.

The phone rang.

Wayne answered. "Lynne? Oh, thank the One! Are you all right?"

Lynne didn't answer for a moment. When she spoke, her

voice came out in sobs. "I'm fine... Ada's fine... Rita's been shot .. Her arm looks bad... Don't know if it can be saved... Wayne... Leroy... He—He's dead."

Kay burst into tears, and I held her, barely holding back tears myself. A DSS agent was telling Wayne something about a craft off the coast of Florida, but I could not comprehend what he was saying. I was too numb to take in anything. I was barely conscious of the sound of the crowds beginning to file out of the Council Chambers. I barely noticed anything except Kay's arms around me, her tears staining my uniform. I held her tightly until her crying ceased.

Once we separated, I realized that Wayne was also crying, his head on Janet's shoulder while Jack patted his back. Once he had come back to himself, he kissed Janet and stood.

"I'm sorry, Ben. Did you say something about the vote?"

Ben smiled. "The Galactic Union has voted to accept the Sol System into the Union. It appears that our roles as *Umea Bakearen* are coming to an end, brother-cousin."

Wayne nodded. "Good."

"I'm sorry about your people."

"Biggs was a good man. I still can't believe he's gone."

I put a hand on Wayne's shoulder. "He died the way he always hoped he would, Wayne. There's nothing he wouldn't have done to keep you and Lynne safe. I'm going to miss him, too. At least he saved Lynne, and Ada. I kind of wish he could have taken Remington with him."

Wayne smiled, in spite of himself. "No, that would have been far too quick a death for the good professor. He's worth more to us alive. He has information."

"He didn't sound terribly eager to spill it."

"I think he will, once he realizes that they can't touch him."

"Where are you going?"

"Whoever had Remington kidnap Lynne desperately wanted to keep me from interfering with the Vega admission vote. I'm going to go in and interfere."

"Flush 'em out. Do you need us with you?"

"No, they can't touch me in there. Make sure no one gets near my folks."

"Got it."

Wayne returned to the Council Chamber with Janet and Jack.

"Leroy Biggs was a good man," said Fowler. "He and I

were partners for a long time."

"I know, Dirk. I'm sorry."

"You know there's going to be an investigation, right? There always is when an agent dies. The fact that he got himself captured isn't going to make things any better."

"It wasn't his fault," I said. "Remington spiked the eggnog."

Fowler raised an eyebrow. "You think that's going to help? Leroy shouldn't have been drinking while on duty in the first place. And he certainly shouldn't have let any of the other guards drink on duty."

"It was after the attack on our ship," said Kay. "Maybe they all assumed the danger was past."

"Also not good. He should have been more alert after the attack, not less."

"Damn," said Kay. "You're right."

"DSS is probably going to scrutinize the whole team. They're going to turn up the heat on everyone."

"I'm not afraid," said Kay. "We'll take whatever comes."

Dirk looked from me to Kay. "Uh-huh. I figured as much. I saw how you two consoled each other. Don't get me wrong. I'm not judging you. Heck, I met my wife working in the field. But DSS is going to hang you out to dry if it comes out."

I nodded. "We're ready to accept whatever happens."

"We'll all agree that this conversation never happened," said Fowler. "I'm going to take the next flight I can back to Earth and see if I can't find some way to insulate you from the witch hunt. You're all fine agents, and sometimes there are more important things than rules."

He shook hands with each of us, said goodbye to Robert and Doris, and walked away.

Kay watched him leave. "I would not have expected that from him. He's always been a big stickler for the rules."

Robert put his hands on our shoulders. "I think years of associating with me have 'corrupted' him. We always used to have long debates over what happens when doing what is right isn't necessarily the same as doing what is required. Or legal."

There was a loud roar from the crowd in the Council Chambers. We immediately looked to the monitors to see what was going on. Within moments, the Polaran delegation stormed past us, followed by groups of delegates from other systems I simply could not identify. None of them looked very pleased.

When Wayne and Ben came out of the chamber, we asked

what had happened.

"Polaris was behind it all," said Wayne. "They accused Vega of attacking our ship, and then firing on their vessel when it responded to our distress call. They even offered their damaged ship as evidence against Vega."

I scoffed. "The bastards. No wonder they wanted you to keep out of it."

"Once I testified that the Vegans were the ones who answered our distress call, the vote was overwhelmingly in favor of readmission. So less was so mad, he withdrew Polaris from the Union. A whole bloc of delegates walked with him. They're going to declare war on Vega."

"Why?"

Wayne shrugged. "No idea. I'd assumed they were all about keeping us out of the Union, but they really seemed to have it in for Vega."

***

Lynne surprised Wayne about a week later when she showed up in the food court dressed as a very pregnant X-wing pilot. Wayne jumped up and ran to meet his wife. "Lynne! What are you doing here? Never mind—I don't care. I'm just glad you're here."

The crowd applauded as they kissed. Kay wiped a tear away from her cheek and punched me in the shoulder.

"What the hell did you do that for?"

"Because kissing you in public would be unprofessional."

I rubbed the bruising spot. "And punching me is?"

Kay smiled. "I'll make it up to you later."

Chapter 27: Changes

Leroy Biggs was buried with full honors at Arlington.

We all went to the funeral, even Rita. Her heavily-bandaged arm rested in a sling. While we waited for the ceremony to begin, she told us that she was able to move her fingers. "The docs say that means I probably won't lose my arm. They did warn me that I probably won't regain the full use of it, either. It looks like I'll be a desk jockey for the rest of my career. However long that is."

Kay kissed her. "Maybe you'll be our boss."

Rita shrugged her good shoulder. "Maybe. I doubt it, though. They're none too happy about the whole kidnapping. If we'd shunned the eggnog, we might not have been taken. I swear, Wayne, we thought the attack on your ship was the end of it. I'll never make that assumption again, I promise."

"No one's perfect," said Wayne. "We all thought that was the end of it. I credit you both for saving the lives of my wife and my grandmother. If I blame anyone for anything, it's Remington."

"What's going to happen to him, anyway?"

"He'll stand trial. Maybe he'll be more willing to talk, now that Polaris can't threaten him."

"Is his testimony even necessary anymore? Polaris declaring war on Vega seems to be all the evidence we need."

"We can't blame the entire system," said Wayne. "Not all Polarans are guilty. Remington will be able to tell us who his handlers were."

**

Dirk met us at the door to our old squad room when we reported back to the DSS office. "I hate to be the one to tell you this, but you're all on administrative leave until further notice. I'm going to have to ask you for your badges and your sidearms."

"Can't say we weren't expecting it." I handed mine over. "Any chance we're ever getting these back?"

Dirk nodded. "This is standard procedure when a team member dies. Don't think the Agency is going to throw any of you under a bus. Especially you, Diego. Leaked footage of your piloting during the attack on Freed's ship is spreading like wildfire."

"Footage? From where? The only ships in the area were ours and the Polarans', and they destroyed theirs."

"Between on board flight recordings and the Vegans' long-range scans, someone built a simulation of the entire incident. You're being called this system's greatest pilot."

Kay scoffed. "Aw, hell, you shouldn't have told him that. There'll be no living with the man from now on. Lucky-ass coin flip, Diego."

I raised my hands and stepped back. "I said nothing!"

"If you're wise, you'll keep it that way."

"I'm sure you're all going to be reinstated," said Dirk. "Think of this as a vacation rather than a suspension. Just keep your phones on you, so the DSS can contact you whenever they have questions."

Outside, Jack shook his head. "They can call it what they want to, but it still sucks. I'm not sure I even want to go back after they clear us."

"With your wife's income," I said, "You'd never have to work again, if you didn't want to."

Kay gave Jack a grin. "Yeah, Mister Living-at-Wayne-Manor."

"Aw, come on, guys. That's not why I married Janet."

"It's cool, bro," I said. "You know we're just kidding."

"What are you two going to do with your 'vacation,' anyway?"

Kay hooked her arm around mine. "I'm taking Tony to Denver to meet my folks."

Jack smiled. "Well, don't do anything I wouldn't do."

"Heck," I said, "I don't even want to do some of the stuff you would do."

***

Kay's family were all pretty friendly to me. Her youngest brother, Karl, greeted me first. "We've heard a lot about you, Tony. Kay says you're almost as good a pilot as she is."

"Almost as good, huh? That's higher praise than I usually get from her."

"Gotta keep you humble," said Kay. "You're far more

tolerable that way."

I harrumphed.

Karl laughed. "I wanted to be a fighter pilot, too, you know. Unfortunately, I failed the eye test. I'm still in the Air Force ROTC program at Georgetown, though."

"Georgetown? I'm an alum there. Good luck with it."

"What's it like? Going out into space?"

I thought for a moment. "Well, the first time was really exciting, but once you get used to it, it's kind of routine."

Karl nodded. "Sounds like sex."

Kay slapped the back of her brother's head. "As if you'd know."

"I'm not a kid anymore, Kay."

Kay looked at Karl and sighed. "Damn, you're not, are you? I've been away for far too long. Are Mom and Dad home?"

"They're in the kitchen, prepping supper."

I looked at my watch. "It's only two. What could possibly take that long to cook?"

Karl grinned. "You'll see."

***

Kay's parents were in the process of butchering a large deer. Mrs. Moss was feeding strips of venison into a large meat grinder, while Mr. Moss turned the crank. Once the current strip was through, they paused to greet us.

Kay hugged her mom and dad and introduced me. "This is my partner, Tony."

Her father nodded politely. "Please, call me Hugh. I'd shake your hand, but I'd have to wash up first."

"I totally understand. Looks like you've got a lot to do, yet."

"Have you ever hunted, Tony?"

"Me? No. I'm a strict vegetarian."

"Oh! Uh, I hope this doesn't offend you."

Kay swatted the back of my head. "That's bull, Mr. Corn Dog."

"Not bull; venison." I smiled. "Sorry, I couldn't resist the joke. Not a very good one, I'll admit. No, I've never hunted, but my family used to get a lot of venison from a neighbor who did."

Kay's mother, Katherine, smiled. "It's good to be friendly with your neighbors. Where are you from?"

"I grew up in New Jersey."

"You don't sound like you're from New Jersey."

I smiled. "I get that a lot. I grew up in Monmouth, one of the towns that make it the Garden State. Most people think all of New Jersey is a suburb of New York."

Kay's older brother, Kevin, raised his hand. "Guilty. Sorry, man."

I waved it off. "No offense taken."

Hugh started turning the crank again. "We're making chili tonight. You're welcome to stay for dinner. How long you in town for? I hope we can convince you to stay awhile."

Kay sighed. "Actually, we're kind of, well, suspended."

"Oh, Kay, I'm sorry!" Katherine wiped her hands on a towel and gave her daughter a tight hug. "What happened?"

We shared the story of Remington and the kidnapping, and Biggs' death. "It's standard procedure to investigate after an agent dies. Since we all worked under Biggs, we're on leave until it's done. Neither of us had anything better to do, so Kay invited me to come see your farm—and your planes."

"So you're a pilot, too, eh?"

Kay nodded. "We crossed paths once or twice during Desert Storm. Joined DSS around the same time, too."

"Is that so? Tell me, Tony, do you think my daughter should have been allowed to become a fighter pilot?"

I nodded. "Damn right. I daresay she's almost as good a pilot as me."

"Almost as good?" Kay glared at me.

"Okay, okay! Kay got higher marks than me in most of the Aldebaran trials. We were both in the top ten, though."

Katherine sat down and looked hard at us both. "It's really true, then. You both have been to outer space? Other planets?"

"Yeah, Mom. It's all true."

***

The Moss family had several spare rooms in their huge farmhouse, and they graciously offered me a room. "Any friend of one of our children is a friend of the family. You just holler if you need anything."

"Thank you. You are too kind."

Kay took the room across the hall from mine. "This was

my room when I was little."

The Moss family gave me the grand tour of the farm. The owned a couple hundred acres, with pastureland for livestock. When we reached a large barn, Kay motioned for me to follow. "I want to show you something in the stables."

The family had a full gym, complete with a boxing ring and a martial arts mat.

"Wow. You folks sure must like to fight. Explains a lot."

Kay looked at me. "What is that supposed to mean?"

"Every time I make a joke, you usually swat the back of my head. You even swatted Karl."

"Not every time."

"No?"

"Okay, most of the time, I guess. Anyway, after dinner, we can spar out here. If you're feeling up to it."

"It seems a little cold."

"Not a problem," said Kay. "It's heated."

"Nice. Your folks' freight biz must be pretty successful."

"Between that and the farm, we've always been pretty self-sufficient."

After dinner, the family came out to watch us demonstrate some of the Aldebaran martial arts we'd learned.

We were always pretty evenly matched. I had greater endurance, so if we went at it for longer than an hour or so, I would gain an advantage, so we generally stuck to a half-hour routine, just to be fair.

We bowed to Kay's family, then to each other, then we began to fight. Neither of us successfully landed a hit for the whole time.

Hugh whistled. "You both are really aggressive. It's amazing that no one ever gets hurt."

"We've only once actually tried to hurt each other, Dad. Tony said something that set me off."

"What was that?"

Kay looked at me. "It doesn't matter anymore. We settled it. I won the fight."

"I yielded."

"Same thing."

"Hardly."

Hugh laughed. "Well, it sure sounds settled. Feel free to use the equipment any time."

"Thanks, Mr. Moss... uh, Hugh. I'm sure we'll put the gym

to good use. It'll give us something to do with our spare time."

Kay grunted. "We do have a lot of it, lately."

***

Sparring every day became a matter of routine for us. We weren't about to sleep together. We had appearances to maintain.

After about a week, though, I was getting tired of pretending that Kay was nothing more than my partner. I made a decision, and I didn't care whether or not it would mean our careers. I made an excuse and headed into town to find a jeweler.

My plan was to propose to her the next time we sparred. I'd pin her to the mat, and then slip the ring on her finger while I was helping her up. The only part I wasn't sure about was actually getting her pinned to the mat, but if I pulled it off, it would be a moment to remember.

Karl watched as we entered the ring and bowed to each other. "Get him, Kay, you can do it!"

I smiled. "You have seen us fight, haven't you? I doubt either one of us could—OOF!"

Kay had knocked the wind out of me. "What's wrong, Tony? I thought you were ready!"

"I was talking to your brother!"

"We already bowed. You're not supposed to get distracted by stuff outside the ring."

I gritted my teeth and winked at her. "Oh, it's on, then!"

We fought as furiously as we had when Kay was really mad at me. I was beginning to wonder if I had actually done something to upset her.

I began to think maybe this wasn't such a good plan, after all. I realized that there was the off chance that I might not actually be able to pin her.

It was getting close to time. If I didn't make a move soon, I was going to have to come up with a plan B, and I hadn't been that great planning A to begin with.

Finally, I saw an opening. It looked like Kay was going for a kick. If I could get behind her left leg, I could throw her. I made my move.

But Kay didn't kick. She planted her right foot down, and instead of planting my leg behind her left foot, I ended up driving my heel through her right knee.

Kay cried out and went down.

"Oh, god! Kay, I'm sorry!" I stood over her. "Are you all right?"

With her uninjured leg, Kay swept both of my feet out from under me, then used the momentum to roll on top of me. "Pin. I win! Dammit, Tony, how many times has Van Dam said to never let your guard down until the fight is over?"

"Sorry, Kay, I didn't mean to..."

Kay silenced me with a far more passionate kiss than I felt I deserved.

Karl was shouting at me as he ran toward us. "That was a cheap shot, Diego! I thought you were... oh, pardon me!"

Kay released me. "I guess the jig is up, Tony. Relax, Karl! It was an accident."

I sat up. "I would never hurt your sister, Karl. I love her."

"You two are in love? I didn't think that was allowed."

"Strictly speaking, it's not." I helped Kay stand. "Can you walk?"

She tried to put weight on her knee and shook her head. "Nope. It's bad. What were you trying to do, anyway?"

I picked her up and carried her to a bench. "I was trying to pin you. There's something I wanted to give you." I reached into my pocket... but there was nothing there. "Shit. I lost it!"

"Lost what?"

Karl bent down and picked something up off the mat. He handed me the ring. "Is this it?"

Kay looked at the ring, and started shaking. "Tony, is that what I think it is?"

"This isn't the way I wanted to propose to you, but what's done is done. Will you marry me, anyway?"

Tears started streaming from her eyes as she nodded and held up her hand so I could slip the ring on her finger. We kissed as Karl ran into the house to tell the family. When Kay could talk, she confirmed it. "Yes, I'll marry you, Tony. Now, would you please take me to a doctor?"

Kayla's parents came running out of the house to congratulate us. Katherine hugged her daughter, while Hugh shook my hand. "I had my suspicions that there was something going on between you."

"Yes, sir. We've had to keep it quiet, because DSS would separate us. With the current investigation going on, I figured it was a matter of time before they found out, anyway."

"If you lose your job, how are you going to be able to support my daughter?"

I smiled. "Kay and I are currently the only Terrans with interstellar flight training. Neither of us should have any trouble finding employment somewhere."

Hugh nodded. "I see where that would be a benefit. You seem a decent fellow."

"It's taken me some time to become so, sir."

"Humble, too. I like that. Welcome to the family, Tony."

Katherine hugged and kissed me. Both parents started asking us questions until Kay began to cry. "Mom! Dad! I'm glad you're happy for us, but I really need my fiancé to take me to the hospital!"

I gave Karl the keys to our rental car, and he drove right up to the door. Hugh and I helped Kay get into the back seat, and Katherine gave her an ice pack. "Do you need us to do anything?"

"No, thanks. I can take it from here."

Kay smiled. "When we get back, we'll answer all your questions, I promise. I love you, Mom and Dad. You, too, Karl."

***

The attending ER doctor called in an orthopedic specialist, who happened to specialize in sports-related injuries. He checked the x-ray, then asked Kay what happened.

"We were sparring. My fiancé was attempting a throw, but my knee got in the way." Kay seemed to enjoy using the word. I found myself enjoying it, too.

The doctor nodded. "That's consistent with what I see here. There is a fracture of your medial epicondyle."

"That sounds bad."

"Most medical terms do. It's the little bump on the inside of your knee. It's a rare injury. Usually when the knee collapses, it bends outward. Your knee bent inwards when Mr. Diego kicked you. Fortunately, there seems to be no need for surgery. Stay off of it for six to eight weeks, wear an immobilizer, and use the crutches we give you. Good day, Ms. Moss. Mr. Diego."

Once he was gone, Kay chuckled. "Nice move, Tony."

"I'm really sorry, Kay."

"I forgive you. If you feel the need to do penance, I'm sure we can work something out."

I bowed. "I will be at your beck and call, my love."

***

With her knee immobilized, the only way Kay could sit in the car was in the back seat behind me with her leg propped up on the seat beside her. "I've never had a chauffeur before."

"Don't get too used to it. I'd much rather have you riding shotgun, where I can look at you. I like looking at you."

"I love you, Tony. Now that we're engaged, I wonder if my mom and dad would mind letting us share a room."

"Uh, I'm not so sure about that. It's bad enough I broke their daughter's leg. I'm not sure how they'd react to me sleeping with said daughter under their roof before we're married."

Kay laughed. "Coward."

"Damn straight. Do you think they'd be offended if we got a hotel room?"

"Probably. I guess we're going to have to be chaste then. At least, until we head back east. It's just as well. I'm not exactly sure how much fun in bed I'd be."

"We'll manage. I have had experience with just such a challenge, if you'll recall... and then don't hate me for bringing her up."

Kay laughed. "Nice recovery, lover. I can't hate you, though I am a little jealous that she got you before I did."

"She wasn't my first, either, love."

"I know, but she was the only one I ever saw you with."

"All anyone else ever got was my body. You have my whole self."

"When you put it that way, I definitely think I got the better end of the deal."

***

Back at the Moss homestead, Kay sat at the table with her leg propped up on my lap. We answered all of her family's questions, even those that were less comfortable to answer. There was one question I hoped wouldn't be asked, but I was ready for it when it came.

Hugh was the one who asked it. "Have you slept together?"

Kay's face turned red. "Dad! That's our business!"

I grasped her hand. "It's okay, Kay. If I was a father, I think I'd want to know, too. From the moment I first met your daughter, I was physically attracted to her. But we never had sex. Not until a few weeks ago, and by then I had already made up my mind to marry her."

Hugh looked me in the eye. I wasn't sure if he was going to kill me or not. I held Kay's hand and waited for the worst.

It never came. Hugh finally smiled. "That's a good answer. If you want to share a room under our roof, you have my approval. I will warn you, federal agent or not, if you break my daughter's heart..."

I nodded, and smiled. "I would expect nothing less from a man who loves his daughter. I never will, sir. I am really sorry for breaking her leg, though."

Hugh began to laugh, along with the rest of the family around the table. "You are always welcome in this house."

That night, Kay and I shared a room, and a bed.

***

We were called back to D.C. a few days later.

Jess looked up from her desk. "Jesus, Kay, what happened to you?"

"Sparring mishap. I zigged, expecting Tony to zag."

Jess glared at me. "Tony..."

Kay laughed. "It wasn't all bad." She held up her had with the ring.

Jess squealed. "Well congratulations! It's about time. When did it happen? I need a date and time, to the nearest hour."

"Last Thursday. About, what, four?"

I nodded. "Yeah, I think so."

Jess checked a chart. "Hah! I win the pool!"

Kay laughed. "People were taking bets?"

"I'll be sure to use at least part of the winnings on your wedding present. I will be invited to the wedding, right?"

"Of course! It won't be a huge wedding. We don't want a long engagement. I do want to be off crutches before I walk down the aisle, but we'll keep you in the loop."

"That's all I ask. Congrats, again. We'll talk after your meeting with Fowler. Good luck."

Dirk let us in and motioned for us to sit. "Welcome back, agents. Let's get right to it. The good news is I plan to reinstate the team. Or what's left of it. Rita's on indefinite medical leave, and Forbes turned in his resignation last week."

I gasped. "Jack quit?"

"He's taken on a job as head of security at Ambassador Freed's home."

"Wow."

"The other news is that there are going to be a whole lot of changes around here."

Kay frowned. "What kind of changes?"

"Well, the Sol-Deneb Treaty is done, for one. Wayne Freed is no longer as essential to our planet's survival as he used to be."

"Are you saying that after all Wayne's done for us, we're just abandoning him?"

"Calm down, Agent Moss. I'm not saying that at all. This country-hell, the whole planet-owes the man a debt of gratitude. But his safety is no longer solely our concern. The United Nations, not to mention Denebian DipSec, wants to have a say in how security is handled for Ambassadors Freed and Elan."

Fowler took a breath and sighed. "Our department is no longer top secret anymore, either. That means more bureaucracy, and more scrutiny. The State Department wants to avoid any further screw-ups, especially now that everyone's watching."

"Screw-ups? Is that how they see us?"

"Not officially. Ambassador Freed has publicly praised the team for bringing his wife and grandmother home safely. That makes the team pretty much untouchable. Officially. But there are higher-ups who are livid that the whole kidnapping took place. They are going to be watching us like a hawk."

"Understood."

Fowler gestured to Kay's left hand. "Nice piece of jewelry you got there. Do I know him?"

"I should think so," she said, taking my arm.

"I figured as much. Congrats, both of you. And, I'm sorry. Rules are rules, even if they suck. One of you will have to transfer out."

I nodded and handed Dirk my badge. "We knew this was coming. It's been a pleasure."

Kay turned in her badge as well. "You can't break up a good set."

Fowler sighed. "No, you can't."

Chapter 28: A New Beginning

We got married at Wayne's villa about a month and a half later. Kay was still recovering, and she used crutches right up to the moment her father helped her limp down the aisle. She wore a hinged knee brace which her gown couldn't hide entirely, but to me she was still the most beautiful bride ever.

After we exchanged our vows, and the Chaplain pronounced us husband and wife, we kissed, and I picked up my bride and carried her back up the aisle as our friends cheered and wept. She sat on a stool in the receiving line to greet all our guests as they filed past.

Lynne was carrying her newborn son, Luken, as she congratulated us. "I knew you'd end up together."

When Wayne got to us, he kissed Kay and shook my hand. "I've heard about your being forced to resign at DSS. I'm sorry about that."

"We weren't forced, exactly. We just didn't want to be sent in opposite directions."

"If you both wouldn't mind working for me, I have need of a couple of pilots. I'd pay a competitive salary. Actually, I think we'd set the standard, since you'll be Earth's first privately-contracted interstellar pilots. I'll also give you one of our guest cottages, just like Jack and Janet."

Kay kissed him again. "You don't have to do that, Wayne."

"No, but you're my friends. Lynne and I still have plenty of adventures ahead of us, and it wouldn't be the same if you both weren't a part of it."

I frowned. "I'd love to, Boss, but I still have a few years left on my ROTC contract."

"I'll buy out your contract, if it's all right with you. Serving your country is a noble pursuit, of course."

I didn't have to think very hard about it, and neither did Kay. "You've got yourself a deal, Boss."

"You don't have to call me Boss. You're my friends, Tony."

"I know. But it feels right."

"What my husband means is that we both have a lot of respect for you, Wayne. We are your friends. We both love you, even though Tony's too macho to say it in so many words. That's what it means when he calls you 'Boss'."

Wayne looked at Kay, and at me. "I can't tell you what that means to me. I love you both, very much. Come see me after your honeymoon, and we'll work out the details. Congratulations. I hope you have many happy years together."

Kay used her crutches for the rest of the evening, though she left them behind when we shared our first and only dance of the evening. I don't suppose you could really call it a dance, since she just stood balancing on her good leg holding me while I did a few steps around her, but we were together, and that made it work. When the music was over, we kissed, and I carried my wife back to our table.

When at last we were finally alone in our bedroom, I helped Kay get undressed and carried her to bed.

"I could get used to this," she said. "How much longer do you think I can milk this knee injury?"

"My love, you don't have to milk it. Whenever you want to be carried, just ask, I will do it."

"I love you, my husband. I feel like I always have. I know I always will."

"I love you, Mrs. Kayla Moss Diego. How would you like to spend our wedding night?"

Kay smiled, hunger in her eyes. "I'll give you one guess."

I was right.

###

Author's Note

I hope you've enjoyed this recounting of the events in A Time to Build from Tony's perspective. I hadn't originally intended to tell Tony's story, but once I realized how important Tony is to Wayne, I knew that he deserved his own book. He has come to mean nearly as much to me as Wayne.

About the Author

Rick Rossing lives in Connecticut with his wife and son. In addition to writing, he crafts with duct tape, cooks pretty decent food, and sings. Sometimes, in front of other people.

Made in the USA
Middletown, DE
01 November 2016